THE FREEDOM TO KILL

J. W. Nicholas

Cover photography: Scott Liddell

ISBN: 0692313842
ISBN 13: 9780692313848
LCCN: Copperthwaite Books—Kansas City, MO

A Copperthwaite Book

To all the unclaimed daughters.

"The first lesson a revolutionary must learn is that he is a doomed man."

—Huey P. Newton

"Truth uttered before its time is always dangerous."

—Mencius, 372–289 BC

Nicholas Winterstein returned many years later to the house where he had been born and raised, and he committed three murders there. A city notice, printed on yellow paper, had been taped to the front window: UNFIT FOR HUMAN HABITATION.

Inside, a young black man lay on the living-room floor in a pool of blood, a bullet through his forehead. An open black satchel, stuffed with cash, was next to him. At the kitchen entry, a police officer lay facedown with a bullet through the back of his head; his service pistol still in his outstretched hand. A second officer lay just inside the entry of the back door; the bullet had entered between his eyes and exited the back of his head. Winterstein stood over him, a nickel-plated revolver in his hand. He examined his shoes, his woolen slacks, and his cashmere pullover for traces of blood.

He stepped over the dead officer and looked again at the young black man. The house was empty of furniture. He opened his revolver, removed three empty casings, slipped them into his pocket, and reloaded the cylinder. He removed his horn-rimmed glasses, folded them, and slipped them into his pocket with the casings.

He went to the front window and looked toward the driveway. The white SUV he had driven was in front of the detached garage. Behind the SUV were two police cruisers with their engines running. The house was out of view of the cameras mounted on the dash of each cruiser, but the SUV was not. He pulled a white curtain from the window, shook the dust from it, and wrapped it around his head and face with an opening to see.

Careful to avoid the blood, he stepped over the dead officer and left through the side door. As he approached the SUV, he knew he was in full view of the camera on the first cruiser. From the house next door, an elderly woman watched him through the window as he opened the SUV's driver's-side door. Their eyes met.

He started the SUV, pulled forward, made a slow U-turn on the front lawn, and drove onto the street. He removed the covering from his head and face. Several blocks away a police cruiser raced past him from the opposite direction, its red-and-blue lights flashing and siren wailing. He watched in the rearview mirror. Another cruiser approached from the other direction. They both turned toward the house. He drove on, just below the speed limit.

He turned south on Gratiot Avenue and crossed Eight Mile Road into Detroit. On a side street, littered with abandoned houses and burned-out shells, he parked the SUV and wiped down the steering wheel and door handles with the white curtain. He left the key in the ignition and the front windows down. He crossed the street to an abandoned house. At the head of the driveway, he slid the garage door open. He backed out onto the street in a black Volkswagen and drove east toward Grosse Pointe.

The house where Nicholas Winterstein was born and raised had been built in 1944 on a one-acre lot without trees, a sewer, or a drainage system. The ground lay below street level, and during the spring rains, the lot often was flooded from the street to the front of the house. The house had been built without a foundation, building permit, or blueprint. Several years passed after its completion before the county tax assessor knew of its existence.

Arthur Reichmann erected the walls, roof, doors, and windows during the summer of 1944. He worked evenings and weekends. He used a hand brace to drill holes through the studs and ran electrical wiring to the outlet boxes in the utility room, bathroom, kitchen, living room, and bedroom. He measured, cut, and fit the plumbing for the bathroom and installed a metal shower stall and stool. The kitchen counter was made of reclaimed plywood, covered with a piece of linoleum, and finished with a metal molding. The sink was secondhand, and the plumbing was pieced together from odds and ends. He placed an oil-burning stove in the corner of the tiny living room with a copper tube leading through the wall to an outside fuel tank on metal stilts, which also provided fuel for the hot-water heater in the utility room. The house was for his daughter.

Five days a week, Arthur worked a ten-hour shift at the Chrysler plant on Lynch Road in Detroit. His daughter, Cheryl, was expecting a child in January. Her husband was in the US Army Air Corps in the South Pacific. Arthur didn't care for his son-in-law, young Joseph Winterstein. He found him to be disrespectful and somehow slothful and sloppy. The rumor that his son-in-law was half Jewish did not contribute to his dislike of him, but neither was it an endearing trait.

Reichmann lived just down the road on ten acres of land with an orchard of cherry, apple, peach, and plum trees. Two acres were cultivated with vegetables, currants, strawberries, and raspberries. There was also a chicken coop within a fenced area. Inside the chicken yard was a tree stump stained with dried blood. A fenced path connected the brooder coop and a henhouse for laying eggs; just beyond that stood Arthur's workshop. Every building was covered in clapboard siding and painted white with green shingles on the roof. He had dug his own well, enclosed it with a pump house, and added an electrical pumping system. For his own use, he also had built a round-bottomed boat from odd pieces of wood. He had caulked and stained the hull with an oil-based material. Then he had crafted an inboard engine with a single piston and connected it to a prop he'd forged from reinforced sheet metal. With a welding torch and drill, he had together a trailer for the boat and hauled it to a log cabin he'd built and varnished blond on the banks of the Au Sable River. Spending time at the cabin and fishing were his only recreation.

The house was finished by Thanksgiving 1944, and Cheryl Winterstein moved in. She expected her husband to return home before Christmas, but he sent a letter indicating that his return had been delayed until midsummer. Cheryl's mother, Mary Reichmann, insisted that her daughter remain at the family's home until young Joseph returned from the army, but Cheryl refused. She was uncomfortable around her father. When she was ten years old, he once had forced her hand to his erect penis, to rub and fondle him until he ejaculated. On another occasion he'd tried to coax her into sucking his penis. She'd refused and run out of the workshop. From then on she was careful never to find herself alone with him.

She never mentioned any of this to her mother, but unfortunately she told her young husband, Joseph Winterstein, whose violent temper was unknown to her.

The Warren Police Department report lay on the desk of Nicholas Winterstein in his private study. It stated that two officers and an unidentified black male had been fatally wounded in a vacant house on Frazho Road. All three had been shot through the head at close-to-medium range. Both officers had had guns drawn, but neither weapon had been fired. Evidence did not indicate any form of struggle. There was no mention of the black satchel stuffed with cash.

Attached to the report was the statement of Mavis Corley.

Squatters come in and out all the time. Sometimes regular folks stop—you know, folks dressed normal—and walk around and look. But I never seen that van before, the one was there when the shooting happened. That police car, the one parked in back of the van—after I called—wasn't there but a few minutes when the second one got here. That's when I heard the second shot...No...that was the third shot—yes, the third. I guess that's when those nice young officers got killed. It's such a shame. Their families must be awful upset.

Well, that Arab come out the front door. He had a turban on, like you see in the news. He walked past this very window and looked right at me. I could see straight in those Arab eyes—cold as blue ice, they were. He got in that van and drove right up on the lawn and on the street, and off he went. You wouldn't think you'd see terrorists in this neighborhood. Not the way it's changing so fast, with the colored moving in.

The national media gave the story a great deal of coverage in an effort to promote gun control, while local networks covered the losses of the families. Officer Heron was survived by his wife and two children, and Officer Livens by his wife, his parents, a brother, and two sisters.

The officers' funerals were broadcast live on the local stations. Motorcycle officers escorted the hearse through the streets and to the cemetery. The grieving widows and children stood at the gravesides. A small boy placed his baseball mitt on his father's casket and stepped back to his mother's side. As the news reporter whispered her comments into the microphone, Nicholas Winterstein set the TV to mute. It never had been his intention to kill the officers. They'd shown up at the wrong time.

A priest spoke at the grave sites. He sprinkled holy water and made the sign of the cross. The flags, draped over each casket, were folded and handed to the widows. The chief of police came forward and spoke to the women, his hand on the boy's shoulder. As the mourners dispersed, the camera focused on a city council member thought to be under investigation for corruption. The young female reporter approached with her microphone, but the councilman shook his head and refused to speak. She followed him until the chief of police intervened. She stopped and looked back at the camera.

For nearly a week, the news media had covered the murders with follow-up stories at the crime scene and interviews from the Arab community in Dearborn, until the story was displaced by reports of alien fish in Lake Huron.

As a child Joseph Winterstein was slight and easily moved to tears. Other children bullied and made fun of him because of it. His mother needed only to look at him, and he'd start to cry. She called him "*huhn geherzt*," chickenhearted. His father always had been a shield against his wife's method of child rearing. She thought the back of her hand was necessary to raise a child.

One day little Joseph saw his mother and relatives crying and comforting one another; he heard talk of the funeral and the wake. He didn't understand this, but he somehow knew his father never would return. There was no longer any protection from his mother. His four sisters tried to comfort and protect him, but they too were at her mercy. His older sister, Magdalena, often warned, "Joey, hide. She's after you." What he had done wrong was always unclear as his mother held him by a handful of hair and cursed in German, the only language he understood until after his first year of school.

Those first years were painful. His lack of English caused tears of confusion. The teachers often called upon his sisters to translate his sobbing words. At home his mother ignored English, and as the children grew fluent in the new language, they used it to keep secrets from her. In school they changed the spelling of their name to sound more American. It was many years before their mother gave in to the need of English.

His mother often took young Joseph to the grocer and butcher shop to give voice to her barter. His young mind had taken quickly to the new language. His mother pointed to a meatless bone and offered two pennies. The butcher said no; it was worth a nickel. Joseph explained that she had only two pennies and that there were six of them to feed. As the butcher wrapped the bone in a sheet of newspaper, he complained that he would end up in the poorhouse. Joseph's mother placed the package in a straw shopping bag mended with twine.

The early years passed, and Joseph grew into the sturdy frame of adolescence. The boys who once had bullied him were now few, and after a school-yard fight that ended with a broken nose, there were none. Through young adulthood he favored not the Semitic appearance of his father but the fair, Hungarian ancestry of his mother. He was blond and blue-eyed with a well-muscled physique, of which he was proud. From a squatting position, he could throw out a runner trying to steal second base and never have to remove his mask. In the fall his short, powerful stature plowed through would-be tacklers with ease. His Hollywood-handsome looks and smile made him the prize of teenage girls. On the night he asked her to dance, Cheryl Reichmann thought she was the luckiest girl at the party.

By the time of the Second World War, he was slim-waisted, with thick forearms and fists. He was inducted to the air corps and trained as a pilot. While he waited for deployment to the South Pacific, Cheryl Reichmann wrote to him and said she was pregnant. She traveled to South Dakota, and they were married in Rapid City. A week later he received word that he was to spend the remainder of the war in the South Pacific.

Near the end of the war, he was stationed on an island that kept a prisoner-of-war camp. The men of his squadron played softball bare-chested in cutoff shorts and laced boots. A Japanese prisoner who spoke English taunted Joseph for days from behind the fenced-in yard. He taunted him with thrown kisses and laughter. Joseph ignored him at first, but in a burst of anger, he tore open the wire door to the prison yard and went after the man. The armed guard simply watched. The attack lasted only seconds, and then the prisoner lay in the sand, bleeding from the nose and mouth. Everyone thought he was unconscious, but he was dead.

The war was over, and everyone was going home, but Joseph was detained. There were "formalities" to clear up, the colonel explained, regarding the death of the prisoner. Joseph's discharge would be delayed a few days—nothing to be concerned about. It was merely a delay, but the delay stretched into months. There wasn't any need to be concerned, he was reassured a second time; the colonel took his hand and held it, as if to show sympathy. It was just a matter of documenting the incident of the prisoner he had killed, the colonel explained, in case there were questions. The incident was now referred to as a *killing*. The colonel again took his hand to reassure him. Joseph thought it odd that the colonel would hold another man's hand in such a manner, but he said nothing. Then he was told that certain papers and files had been lost or mishandled, and the delay continued.

Joseph wrote to Cheryl every week. He promised to be home soon, but a month passed and then another month and then a few months more. He assured her that he would be home by midsummer, but the delay continued into the following year.

Mary Reichmann begged Cheryl to spend Christmas with them, not in this empty house and seven months pregnant. But Cheryl was determined; she would decorate a tree, spend New Year's here, and give birth to her first child in this house. Her mother didn't understand this stubbornness, and she continued to argue against it. Arthur Reichmann never offered a word to the argument. While mother and daughter went back and forth over Cheryl's refusal to come home, Cheryl glanced at her father and saw a strange, vacant look on his face, as if he were unaware that he was the reason for her refusal to return home. In her heart she wished to see a sign of regret, some remorse for what he had done, but she saw only emptiness, if not a distant grin only he understood.

Cheryl spent Christmas Eve and Christmas dinner with her parents, but each night she returned to the tiny, half-furnished house, with only a radio for company. There she wrote letters to her young husband far away in the South Pacific. Her mother arrived on New Year's Eve, carrying her own beer to help her and her daughter see in the New Year while listening to Glenn Miller on the radio.

By the middle of January, Cheryl thought the child would never come, and then her water broke while her mother was visiting. Mary hurried across the street to the Stalls' and phoned Dr. Rosenheim. He arrived thirty minutes later to deliver a male child. Cheryl and Joseph had discussed names through their letters and decided that if the child was a boy, they would name him Nicholas.

A year before the murders on Frazho Road, Nicholas Winterstein awoke at five o'clock in the morning, sat down at his computer with a cup of black coffee, and logged in to *The Detroit News* website. The lead story was about a raid by the Detroit Police Department on a Mexican drug ring. Fifteen officers had surrounded an empty warehouse and entered from opposite sides to face one another across the darkened space inside. Gunfire erupted, and seven officers were shot and killed by their fellow officers, with several more wounded. There were no drugs or gang members to be found. The chief of police said he would conduct an investigation to determine why so many officers had been in the line of fire. When asked why there had been no arrests made or narcotics recovered, the chief said he would look into those details too.

Nick poured a second cup of coffee and logged in to his e-mail account. He deleted half without opening them then opened only personal or work-related mail. One message informed him that someone had been researching his name and background. Since he was an attorney, this search would have seemed fairly normal, but a forty-two-year-old female outside Baltimore, Maryland, had initiated it. If the location hadn't been Maryland, he would have thought little of it. But Maryland gave him pause, a moment to think back to his youth, to his second year in law school. He remembered a girl named Janice. She had been sweet and wholesome, a girl anyone's parents would have loved, but there hadn't been anything exciting about her. Because of her youth and her need to please, she was easy to bed. She had been seeing a young math student when Nick met her. A few months later she told him she was pregnant. He was defensive and denied the baby was his. After all, she had been seeing the math guy too. She was hurt, and he saw the pain in her face. She said her parents were taking her back to Baltimore at the end of the week. She looked at him once again. He later admitted to himself that the baby *was* his; he'd carried a sense of guilt through the years.

The sun rose above Lake Saint Clair. He put on his running clothes and went out the side door. He seldom varied the course he ran. It took forty-five minutes. It was a good time to think, to go over cases, to consider arguments, but this morning he was curious about this strange female from Baltimore who was researching his background. Maybe the search had to do with Janice, with the child she had borne. He never had known whether it was a girl or boy, dead or alive. Janice had disappeared from all but his memory.

At the end of his run, he was sweaty but not winded. He felt good. With his hands on his hips, he looked around as if in thought. The early leaves of spring were mint green in the morning light. The grass glistened with dew.

He showered and dressed for the office. He opened the garage door with a remote on his key chain. A black Volkswagen was parked next to a cream-colored Lincoln. He backed the Lincoln out and followed Jefferson Avenue to his office in the city. The nameplate on the front of the building read, WINTERSTEIN & ASSOCIATES, ATTORNEYS AT LAW, but the associates were long gone. The firm consisted of Nicholas Winterstein and Helen Wincraft, a paralegal. Winterstein had eliminated the partnership years ago. There had been a conflict in philosophy, in an elemental understanding of the law. Winterstein knew the law is whatever you make it up to be; there is no math involved. His partners, however, had believed the law is an objective force, a universal signpost to right and wrong, without which you have chaos and anarchy. "But you don't know that," Winterstein had argued. "You're simply repeating something you've heard." At first it had been an argument to have over a drink, but then it became an inconvenience, and then, toward the end, it put the firm at odds with itself. Nick approached a case one way, and the partners approached it from the opposite end. The impact became economic. He now worked alone.

Helen, his paralegal, was already at the office. He enjoyed the faint scent of her perfume in the air, the feeling of completeness only a woman could add. Her computer was logged in to Scottrade's website. She was smart, attractive, and in her early forties. He'd met her at an indoor pistol range, where he'd first noticed the curve of her hips, the arch of her buttocks. Her stance with the pistol was relaxed and correct. At fifteen yards she placed a grouping of six rounds within two inches of the bull's-eye. As she reloaded the clip, he saw her profile and a three-quarter view of her face. Her features were angular, attractive, familiar. She noticed him staring, and he looked away. He didn't want it to appear as though he were trying to pick her up. Then it came to him who she was, where he had seen her. It had been on the evening news. She had been a high-school teacher in the suburbs who had been arrested for having sex with a fifteen-year-old boy. The case had gone to trial, but in the middle of it all, the boy recanted his story. He now swore that he had made the whole thing up. But because of the way he looked at her from the witness stand, with the longing of a young boy in love, no one believed him. Most everyone believed her to be guilty, but in the end, the case was thrown out. The district attorney had screwed up, but before it was over, he managed to stick Helen with a weapons offense. She served nine months of an eighteen-month sentence. It was better than living as a registered sex offender.

Then Nick saw her a second time at the pistol range. It was early morning, and she was the only one there. As he entered the firing area, she looked toward the door as though she had sensed his presence. Without stopping he acknowledged her with a nod and went farther down the line. He had a .40-caliber pistol that didn't fire true to its sights. The defect concerned him.

A week later he saw her at Starbucks. He noticed her come through the door. She ordered coffee, stopped at the counter to add cream, then looked for a seat. When she saw him, she stopped. He motioned with an open hand to the armchair next to him. She hesitated then came forward and sat in the oversize leather chair. She set her coffee next to his. He introduced himself, and before she could respond, he asked how she was getting along since her release from prison. The question caught her off guard. She looked down at her lap, smoothed her skirt, and answered that it had been hard. She couldn't find work. Background checks followed every place where she had applied. She'd sold a number of her stocks piecemeal from a very meager portfolio to pay her utilities, rent, and tuition. She was now enrolled in a paralegal program at Wayne State. The law seemed like a good fit; it was a sandbox without conscience. Nick smiled. He revealed that he was an attorney and had offices only a few blocks from here. She appeared unsurprised.

They met again at Starbucks then another time after that. Helen grew comfortable with him. She revealed details of her past as though she needed to hear them aloud to make sense of her own behavior. At age fourteen she'd had an affair with a much older man. He was married and had a daughter who was a year older than Helen. The daughter didn't know Helen from any other girl in the school, but Helen knew her. The daughter was very pretty and popular, a cheerleader. Helen often saw her in the halls, the cafeteria, as well as after school, when the girl's father sometimes picked her up. That was how Helen first saw him. The graying temples and exotic eyes smiled at her. He asked whether she needed a ride. Without speaking, unable to find words, she got into the backseat. His daughter was in the front. She neither spoke nor turned to acknowledge Helen. He took his daughter home first then asked Helen where she lived. She gave the address of a small apartment complex. She lived alone with her mother. She had no idea who her father was. Her mother said he could have been any number of boys; she simply didn't know.

The affair between young Helen and the older man went on for more than a year. Helen gave her virginity to him and learned all the intimacies of lovemaking. Then it ended. He was an attorney for General Motors and was transferred to New York. He said he would be in touch, but she never heard from him again. Nick sensed a melancholy in her voice as she recalled the past, but her tone was never bitter. Perhaps she had a deeper understanding of the human heart than bitterness allowed.

In the weeks to come, she and Nick often met at Starbucks. It was an unspoken agreement; one simply knew the other would be there. Finally one morning Nick invited her to view his offices. They were on the fifth floor. The first room served as both the reception area and office. A thick oriental rug of red and gold with black trim covered the floor. To the left was a large conference room. Nick's office was to the right, with another oriental rug and a cream-colored sofa upholstered in wide corduroy. Helen expressed pleasure in what she saw. It was so beautiful, she said, her hands clasped together.

Nick offered her a job.

"Are you serious?" she said, turning to face him. Tears welled up in her eyes.

The child was born premature and breech. When he was handed to Cheryl, she was startled to see that his left leg and neck were deformed. Dr. Rosenheim reassured her that within a few weeks everything would appear normal.

"Babies are like rubber," he explained. "You can twist and turn their little parts, and they come right back."

But the baby's head, tilted to the right, did not straighten, and the left knee was still drawn back weeks later. A consultation between pediatricians and surgeons followed, and minor surgery was recommended to "free things up."

"But what does that mean?" she asked. "And what is involved?" And of course she had to discuss it with her husband first.

Mary Reichmann argued that the delay was unnecessary and risky, and what could the husband have to say? He was a half world away. Arthur Reichmann offered nothing to the discussion. Infants and the human heart were foreign to him. Cheryl accepted her mother's decision and was grateful for her courage. She worried now about the child, not about the decision to allow surgery.

The procedure was successful, and the small incisions healed without a mark left behind. The child's head was no longer tilted to the right, and his neck had a complete range of motion. The same was true for the left knee, but Cheryl worried there was an unseen deformity. She'd heard stories of breech babies having mental deficiencies and personality disorders. She watched her baby too closely for signs of abnormality, until simple drooling became a worry.

Dr. Rosenheim said that if the brain had been deprived of oxygen during a breech delivery, such problems could appear, but he didn't think this was the case; at least he was relatively sure of it.

At two months the child was uttering a series of sounds with a distinct cadence. At first Cheryl thought it was cute, but the strings of sounds grew more varied, as if they represented a language of some kind. Dr. Rosenheim said it was too early to test for autism, and anyway he didn't think that was the case—at least not yet.

At five months the child crawled naturally enough and displayed an extraordinary curiosity while uttering the strange sounds Cheryl thought contained vowels. Dr. Rosenheim said the child might be an idiot savant, but that wasn't all bad, because he could be used to calculate numbers and therefore could earn a living.

Mary Reichmann was furious at such nonsense and forbade her daughter to see Dr. Rosenheim again. "'Different' is not crazy! Just look at your father."

With time and her mother's reassurance, Cheryl no longer saw "different" as negative. Her son did display a range of odd behaviors, but the more time she was with him, the more normal he seemed. He often crawled under the house among the cinder blocks to play in the white sand with his truck and babble with the strange, language-like noise. At first Cheryl tried to ignore it. Hopefully he would grow out of this strange language he used and appear normal to his father. But in time it was Cheryl who changed, not the child. She heard the language so often that it started to make sense to her. She repeated the words and began to understand the verbs, realizing that the adjective followed the noun. But where had the language come from? And where might it lead?

She looked at the child and worried her husband might not be so accepting.

"You had a personal call," Helen said. "At least she said it was personal. I asked if she wanted to leave a message, and she hung up."

"No name?"

"No. It was a Maryland area code."

She returned to her desk, and Nick heard her phone ring again. Several minutes passed, and she was still on the phone. She had a taste for young boys, and it seemed she had her hands full with this one. She complained that it was like trying to housetrain a puppy.

Nick went through his e-mails. With his years of experience, finding clients wasn't difficult, but finding those with deep pockets was far more rewarding and had left him comfortable in life. Several e-mails he didn't bother to open. He simply forwarded them to Helen. At the bottom of his in-box was the name "Judge Goodwin Marshall." He had been mentioned as a possible candidate for the Michigan State Supreme Court on the Democrat ticket.

He opened the e-mail: "Winterstein, please call me—313-582-9888. Do not leave a voice mail."

Nick closed the e-mail and went on to the other messages. One concerned a suit against an insurance company, and another was a possible wrongful-death suit. Several minutes later he reopened the e-mail from Judge Marshall. Nick didn't know him personally, but he knew of him through several biographical pieces he'd read.

One stated that Marshall was originally from Baltimore, Maryland, but when he was eight years old, his mother had moved them to Detroit after her white, common-law husband had abandoned them. His mother had worked as a domestic in Grosse Pointe, while his aging grandmother had taken in laundry. Young Goodwin went through the Detroit school system in the early 1950s. The school he attended was largely white, and it was there that he heard the term *mulatto* for the first time. At first the word confused him. It didn't feel like name-calling, and it had a pleasant-enough sound, but neither did it feel like a pat on the back. He remembered his father being white, but he didn't *think* of him as white. He'd just been his father, someone he'd loved and looked up to, but he now saw these students as the same as his father, and their whiteness somehow was associated with the pain of abandonment. The word *mulatto*, the author of the article pointed out, became uncomfortable for young Goodwin to hear, but that changed.

By the time he entered high school, Goodwin had learned to avoid white company in order to gain acceptance among the darker-skinned students. His light skin and intellect provided easy movement within his own race, as long as he didn't venture too far down the social ladder. The young girls he dated were of fair complexion, while he satisfied his sexual needs in the darker corners of the neighborhood, where females admired his hazel eyes and fine hair. The life of a mulatto, he realized, came with certain rewards.

While at Wayne State University, he first glimpsed the tool of politics as a method of control. The Young Socialists of Michigan worked to recruit him. Although he never joined the party, he participated in organizational events. Their method of fund-raising left

an impression through its simplicity and effectiveness: the party organized a meager soup kitchen and then pressured local merchants,
through threats of boycott and negative publicity, to contribute to
their cause of feeding the poor. Contributions were then funneled
into the party's general fund. Goodwin saw this act as petty extortion,
but it worked without complaint from the victims.

From Wayne State he then attended the Detroit College of Law,
where he polished his views on civil rights. This seemed like a lucra-
tive area. His first published article concerned black unemployment.
It was a safe enough political stance and a yet-unknown portal to
his future. The Nation of Islam soon contacted him, but he found
their unorthodox sense of dignity appeared feigned and stiff. After
a third meeting, Goodwin realized these people were on the mere
fringe of reality. They served him no purpose, yet he was careful not
to antagonize them; this was a time to build bridges, not burn them.
He maintained a quiet, nearly secretive relationship with the radical
group throughout his early years.

Once he had passed the bar, he successfully litigated a number
of civil-rights cases. Regarding the case of a terminated employee,
Jefferson v. Ford Motor Company, uncontested by the union, the press
referred to Goodwin as the Robin Hood of civil rights. This victory
and a similar one against Chrysler led to his closer association with
the National Association for the Advancement of Colored People
(NAACP) and to his future appointment as general counsel for its
Detroit chapter.

Goodwin felt at home within the social structure of the NAACP.
He quietly viewed it as a club for mulattoes, the patrician ancestry
of slaves, and now the political slave owners of power. There he met
his future wife, Angela, a young woman of fair complexion with a
disarming talent for fund-raising. Her manner was charitable, never
political.

During his first year at the NAACP, Goodwin met Jessup Carthage,
a Chicago activist. Carthage was accused of adding human feces to a

jambalaya at an exclusive restaurant hosting the Sons and Daughters of the Confederacy. A white dishwasher and a bus girl claimed to have witnessed his act and said they later retrieved a wax-paper bag from the trash and smelled it. They reported his behavior to management, and Carthage was fired, although no criminal charges were pursued. It wasn't until the next day that management searched for the wax-paper bag but couldn't find it. Carthage was soon on the streets, screaming racism and threatening boycotts and legal action. The American Civil Liberties Union investigated his claims but later refused to get involved. Goodwin Marshall heard of their decision through a personal phone call. With little hesitation he filed suit on behalf of Jessup Carthage, but the case was settled out of court. The defendant could not produce any hard evidence but merely the interpretation of an event by two witnesses, one of whom had a criminal record. The restaurant offered Carthage a generous severance package, which he accepted.

Through the years Goodwin Marshall and Jessup Carthage developed a working relationship, but it never reached the social level. The inner members of the NAACP viewed Carthage as a live cannon on a crowded street. Marshall, on the other hand, never expressed a public view of Carthage but pursued a quiet business relationship with him. It was the reason behind his e-mail to Nicholas Winterstein.

I n June 1945 Cheryl Winterstein received a letter from her husband. He would not be home this summer, but he guaranteed his return in eighteen months. Colonel Shelby presented the delay as a "voluntary extension of service." It was in writing, Joseph explained, and Colonel Shelby had signed it.

Cheryl sat down at the kitchen table and read the letter again. Her disappointment brought her near tears. Nicky was on a blanket on the living-room floor, but he now crawled off to the kitchen entrance. Cheryl watched him come toward her. Her husband sent money every month, but she didn't use it. There would be reason enough for that when he returned until he found work. She noticed the radio wasn't playing. How long ago had it stopped? She turned the knob. The radio was still on, but there was no sound. She switched the knob back and forth then slapped the top. There was a slight static then nothing. *Oh, great!* She looked back at the letter on the table then at Nicky, who now was headed toward the utility room.

Her mother said not to worry about the radio; her dad could fix that. Mary almost always arrived with one or two bottles of beer wrapped in a towel and carried in a straw basket with a handle. An open pack of Chesterfields lay on the table. The cigarettes were to hide the smell of beer from Mary's husband, yet she still had a strong will of her own. Early in their marriage, Arthur had cheated on her. She'd found out and announced to his face that she would do the same: what was good for the gander was good for the goose! This ultimatum had ended his infidelity.

Cheryl's father arrived the next day. She heard his knock and, through the window, saw him standing at the front door with a cardboard box held together with brown twine that formed a handle at the top. For a moment she stared at him. He stood there with that same distant grin; she felt uncomfortable.

She went to the front door to let him in; their eyes did not meet. He opened the box and removed a Philco radio. The shiny case had been newly varnished. He set it on the end table and plugged it in. It took a moment to warm up. In her heart she was grateful and looked for forgiveness, but the memory was indelible. She could not bring herself to kiss him on the forehead or cheek. She simply thanked him.

Arthur Reichmann packed the old radio in the box and took it to his workshop. He replaced one of the vacuum tubes and reattached a wire. He plugged the radio in and turned the dial to *The Goldbergs.* They were funny and resourceful. Unlike his son-in-law, the blond, blue-eyed Jew, the Goldbergs could manage the necessities of life. His son-in-law was cut for failure. Reichmann stood in the shop doorway and looked out at his cultivated, meticulous garden. A wet summer had given an early harvest.

Cheryl and her mother canned cucumbers, string beans, tomatoes, and carrots, as well as fruits from the orchard. Roots and potatoes were stored in the pump house. Dozens of eggs had been collected through the year then hard-boiled, pickled, and sealed in jars. After they had used all the canning jars, there was still produce left over.

From her father's garden, Cheryl collected vegetables in two wagons, one tethered to the other, with Nicky in a sling attached around her neck and waist. She pulled the wagons to the corner of Groesbeck Highway, where she sold the produce. She was there for the morning traffic and returned in the afternoon. She enjoyed the conversation with her customers and the flattery of the passing truckers as they honked and waved out the window. In six days she earned enough to cover her electric bill through the winter. Her mother refused any money. It was hers! Cheryl had earned it.

The following year Cheryl was determined to plant a garden of her own. She had nearly an acre of unused ground behind the house. She mentioned the idea to her mother, and in the early spring, her father arrived with a hand tractor he had built. It was a small Briggs & Stratton engine mounted to a wooden platform with a bicycle chain and sprocket; the handlebars and plow once had been used behind a horse. The ground was moist and easy to furrow. Cheryl and her father worked three days together, but in that time, they didn't speak more than ten words to each other.

The spring rains were abundant, and the produce flourished. To the corn, tomatoes, cucumbers, beans, and carrots, she added watermelon and cantaloupe. She expressed her excitement in her letters to her husband. She described how healthy her vegetables looked and how the ground had remained soft and black from all the rain. When he wrote to ask whether her father had helped, she avoided the answer by explaining how the extra money helped with the electric and heating fuel. It might even add to their savings.

As the vegetables came into season, she once again sold her produce at the corner of Groesbeck Highway. She spread a blanket well back from the road for Nicky, where she tethered him to a rope around his waist and staked it to the ground. He was getting too big to carry in the sling for long periods.

The truckers still honked and waved. She felt pretty again. A new Ford convertible came to a shiny stop ahead. The driver put it in reverse and backed up to her wagons. The car was beautiful, one of the first models produced after the war. The young man wore a yellow tie with a black print, held snug with a collar pin. His hat lay on the seat next to him. Cheryl felt giddy; he was so handsome. Nicky crawled toward the tall grass, but the rope restrained him. The young man patted the front seat and asked if she'd like to go for a ride. Her eyes opened wide, but she then realized what his offer implied. It was a nice car, but she couldn't—maybe some other time. He looked toward Nicky. The kid looked retarded—babbling and tied to a stake. The young man put the car in gear and sped off, the back tires kicking up gravel. The shiny convertible and the handsome young man had been so exciting at first sight, but now, as the car disappeared in the distance, Cheryl felt cheap.

Toward the end of the season, she sold the melons. She would cut a watermelon in half, cover one side with wax paper, and cut the other side into sections for tasting. The watermelons as well as the cantaloupes were gone in a few days.

One morning, with a cup of coffee held in both hands, she stood looking out the kitchen window in front of the sink. Her garden was empty. Her father had cut the cornstalks low to the ground. Brown leaves blew from the trees, and she thought of next year's garden.

Nicky turned two in the middle of the winter. Cheryl wrote to her husband every week. She wrote of Nicky and of how he never had seen his father. She wondered how he might react to the first sight of him.

Joseph was still in the South Pacific. He was sunburned and brown. His beard had turned reddish blond. There was no need to shave, as there was but one officer there, and he never shaved either. Joseph helped maintain the aircraft, preparing for the day when he and the rest of the crew would fly them off the island. He worked on the one he had damaged. He'd applied too much pressure to a wrench on a coupling attached to the landing gear, and when the wrench slipped, he had cut his hand. He had then grabbed a hammer and, out of anger, smashed the coupling. Fluid had gushed from the brake line. Joseph had stood there, blood dripping from his hand, as brake fluid covered the ground. His temper still plagued him.

Nick called Goodwin Marshall from his desk phone. He tried to think of why Marshall had contacted him—and why he had requested that he not leave a voice mail. Marshall answered on the third ring.

"Judge Marshall? This is Winterstein."

"Yes." There was a pause. "Thank you for calling."

Nick heard the squeak of leather, as if the judge had stood up from a large chair and walked to another part of the room. Nick waited for him to continue.

"I'd like to meet with you," Marshall said. "But not at my office."

"Where then?"

"I'm not sure."

"How about Starbucks?"

"That will do," Marshall said. His voice wasn't agitated, but neither was it relaxed. There was a lack of confidence to it. "When are you free?"

"Will tomorrow do?"

"Yes, that's fine. What time?"

"Tomorrow morning at nine. There's a Starbucks not far from my office."

"Yes, I know where it is. See you then," Marshall said, and hung up.

Nick turned in his swivel chair to look toward the river. Marshall did not wish to simply pass the time of day. Did he need an attorney?

He asked Helen what she knew of Marshall's recent activities.

"He seems devious," she said, "and there's his buddy, Jessup Carthage. Oh, excuse me..." She rolled her eyes. "*Reverend* Carthage."

"See what you can find on Carthage," he said, "no matter how mundane."

The next morning was gray, with a steady drizzle that gave a chill to the air. Nick arrived at Starbucks before Marshall. From inside he watched the judge arrive and park his white Escalade, but he didn't get out. He sat there for several minutes. The intermittent wipers cleared the windshield. Marshall finally emerged from the car, walked toward the coffeehouse, and pulled open the glass door. He ordered coffee then came toward Nick without acknowledging that he'd seen him. He sat down in the armchair next to him.

"Dismal day," Nick said.

Marshall looked toward the window. Cars with headlights and wipers on passed along the street. "I may need your services," he said.

"You're not sure?"

"I might be charged with insider trading."

"Why come to me? That isn't my area."

"I have a feeling," Marshall said. "I heard your argument, the thin-paper theory."

Nick smiled. "That's what the press called it."

"It was quite clever," Marshall said.

Nick was flattered, but he knew not to show it.

"Are you guilty?" Nick asked.

Marshall hesitated. "The SEC seems to think so."

"Well, are you?"

"That's irrelevant. Are you interested?"

"I'll need more information."

"I'll give you what the SEC has or what they think they have. You can judge from there."

⇤ ⇥

When Nick returned to the office, Helen looked up from her desk, but she seemed not to notice him. She made notes on a yellow pad and continued to read from the computer screen. The information she had collected from public sources covered nearly forty years.

Jessup Carthage had been born in the Deep South to a fifteen-year-old girl out of wedlock. His father, once a prizefighter, had been married for many years to the same woman, with whom he had several children. Jessup, in fact, attended school with his half brother, though the boys never were told they were related. They never spoke to each other, yet the thread that connected them somehow was known to them. Between Jessup and his half sisters, however, the ethereal connection wasn't visible. A lifetime as strangers could have passed between them.

One of the few times Jessup saw his father was outside a bar on a dirt road on the colored side of town. His father wore only one shoe as he laughed and stood about with his friends, while Jessup remained out of view, just around the corner. It was years later before he put all the bitter pieces together.

Jessup also wrote of the tragic scene he'd witnessed in an empty parking lot after a demonstration over whites-only restrooms. Several policemen with dogs stopped his half brother. They told the boy to run then released the dogs after him. The dogs pulled him down and tore at his arms and legs. Jessup saw blood through his brother's shirt. They called the dogs off and gathered around the boy as he lay on the ground. As he got to his feet, a policeman hit him from behind with his nightstick, and the boy went down again. His head hit the concrete hard, and he didn't move. His brother never again appeared at school. Folks said he ran off, went up North with the demonstrators to be free. Although a body was never produced, Jessup knew the boy was dead.

Jessup did well enough in high school to receive an athletic scholarship in football to the University of Michigan, but he lasted only two semesters. He accused the school of racial bias when a lighter-skinned black athlete replaced him at a starting position. This event followed his dismissal from the debate team after his refusal to follow the rules of elocution. Years later the university revised their account of his departure as a "mutual agreement."

He then attended an all-black college in Georgia that had lost its accreditation for academic and financial reasons. He received a certificate of completion in the calligraphy of a diploma.

The incident at the white-owned restaurant and his first meeting with Goodwin Marshall soon followed. The severance package he received was a soon-to-be career path, but first he needed respectability; he needed a title. A doctorate was out of the question. He enrolled in Central Theological Seminary but attended less than a year, dropping out to devote himself full-time to the civil-rights movement. The opportunity to earn money and gain legitimacy was in front of him. When he was at the front of any protest, his name appeared as "Reverend Carthage." Although he was unaffiliated with any church and held no degree, no one questioned his assumed title.

His behavior embarrassed the leaders of the Christian Civil Rights Conference (CCRC). He staged events to promote himself in the name of the movement. He took up the cause of a black prostitute who claimed several white policemen had raped her. As the truth became known, the young prostitute recanted her story, yet Carthage never admitted an injustice had been done. He was indignant that the white officers were not prosecuted and punished. He demanded the death penalty for the rape of a black woman.

The assassination of Martin Luther King Jr. soon followed. Carthage appeared for an interview wearing a bloodstained shirt. He claimed to have received the dying man's last words, whispered in his ear; while on a previous occasion, Carthage had claimed that he was the speechwriter for Martin Luther King Jr. and said that "I had a dream…" were his words. The following week the CCRC expelled him for plagiarism and "other offenses." Carthage then announced that it was he who had decided to separate from the CCRC and that he was organizing the Chicago Christian Leadership Conference or CCLC. With national recognition came closer scrutiny of his personal life. His early background came to light, as did a conversation he'd thought was private. But the incident of "human feces in the jambalaya" and the remark "whining kikes of New York," caught on tape, caused little stir in the media. After an outright denial of the first incident and a brief apology for the remarks caught on tape, it was business as usual. He had become an accepted figure of the civil-rights movement.

Reverend Jessup Carthage and Judge Goodwin Marshall were now seen together at the Detroit offices of the Chicago Christian Leadership Conference.

Helen organized her findings into one large file and printed it out. Nick didn't like reading from a computer screen. She then cleaned up around her desk, turned off the computer, and rinsed her coffee cup in the kitchenette sink before placing it in the drying rack. She stepped into Nick's office to say good night. He was staring out the window toward the river.

"Is everything all right?" she asked.

He turned in his chair. "Are you leaving?"

"Yes. How did the meeting go?"

"Marshall wants me to represent him."

"What's the issue?" She stepped farther into the office.

"Insider trading. I know..." he said, reading her expression. "It's not my area."

"Then why come to you?"

"He said he had a hunch."

She laughed. "What does that mean?"

"The thin-paper theory."

"The what?"

"It was the closing argument I once used in a murder trial. The guy was accused of killing his wife. Much of the evidence was circumstantial. I argued there was enough reasonable doubt to acquit." Nick pushed a sheet of white paper from his desk. It oscillated as it fell lightly to the floor. "I described an incident that once happened in my office." He pointed to the paper on the floor. "Did you see how it fell? I was going through some papers on top of a filing cabinet. The paper I was looking for slipped from the top of the cabinet and fell to the floor. I glimpsed it beneath my left elbow as it fell. When I turned to pick it up, it was gone. I searched and searched, but I couldn't find it. I began to doubt that I'd even seen it fall. Later that afternoon I found it. It lay on top of the hanging files, inside the last drawer from the bottom. As it oscillated toward the floor, it had slipped between the opening of the second and last drawer. The opening between the two was less than a sixteenth of an inch. It slipped through without touching the top or bottom of the opening and came to rest inside. Think of the odds of that happening."

Helen listened with amazement. "And you argued—"

"Yes," he said. "There was more than reasonable doubt. There was no murder weapon. There was no witness. If that piece of paper can slip through that thin of an opening, how can you convict without solid evidence? The jury was out less than an hour."

"And he was acquitted?"

Nick nodded. "Yes."

Helen shook her head and turned to leave but stopped. She stepped back into the office. "Did he do it?" she asked. "Did he kill her?"

"Yes."

J oseph Winterstein returned home in the late spring of 1947. Cheryl had expected him home in the summer, but she didn't know when. There was only his promise in a letter. She went ahead with her vegetable garden. The profit was worth all the hard work. She was bent forward with a rake in her hands when she heard Nicky cry. She turned to see what it was. A soldier stood near the house, looking at her. A moment passed before she realized who it was. "Oh, my God. Joe!"

The rake fell from her hands. Tears filled her eyes as she walked then ran toward him. He let the duffel bag drop from his shoulder. Held tightly in his arms, she kissed the side of his neck again and again.

Nicky quieted down but the toddler then again burst into loud tears. After wiping her eyes, Cheryl picked him up and took him to his father. The boy's hair was whitish blond, his eyes blue. Joseph reached and took his son from Cheryl, but when the boy screamed, he handed him back to Cheryl.

Inside the house Joseph sat on the floor and watched his son gather toys from around the room to show his father. The boy's grandfather had made the toys. They were carved from wood and had wheels that moved. There were trucks and a tractor and a car that resembled the new-model Plymouth. In his heart Joseph was jealous. He didn't like the old man being anywhere near his son, but he kept this to himself.

The boy held out the toys and gave them names, but they were unintelligible. Cheryl explained that he sometimes made up his own words, but she wasn't concerned because he used real sentences when he wanted to. Over the next several years, the language Nick created would grow in complexity. To the listener it sounded like gibberish, but the gibberish contained a subject, a noun, and a verb—structure. In public Joseph found the strange language embarrassing, and only under threats of punishment did Nick cease using it aloud. Joseph was concerned the boy might be slow-minded, mentally damaged. But this worry passed, and the closeness between father and son grew stronger through the months to come.

Weeks after his return from the service, Joseph bought a 1932 Ford Coupe. He paid fifty dollars and promised the rest would come soon. The dealer agreed to it. Nick stood on the front seat next to his father as they drove to the grass airport on Gratiot Avenue. Joseph missed flying, but the money wasn't there for such things. He was just learning the trade of a carpenter. Nick watched the airplanes lift off the ground, circle overhead, and land on the grass, which looked soft and green. At the edge of the runway, the longer grass bent backward from the wind of the propellers as the planes taxied by.

On Sunday mornings the three of them attended Mass. Nick stood on the front seat between his mom and dad. Although he seldom spoke of it, Cheryl was aware of her husband's Jewish blood. She looked at him and wondered what his thoughts were. He had such a strong belief in God and recited stories from the Bible to his son. He told Nick of Abraham and Isaac and of God's command that Abraham sacrifice his son. Joseph sat the boy down on his lap and explained that if God had asked that of him, he would have said no. Nick snuggled close to his father's chest. He was safe there.

Before kindergarten the Catholic nuns gave Nick religious instructions. He learned of mortal sin, the sacraments, and the stories of the Bible. He learned them well, and the nuns praised him. Joseph was proud of his son.

Before Nick started kindergarten, Cheryl came home with a new baby. The baby had arrived sooner than expected. That's why his mother had gone to the hospital to have her. She pulled the blanket away from her little face for Nick to see.

In the spring Kathleena played on a blanket on the grass, while Cheryl and her father cut into the ground for her garden. In good weather Joseph worked Saturdays, but he came home early this day and found Reichmann still there. Joseph saw the distant grin on his father-in-law's face, and it angered him. To keep peace, however, he gave a cold nod.

In the fall Nick started kindergarten. His teacher wore wire glasses and had fuzzy hair. She was also his first and third grade teacher. In the first grade, Candy came to his school. She was his first girlfriend. His desk was at the front of the class, and Candy came down the aisle. She stopped in front of his desk and did a twirl so the hem of her dress fanned out. "I like my dress," she said. "It's pretty." Brown eyes and blond hair smiled at him.

He soon learned that she lived only three blocks away. Nick was in heaven. He rode past her house on his bicycle, a red J.C. Higgins. Riding with no hands was a snap. He had to do something special. He tried doing "no hands" and standing on the seat, but as he passed in front of Candy's house, the bike went into the shrubs and tossed him onto the grass.

The noise brought her father out in a hurry. "What the hell!" He looked down at Nick on the grass. Right behind him stood Candy. She smiled and did a twirl.

The following year Candy contracted rheumatic fever. Even after she passed away, Nick visited Candy's mother. He was always welcome.

Helen received a package from a private courier. The boy was in his midtwenties and had a tattoo of a butterfly on the side of his neck. His smile was more confident than deserved. Helen signed for the package and dismissed him.

The envelope was sealed with a metal clasp. She opened it and removed a manila folder filled with papers. They were from Judge Goodwin Marshall, addressed to Nicholas Winterstein. She leafed through several pages, stopping here and there to read. Her knowledge of insider trading was limited. She logged in to the law library. She looked from the page in her hand to the screen then back again, making notes as she went along.

Helen rearranged the order of the pages according to the date of occurrence and spaced her notes to match. She spent several hours organizing the papers then placed the folder at the corner of her desk. Nick was still out of the office. He was on his way to see a friend, he had told Helen before he had left. Helen had seen the woman only once. She had been in the parking lot below the office windows, waiting for Nick. She had silver hair and wore a white tennis skirt. Her legs looked smooth and well shaped. Nick seldom spoke of her and then only in passing. Helen was curious.

Hours passed, and Nick hadn't returned to the office. It was nearly five o'clock. Helen was reluctant to call his cell phone. She rinsed her coffee cup, turned off the computer, and locked up the office. Before leaving, she checked the security-camera monitor and scanned the outside of the building. Detroit was unsafe, and the police were of little help, if they showed up at all. She had no idea where Nick was, and as she walked to her car, she considered calling him at home.

═╪ ╪═

Nick returned home later that evening. The landline indicated a voice mail, but when he listened to it, there was only silence. He showered, made a cup of hot broth, and sat down in front of the TV in his office. He could hardly keep his eyes open.

He didn't realize he had fallen asleep until he heard the phone ring. It took him a moment to focus. It was nearly eight o'clock. He answered and heard Helen's voice.

"Nick, I need help."

"What happened?"

"I'm in jail." He heard the stress in her voice. "Central precinct, I think." She moved the phone away from her mouth and said to someone there, "Can you tell him where I am? It's my attorney."

The voice on the other end was male and raspy. She was at the central precinct on Woodward Avenue. Helen came back on the phone, and Nick assured her he was on his way. He first took a pistol from his desk, chambered a round, and set the safety. He backed the black Volkswagen out of the garage. It was less of a target for carjackers than the Lincoln.

The officer he met at the precinct was the same one he had spoken to on the phone. Nick said he was Helen's attorney and asked what the charges were.

"Ain't no charges," he said.

"Who brought her in?" Nick asked.

"Bellwether, but he didn't fill out no papers. He just put her in the back."

"I'd like to see her."

"You can take her on out," he said. "Ain't no record of it. Take her 'fore someone go back there an' do her." He laughed.

Helen still had her purse with her. Nick escorted her out of the building. He opened the car door; she got in; and he closed it behind her. He looked in all directions and stepped around to the driver's side. He put the car in drive and heard all the doors lock.

"Did you have a gun with you?" he asked.

"Yes." She nodded. "He took it."

They both knew she was lucky—a convicted felon with a firearm.

"Can they trace it?" he asked.

She shook her head. "No, I stole it."

He waited to hear the rest of it.

"I stole it from a boy. He stole it from his uncle." She looked at him with shame or embarrassment in her eyes.

Nick asked where her car was, and she said she had left it where the policeman had pulled her over.

"What happened?"

"A patrol car came alongside me at a light, and he just stared. When the light changed, he followed me. Next thing I knew, his lights were flashing for me to pull over. He asked for my driver's license, and when I opened my purse, he took it from me. He found the gun and asked if I had a permit. He kept calling me 'snowflake.' I said no, I didn't have a permit, and he reached inside and put his hand on my leg. I grabbed his wrist, but he wouldn't stop. I had to push him off."

A patrol car pulled up behind them. An officer got out and approached the car. Nick rolled down the window, and the officer asked whether everything was OK. Nick said everything was fine. The officer warned him that the neighborhood wasn't safe, including here.

"Keep your doors and windows locked." He nodded good night and returned to the patrol car.

"Where's your car?" Nick asked. He looked in the mirror. The officer was on the radio. For moment Nick worried he had the wrong license plate on his car. He sometimes switched between the real one and a bogus one, depending on his intentions.

"South of here," she said, "near Garfield."

He put the car in gear and pulled onto the street while glancing quickly in the rearview mirror. The patrol car was still parked at the curb.

They found Helen's car on the side of the road at the Garfield intersection. The driver's-side window was down, and the keys were still in the ignition. "Must be a slow night," Nick said. Helen got in her car, and Nick told her to follow him and stay close behind. "Don't lose sight of me," he said.

She followed him to Grosse Pointe, and as Nick pulled into his drive, the headlights fell across the lawn then onto the garage as the doors opened. There was room for a third car, and he motioned for Helen to pull in. They entered the house through the breezeway.

He could see she wasn't herself. Her confidence was shaken. "You can stay here tonight," he said. "There's a room upstairs with a separate bath. I'm just down the hall."

"I'm so sorry, Nick—"

"No, don't go there," he said. "Would you like a drink?"

She nodded. He fixed her a whiskey with ice and added sweet vermouth. He handed her the drink. "We'll talk in the morning."

He showed her the guest bedroom and switched on the light in the bathroom, with its fluffy towels and scented soap. He gave her one of his shirts to sleep in and went to his room.

Nick showered again then went downstairs to the kitchen and fixed another cup of hot broth. He heard the shower running upstairs. He sat in his room and sipped the broth. Helen had been lucky tonight. Things could have gone terribly wrong. He got into bed and turned off the light on the nightstand. Sleep came easy to him. It always had; he was lucky.

He awoke much later. Helen's outline was in the doorway. He sat up. "What's wrong?"

She wore just his shirt. "I feel terrible," she said, and sat down in the armchair in the moonlight, her knees together. She wiped her eyes.

"Are you hungry?" he asked.

She nodded.

Nick slipped into a pair of khaki shorts and canvas loafers he picked up from the floor. From the closet he handed her a cardigan that reached to her knees. "You look cold."

Downstairs he switched on a kitchen lamp and took some eggs and butter from the refrigerator. He placed two slices of French *boule* in the toaster.

Helen picked at the scrambled eggs. "Of all people—I bring my crappy life to you." Tears fell to her eggs.

"Helen, I'm no saint."

"Yes, you are."

He knew the subject had to be changed. "You'll see things differently in the morning." He poured a brandy and set it on the table for her.

She cleared her throat. "A package came from Judge Marshall. It's on my desk."

"We'll go over it later. Why don't you take tomorrow off?"

"I'd rather keep busy," she said, and returned to her room with the brandy.

The next morning Nick was up early. He had coffee, read his e-mails, and went for a morning run. The sun was just above the lake. Noisy blue jays were in the trees, but he couldn't see them. He returned from his run in forty minutes, showered, and dressed for the office. He stopped at Helen's room and looked in. She was asleep. The empty brandy glass was on the nightstand.

He backed the Lincoln out of the garage and down the drive. The sun glistened on the wet grass. Spring was turning to summer.

Joseph was soon a journeyman carpenter. He liked the work, the satisfaction of creating something from wood, although his impatience and bursts of temper still caused him to repair many projects. The lesson of a cool head seemed impossible to learn.

Money was easy to save when there was plenty of it, but it gathered without method. A paycheck in July might go uncashed for weeks, but once it was cashed, it dwindled away. In the lean months of winter, they lived from Cheryl's pantry. The discipline of Arthur Reichmann was the mirror of failure to Joseph. Each man despised the other.

In the snow and cold of February, a second daughter was born, Cheryl-Ann. She was more olive than fair, a reminder of Joseph's Jewish blood.

In the spring Cheryl didn't plant her garden. Joseph didn't want Reichmann there with his hand tractor, his smirk, that distant grin. He would build a garage to double as a workshop to build fine cabinets for extra money—in place of the garden. He used the money Cheryl had set aside for the coming winter to buy material to build the garage.

He laid the forms, poured the concrete floor, and wrote the date in the concrete. He later found his two-inch chisel, half buried in the hardened concrete, and used his hammer to loosen it. The handle to the chisel split in two and left a hole in the concrete, which angered him, so he whacked it again, and now the hole was even larger. Kneeling in front of the hole, with the hammer still in his hand, he stared at the mess.

He attached struts to the framed-in walls, raised and fastened them into position, then removed the struts. He called Cheryl outside to see his progress. He smiled at the standing, upright two-by-fours. He then attached tongue-and-groove siding to the walls. Insulation was needed if the space was to serve as a workshop during the winter months, but there was no money for it. He later used a wood-burning cast-iron stove to heat the workshop, but without insulation the heat quickly was lost.

His plan to work inside when construction was slow was never taken to its end. Joseph was no salesman. He relied on word of mouth to advertise his skills, but still there were no customers, and now there was no money, and the pantry was empty, and there were three children to feed. Cheryl knew better than to point out this fact. She accepted canned goods from her mother and occasionally a few dollars. Seeing his own mistakes put Joseph in a foul mood.

In the spring new construction started, which led to orders for cabinets and finished pieces for decoration. Rough construction was dependable money, but he now saw a chance to earn a name in cabinetry. The orders piled up.

Nick had no choice but to help his father in the shop, and there he often felt the brunt of his impatience and quick temper. In his heart Joseph knew the boy was too young to give a meaningful hand, but he wanted his company. Nick was there to help guide a long, clumsy piece of wood through the table saw, and as the cut inevitably went wrong, his father's shouting anger moved Nick to tears. Joseph knew it wasn't the boy's fault, and his anger was more at himself for not letting his son know it was OK. His son was too slight of frame to handle a full sheet of heavy plywood. He had not the thick power of his father but rather the grace and coordination of his mother's side. In his son's physical manner and habits, Joseph saw Arthur Reichmann.

He gave Nick the task of cleaning up in the shop. When he returned, the floor was swept clean, the sawdust in a cardboard box, and the wood scraps piled neatly near the wood-burning stove. The usable lumber had been sorted by variety: pine, birch, maple, oak, and cedar, with a label in front of each bin. Nails and wood screws were separated from each other and stored in different boxes. The hand tools were arranged according to task and hung on the wall. Joseph gave pause when he saw the shop, but he didn't mention it. He went on with his project but glanced up now and again to see how organized things were.

Nick found the package from Marshall on the corner of Helen's desk. He took it to his office along with a cup of coffee on a saucer. He read through the file and separated it into three sections on his desk then reread each section.

Upon his retirement from the bench, Judge Goodwin Marshall had been appointed to the board of directors of Motor City Brewing Company. The brewery was a local phenomenon that had achieved rapid success and was soon taken public. A Detroit financial institution with connections to a Chicago bank had been hired to conduct the initial public offering (IPO). Work on the IPO was leaked, inflating expectations. It was at this point that Jessup Carthage and Goodwin Marshall took an interest in the brewery.

They first looked into the brewery's minority hiring and found it vulnerable. They suggested to the brewery owners that a vigorous hiring plan for minorities might avoid negative publicity at a time when institutional investors were being courted. The brewery had little choice but to satisfy the reputation of Jessup Carthage. In the end minorities were 32 percent of new hires; a distributorship was marked for minority ownership; Goodwin Marshall was selected for a seat on the board of directors; and a number of nonemployee stock options went to the Chicago Christian Leadership Conference.

As its success grew, the Detroit brewery drew the attention of a large European brewery. The favorable negotiations of a merger had the potential to greatly increase stock value. Although Marshall refrained from trading any stock, the CCLC traded on margin before the announcement of the deal, and their holdings tripled. As the alleged source of the insider information to the CCLC, Marshall was seen as compliant, and now he was at risk of being found guilty of insider trading.

No charges had been filed, nor a grand jury convened, but Nick thought it was just a matter of time. Helen had attached footnotes to several pages, often with references to Jessup Carthage. Nick was convinced the two of them had made money from this. Over time the once-noble civil-rights movement had become an enticement for corruption, an industry unto itself, replete with greed at the sacrifice of the innocent. Marshall was right to feel concerned.

Closer to noon Helen arrived. Nick heard her in the kitchenette. A moment later she entered his office and sat down. She set her cup and saucer on the edge of the desk. She wore different clothes; she'd been to her apartment.

"Thanks," he said. "It's well organized...the footnotes, the references. It helps."

"I feel terrible," she said. "Last night...the whole thing."

"Tomorrow it will look smaller," he said, "and the day after. I've done things that have haunted me for months, if not years. It'll go away. Besides, you didn't do anything. You were in the wrong place at the wrong time."

Helen picked her coffee up by the saucer. "Are you taking the case?"

"It's not my area. It'll require research, a lot of study, a meticulous approach."

"Meticulous." She smiled. "For you that's like getting out of bed in the morning."

"It's in my genes," Nick said with a smile, "but then again everything is."

⇥ ⇤

He asked Helen to schedule a meeting with Marshall, but then he changed his mind. He would do it himself. He wanted Helen to look into the finances of Jessup Carthage and the CCLC.

Helen first created an outline, a method to gather financial information. This required patience. There was no reason to believe his finances weren't disguised. She started with the CCLC.

She heard Nick's cell phone ring, and she heard him answer it. He spoke for a minute or so then stepped around the corner and said he was leaving for the afternoon. At the office door, Nick said he wasn't sure when he'd return. From the window Helen watched him cross the parking lot below. The woman with silver hair was waiting for him in a black Jaguar. He got in on the passenger's side, and they drove off.

Helen put her curiosity aside and returned to her project. She learned that the Chicago Christian Leadership Conference, having met the IRS guidelines, had been granted tax-exempt status as a church. Jessup Carthage was the sole trustee. The ministry consisted of Jessup Carthage, his daughter, state senator Monica Carthage, and Reverend Dillon Hightower. The house where Jessup Carthage lived and the house in which his daughter lived were owned by the CCLC and leased to them, as were the vehicles they drove. She also found that Carthage had a life-insurance policy overfunded by a million dollars; he used it as a personal loan instrument.

The phone on Helen's desk rang. It was Nick. He asked if she would go ahead and call Judge Marshall to arrange a meeting. "I

49

thought I'd get to it, but I can't," he said, then gave her the judge's private number.

Helen wrote the number on a yellow pad. She thought for a moment then dialed the number. Judge Marshall answered on the first ring. His voice was soft and pleasant. His manner surprised her; she had formed an image of a grumpy, angry old man, but his pleasantries dispelled it.

"Judge Marshall, this is Helen Wincraft, Mr. Winterstein's paralegal. He'd like to arrange a meeting."

"Did he have a time in mind?"

"Whatever is good for you, Your Honor. He's at your disposal."

J oseph swept the autumn leaves into a pile with a rake, but the pile was too large, and the wind easily scattered them. His son worked alongside him, but he made smaller piles that were more difficult for the wind to scatter, and then he scooped them into a burlap bag, which was emptied in the garden area and the leaves burned. Joseph noticed the methodical manner in which his son worked, and it irritated him. It was too much like Arthur Reichmann.

A gust of wind swirled along the ground and scattered the pile over a large area. Joseph cursed and threw his rake at the blowing leaves as though it would stop them. Nick was quiet and kept his head down. His father was in a mood.

At the roadside in front of the house, there was a small pile of junk, as there was in front of the houses of the Burkowskis, Steinbergs, and Battelinies. A slightly stooped Negro with graying hair and beard walked alongside a cart drawn by a donkey. He picked through the junk piles. His movements were slow and arthritic. He withdrew a piece of metal from the bottom of a pile and looked closely at it. Nick watched him. "That *nigger* found something," the boy said. To

Joseph's ear, the sound of *nigger* was like *kike*. He swung the rake at his son. The long, flexible claws struck him on the elbow. Nick grabbed his arm; blood seeped between his fingers and ran down his forearm. Joseph saw what he had done to his son and turned pale. Without a word he knelt in front of Nick and held him in his arms. Over his father's shoulder, Nick saw his mother at the screen door, her hand over her mouth.

Cheryl arrived with a towel. She wrapped it around Nick's elbow and took him inside. No one spoke a word.

Joseph retreated to the garage to hide his shame in work. He stood for a moment and stared out the open garage door. He struck a match to light a cigarette then dropped the match to the sawdust-covered floor. At the stove he poured a cup of cold coffee. In back of him the match smoldered then went out. A tiny ribbon of smoke trailed up.

He spilled coffee from his cup and splashed it onto the front of a lined notepad that lay on a bench Nick often used. There was writing on the first page of the notepad. He wiped the pad clean on the leg of his trousers and read from the page: "Dad has his own rules. I think he makes them up as he goes. So does Grandpa."

The black Jaguar turned north on Grosse Pointe's Jefferson Avenue then onto Lake Shore Drive. They stopped to pick up Nick's golf clubs then continued north to the clubhouse. A golf cart was delivered to the Jaguar; an attendant loaded the clubs onto the cart; and the valet parked the car. In the locker room, Nick changed into khaki shorts and golf shoes; Sandy emerged in white shorts and a pink top. Her green eyes smiled at him.

After they drove the cart to the first tee, Sandy stepped off and withdrew her driver from the golf bag.

"Let's make this interesting," she said. He watched her bend over to tee the ball up. "What are you grinning at?" she said, straightening up.

He continued to grin. "Oh, nothing."

"I see that look."

She drove the ball down the middle of the fairway and looked back at him. "How do you like them apples?"

Nick's drive hooked to the right and went into the rough. By the time he was on the fairway, he was already a stroke behind. Sandy's second shot was excellent. Three strokes later they were on the green and tied. They were each facing a long putt. "Tell you what…" she said. "I bet you a sexual favor you don't make it."

It took him three putts to make it. She wet her finger and made a mark in the air. "That's one for me." She grinned. By the end of the fifth hole, Nick was three favors behind. "You're going to be a busy boy," she said.

At the end of nine holes, the score remained the same. He put his arm around her and kissed the top of her head. "I've never been able to beat you."

"You try too hard," she said. "If you ever relaxed, I'd never win."

In his heart Nick knew Sandy was the better golfer—but her words were pleasant to hear.

They both agreed nine holes were enough. The sun was at a lower angle, and the light through the trees was soft. Nick drove the cart along the path toward the clubhouse.

"Look," she said, pointing to a tree they were passing. "On the lower branch. What kind of bird is that?"

Nick slowed down as he looked toward the tree. "American goldfinch," he said. "Pretty, aren't they?"

She looked at Nick. "Take me to dinner," she said. "Someplace different."

"What do you have in mind?"

"Downtown Detroit."

He looked at her as they followed the curve along the cart path. "Are you serious? It'll be dark soon."

"Down by the river." She looped her arm through his and rested her head on his shoulder. "It'll be safe."

"Not always."

They stopped at Nick's to shower and change clothes for dinner. Sandy wrapped a towel around her hair to keep it dry in the walk-in shower. The towel pulled at the corners of her eyes and changed her appearance. The water came from several directions and covered them both. Nick watched it bead and run down her body. From the closet Sandy chose a black skirt, a red top, and a black necklace Nick had gotten her in New Orleans. She brushed her hair in front of the mirror and reapplied her lipstick. Nick was uneasy with the thought of Detroit after dark during the summer months.

They arrived at the Renaissance Center at dusk and parked indoors. There were few cars in the garage. The sensor light on the overhead surveillance camera was out. It seemed none of them were working. They walked to the elevator and rode up to the restaurant. Sandy held Nick by the arm. He looked at her; she seemed happy.

They were seated without a reservation and with a view of the river. The orange glow of the sky reflected on the water, and the moon was visible. Their waiter arrived, and Nick ordered a bottle of Riesling.

"Look how pretty it is," Sandy said, looking toward the river. "It's a shame what's happened to this town."

"Not far from here, Henry Ford tested his first car."

"It didn't look much like a car."

"No, it didn't—the Quadricycle."

"Why do you stay here?" she asked. "Why keep an office in the city?"

"It's hard to leave," he said. "It's like the house one grows up in. As you age there's a need to revisit it, to look at it. It helps define you."

"You could have an office in Grosse Pointe or Birmingham. Someplace safe."

"I'm a risk taker, Sandy, and people don't change. They get older, but they don't change."

They ordered *à la carte*, and their salads came first, followed by the lobster. Nick refilled the wineglasses.

"How's your new secretary working out?" She raised the wineglass to her lips.

"She's really not a secretary. She's a paralegal, and she's working out fine."

"What's her name?"

"Helen."

"Is she pretty?"

"Yes," he said. "I've come to depend on her. She's meticulous and thorough."

"What's her last name?"

"Wincraft," he said.

"Helen Wincraft," she repeated. "I've heard that name before. I know I have."

Nick looked to change the subject. He didn't wish to defend Helen's past against loose judgment. "Here, try this." He dipped a piece of lobster in the butter and held it out on his fork.

"Oh, thank you." She opened her mouth. Her smile was for the pleasure of the lobster. "Nothing else tastes so wonderful," she said. She patted her lips with her napkin. "Have you ever seen freshwater lobster? My God, they're ugly. Like something from science fiction."

Nick refilled their wineglasses and set the empty bottle aside. Sandy didn't want to order dessert.

"What a wonderful meal," she said. "It's been such a nice day."

Once they had finished dinner, Nick paid the check in cash. He avoided using credit cards. He didn't like the card to actually leave his sight. He had been burned once before; the account number had been copied and reused.

"I've heard that name before," Sandy said as they rode the elevator down. "Helen Wincraft. I think it was on the news. I'm sure it was."

The parking garage was strangely quiet. Nick removed the keys from his pocket and activated the remote. The car lights flashed twice, and the doors unlocked.

A few feet from the car, a man stepped out from behind a pillar with a gun. He wore a hoodie over his head. He held the pistol straight out, turned sideways in his hand. He demanded the keys. Nick hesitated.

"Now, muthafucka!"

Nick held out the keys. The man reached forward. Nick had a mere second to make a decision. With the keys in his left hand, the man reached across his body to open the car door. As he slipped between the door and the car frame, Nick kicked the door closed with his right foot. It caught the man's head. Nick grabbed the door handle and slammed the man's head into the door again and again. The gun dropped to the concrete, and the man's knees buckled. Nick pulled him out by the collar and dropped him to the concrete. He picked up the gun, looked down at the half-conscious man, and kicked him in the groin repeatedly.

"Nicky, stop!" Sandy screamed.

He saw the fear in her eyes.

"Get in," he said. "Quick."

He started the car and drove toward the exit. He slipped the gun into the glove compartment. The exit gate was up, and the ticket booth was empty. He pulled onto the street. In the rearview mirror, the entrance to the parking garage receded in the distance.

He glanced at Sandy. "Are you OK?"

She nodded.

He drove to his office parking lot and parked alongside the Lincoln. He took Sandy by the hand. "Follow me back to my place, OK? Keep my car in sight."

She nodded. "I'm OK."

He removed the gun from the glove box and kissed her on the forehead. "I'll drive the Lincoln back. Are you sure you're OK?"

"It's just sinking in," she said. "What happened—what could've happened."

He squeezed her hand. "Do you want me to drive?"

"No, I'm fine—really I am."

On the way back along Lake Shore Drive, Nick glanced often in the mirror. Sandy was close behind. As he pulled into his driveway, he activated the remote, and the garage doors opened. Sandy pulled into the third bay.

In the house he poured two glasses of brandy and opened the front windows in the living room to let in a breeze.

"What surprised me the most," she said, sitting on the sofa, "was your temper. I've never seen that before."

"Temper?" He gave a nervous laugh. "I don't have a temper, Sandy. I really don't."

"That's not what I saw."

Snow blew across the empty garden as Cheryl peered out the kitchen window. Although the garden hadn't been planted for two years, corn stubble protruded above the snow. Joseph wouldn't allow her father to plow the ground, and he never found time to do it himself. The holidays had been meager and cold. Had it not been for the canned goods from her mother and a fresh chicken, there wouldn't have been a Christmas dinner. The winter months always had been fun for Cheryl as a child. She and her brother had matching snowsuits with rubber boots and warm mittens. The house was always warm inside. The oil stove never went out, and there was hot chocolate when she came in from the snow.

The summer Cheryl had turned ten, her father surprised her and her brother with matching bicycles. They were Schwinns, a boy's model and a girl's model, red and chrome. Her father managed money and property very well, while the human heart was invisible to him. He provided for his family as a banker managed his accounts.

Cheryl stirred the pot of beans flavored with bacon fat, onions, and brown sugar. Steam rose from the simmering pot and painted the kitchen window. Her husband was in the shop. He had a project that promised money in a few weeks. Nick was on holiday break from school and helped his father in the shop. She peeled an onion, sliced it, and placed it in the frying pan with bacon fat. She then sprinkled salt on the frying onion, and when the slices were slightly brown, she placed them between slices of fresh bread, cut the sandwiches in half, and placed them on a plate. She then wrapped herself in a cotton shawl that belonged to her mother, and took the sandwiches out to the shop.

Snowflakes blew past her as she stepped through the shop's door and closed it behind her. The custom-made desk her husband was building had taken shape. He was sanding the sides leading up to the desktop. Nick was writing in his notepad, seated near the wood stove. The coffeepot was set at the edge of the stove to keep it warm. Everything in Nick's vicinity was neat and orderly.

Her husband blew sawdust from the desktop, wiped it with his hand, and resumed sanding. The desk was quite handsome, with straight lines and intricate molding. Cheryl felt pride in his crafts-manship—so long as he didn't destroy it through his temper before it was finished.

As she returned to the house, she stopped a moment in the cold and looked at her garden, which was covered in winter. She promised herself that she would see it planted in the spring, even if she had to dig the ground with a shovel.

By early spring there was more money. The cabinetry business had increased through word of mouth. Cheryl set a few dollars aside for the planting of her garden, and with less pressure to find work, her husband's mood was much better. He agreed to allow Arthur Reichmann to cultivate the ground for planting. With paper and pen-cil, Cheryl figured the amount of land allotted to each vegetable, the amount of produce to be canned, and the portion to be sold. This year she would allot more ground for melons and corn. The return was much better than for root vegetables.

Her husband and son returned early on a Sunday evening to find Arthur Reichmann still there with his hand tractor. The ground had been cultivated in straight lines with white twine staked into sections to mark each plot's use. Nick exclaimed how great it looked, so geometric and perfect.

Joseph looked at Arthur Reichmann without a word

Nick met Goodwin Marshall at a café in Grosse Pointe. Nick suggested they sit at an outside table, but Marshall insisted on the air conditioning inside. At a table in the center of the room sat a man in the attire of the Nation of Islam. He looked up at Marshall. The two men stared at each other for a moment; then Marshall said he'd changed his mind and wanted to sit outside, if Nick didn't mind.

Seated outside, Marshall glanced down the street, then at his watch. He expressed impatience for the waitress to arrive. Nick asked whether he knew the man inside, and Marshall said no.

Nick could see he was lying.

Marshall asked whether Nick had reviewed the package he sent to his office. He still avoided eye contact.

"It doesn't look good," Nick said. "Did you pass information to Carthage?"

Marshall didn't answer.

"You're both in deep," Nick said, "even if you didn't trade anything yourself. How much did Carthage trade?"

"Several million dollars. Maybe more."

"Maybe? What did you get out of it?"

Marshall looked away.

"The feds will look into everything you've ever touched, Judge. Everything."

Marshall looked at him.

"Once this is public," Nick added, "it gains a life of its own. It's like a sex-abuse case; *everyone* claims to be a victim."

"How do we defend against it," Marshall said, "if there's an indictment?"

"There will be," Nick said. "It's too juicy for them to let go. But remember, above all else don't answer questions or discuss it with anyone." Nick watched him to see whether the situation was sinking in. "Judge, please—look at me. Say nothing. To anyone."

Marshall's cell phone rang, and he looked down to see the number. "Excuse me a minute," he said, getting up from the table. He walked a few yards away to answer it. He kept his back toward Nick as he spoke.

The waitress asked Nick whether he would care for more coffee. He said yes, just a half cup. A moment later she returned with a fresh cup and asked if there was anything else. He said no, and she left the check on the table. Marshall was still on the phone. Nick wondered how much Carthage actually had made on the trades and how much had come back to Marshall. Nick didn't think he'd find out until the SEC came up with an actual number. He knew Marshall wouldn't divulge it.

Marshall returned to the table. "I have a favor to ask," he said.

Nick waited.

"You know Monica Carthage, the state senator?"

"Jessup's daughter?"

"Yes. Her son is in jail. He was picked up for possession of marijuana. She can't pick him up at the precinct. Jessup asked if you would do it."

"That's who you were talking to—Jessup?"

"Yes. His name is Michael. Michael Carthage. He's at the Macomb Street station."

The meeting with Marshall wasn't going well. Marshall seemed too distracted to focus on much of anything, so Nick agreed to help. He'd send the bill to Jessup Carthage.

He shook Marshall's hand and said again, "Remember, Judge, don't talk to anyone, *please.*" Marshall knew the law well enough not to convict himself by talking about the case to the wrong people, but there was something Marshall wasn't sharing, something he was holding back. Nick watched him walk toward his car. There was a quality or sense of tragedy that opened his heart to him. Marshall got into his Escalade and made a U-turn on Kercheval to head back to Detroit.

━◄╂ ╂►━

Walking to his car, Nick remembered having seen Michael Carthage on the news a few times. He once had been taken into custody in connection with what had been termed an incident of "youth violence" in which a prostitute had been murdered. He'd been fifteen at the time, and because of his age, little information was made public. But in time, as the story surfaced, it came to seem that he had been robbing prostitutes, and this particular one had resisted. The incident somehow was placed on the consent calendar in the juvenile system and eventually disappeared.

A few years later, Nick saw young Carthage on the news again. He spoke of the New Black Panthers of Detroit and his support for them. He rambled on about Huey Newton and Bobby Seale. His knowledge of Huey Newton had come from the lyrics of Tupac Shakur and from a family rumor that his biological father somehow was related to Huey Newton, if not his actual son. Michael's message was one in which drugs were seen as a financial means to a political end. The philosophy of Huey Newton was evident. Michael referred to himself as a revolutionary; he liked the sound of it. He used the phrase many times after that, as though it were a toy, an action figure, to wave about and play with. He rejected the political methods of his maternal grandfather as being "too white" and was drawn to the romance of his father's violent end. His father had been shot execution style in a downtown nightclub in what was thought to be a drug deal gone wrong.

At the Macomb Street station, Nick parked in a no-parking zone and went inside. He explained who he was and asked to see Michael Carthage. Again there wasn't any paper work, and the officer was unsure where they had put young Carthage. It seemed odd that he had been arrested for marijuana and, given his family name, that he even had been arrested at all—but then Nick realized that Carthage had not actually been arrested, as Helen had not been "arrested."

Someone finally produced Michael. At first sight Nick was surprised. He was younger looking than he had expected, maybe twenty, with a hidden arrogance and a disarming smile. The officer next to young Carthage told him something and pointed out Nick across the room.

Carthage came forward to shake Nick's hand. There were many faces behind the smile. "Mr. Winterstein," Carthage said, hand extended. "My mother send you?" Aside from the smile, there was the image of Jessup Carthage as a much younger man. But the smile and the boyish appeal were Huey Newton, as though he'd just stepped from a news clip in black and white. It was uncanny.

"Your grandfather sent me," Nick said. "He sent word through Judge Marshall."

Nick was given a form to sign. He said nothing, signed an illegible name at the bottom of the form, and left with Carthage through the front door.

"You work for my mother?" Carthage asked. There was a maturity that seemed beyond his years, yet something was out of place, like a

collage of blue with a smudge of red in the background. At first you
don't see it, and then you do—your eye is drawn it.

"No. As I said, your grandfather asked me to help."

"So you work for him?"

"No—do you have a car someplace?"

Carthage gave an address on Hurlbut near Jefferson. "I keep my
ride hidden." He laughed. "You never know who's lookin' to find you."

"Is that a problem?" Nick asked.

"Not if they don't find you." His head slightly cocked, he looked
at Nick. "So you a lawyer? You supposed to hold my hand?" He
laughed.

"No." Nick glanced at Carthage. "I drop you off, and that's the
end of it." Nick unlocked the car with the remote, and they got in.

"Glad to be out of there," Carthage said. "Know what I mean?" He
ran his hand along the top of the dash. "Nice ride," he said, as his hand
continued along the dash, then down and over the glove-box door. He
pushed the latch with his thumb, and the door popped opened.

"What's this?" He removed the pistol.

"Put it back."

Carthage hesitated, and Nick grabbed it from his hand. He
pushed the gun back into the glove box and closed the door hard.

"Don't be disrespectin' me like that, man. You don't do that
shit."

Nick said nothing, put the car in gear, and drove forward.

Hurlbut was a one-way street, and Nick approached from the west.
He pulled up in front of a three-story house with empty lots on either
side. The upper floors were boarded up, and the siding had been
charred from a fire. Two cars were out front: a white Dodge SUV and
a Buick.

"Is this it?" Nick asked, and stopped the car.

Carthage got out and slammed the door closed with his foot. "You
got you an attitude, Mr. Lawyer." The smile was gone. "I don't forget
that shit. Maybe you wanna say how sorry you are?"

Nick put the car in gear and drove off. He looked up in the rear-view mirror to watch Carthage. Despite the smile and the charm, the young man was capable of cold violence. Nick could feel it.

When Nick arrived back at the office, the incident with Carthage was still in his mind like an insult, a slap in the face. Helen was at her desk. There was a search screen on her computer and a page of notes on a yellow pad in front of her. Nick passed her without saying a word. In the beginning she'd worried that such behavior was because of her, but in time she had learned to read him better. There was no need to feel paranoid. There always followed a reassurance of her importance to him: an offer to pour her coffee or an invitation to lunch to discuss a legal or personal matter.

She heard the faint sound of music coming from his office. It was Johnny Mathis. Was he thinking of his friend, Sandy? Perhaps they'd had a fight. Helen had grown curious about her. She had researched the name "Sandy Wellington" on Zabasearch.com, Classmates.com, and Google.

From Zabasearch she found that Sandy Wellington lived in Birmingham and that she and Nick were the same age. She had attended Seaholm High School, and her maiden name was "Vermeer." She had once been married to Edward Wellington of Wellington Manufacturing and had two children, one of whom—her son, Edward Jr.—lived in Ann Arbor; the daughter lived with her and was on probation for repeated shoplifting.

It appeared that Sandy had filed for divorce only months before her husband's sudden death. The cause of death was listed as heart failure. Her brother-in-law had then contested control of the business. The dispute lasted several years, and in the end, Harry Wellington took control of the business with full support of Edward Wellington Jr. A local newspaper suggested the court battle had caused irreparable damage between mother and son. When asked outside the courthouse whether she was still on speaking terms with her son, Sandy had replied, "No comment."

The phone rang, and Helen looked to see which line it was. She answered, "Winterstein and Associates."

The voice on the other end sounded familiar. She looked at the number on caller ID, which showed an area code in Maryland.

The woman on the other end asked to speak to Nicholas Winterstein.

"May I ask who's calling?" Helen said. She listened in utter surprise. "Yes," she answered. "Please hold."

Helen stepped around the corner to Nick's office. "You have a phone call," she said. "Line two."

"Who is it?"

"She said she's your daughter."

B y midsummer there was enough money to save, but Joseph didn't think in terms of saving money. He thought of ways to spend it. He was busy ten hours a day and a few hours each evening in the shop, while Cheryl received a hundred new canning jars from her mother for a total of nearly two hundred. With a hammer and crowbar, she removed one side of the storage pantry in the utility room and convinced Joseph to increase the number of shelves to twice its size. The extra produce she would again sell, but this time she had arranged to sell it to a small neighborhood grocery store owned by a Lebanese immigrant. Joseph agreed it was a good idea, but he wasn't listening. The bleakness of winter was the farthest thing from his mind. At the Gratiot Airport, there was an airplane for sale, an Aeronca Champ.

Aeronca aircraft first had been built before the war, and Joseph had flown one in Hawaii. He didn't discuss with Cheryl his intentions of buying it. Used aircraft only seemed to appreciate in value, and this became his savings plan. But once he had purchased the airplane, Cheryl pointed out the cost of maintaining it. This wasn't like a car, which he so often drove without oil until the engine seized up. This was an airplane.

In the end she resigned herself to the fact that her husband would do as he pleased. He wouldn't listen to reason, certainly not from her, so she let it go and looked for additional ways to save for the coming winter. But their disagreement over the airplane reappeared. Joseph insisted that Nick learn to fly. Cheryl turned pale at the thought of her son flying in that airplane. But again her husband turned his back on her argument and did as he pleased.

The Aeronca Champ had two seats with dual controls. Nick fell in love with it. The first time he flew with his father, he stuck his hand out the window. The air blew so hard it pushed his arm back.

Learning to fly came easily to Nick. At twelve years old, he knew no fear, only excitement. He first learned to take off and to do a power-off stall, then how to fly the pattern and how to land. Flying was no harder than riding a bike. He read *The Pilot Operating Handbook* from cover to cover, and everything he read stuck like a photograph. Whenever he and his father arrived at the airport, Nick was always the first to check the oil and perform the preflight inspection.

His father taxied down the grass runway, turned into position, and pushed the throttle to full power. The airplane started down the runway, gathering speed, then lifted off the ground. Gaining altitude, they banked left then flew west for two miles, over the house on Frazho Road. Nick saw his mother's garden below. The corn was tall and green, and the red tomatoes were visible on dark vines.

On their return to the airport, the door on the pilot side started to vibrate and came loose at the hinge. His father seemed unconcerned and held the door closed with his hand. On the ground they found a stress fracture along the hinge. The pin was gone. His father threaded a piece of wire through the hinge to hold the door in place and left it at that.

Later in the day, Nick rode to the airport on his bike with a notepad and a pencil. He pressed a piece of paper to the hinge and traced around it, then made marks where the screws went. On his way back, he stopped at his grandparents' place. His grandmother was in the kitchen, rolling dough out on the kitchen table. Nick asked where Grandpa was, and she said he was out back, maybe in the workshop.

Nick rode his bike along the concrete walk to the last building at the end. His grandfather was in the shop; he didn't hear Nick approach. Nick watched him insert quarters through a small opening on the top of a five-gallon drum. From the sound of the quarters as they dropped, the drum seemed to be nearly full of coins.

Nick showed the drawing of the hinge to his grandfather and asked whether he could make one like it. His grandfather studied it for a moment then took a glass jar full of hinges from a shelf. He placed a hinge over the drawing then used the electric grinder to match the hinge to the size of the drawing. He drilled new holes and filed the edges smooth.

Nick returned to the airport and removed the broken hinge with a screwdriver then replaced it with the new hinge. The next day he painted the new hinge with model-airplane paint to match the color of the door. He was eager for his father to see the repair, but when Joseph saw the new hinge, he knew it was the work of Arthur Reichmann. He didn't speak to his son for days—not until Nick went to him in tears and begged his forgiveness.

It was Nick's first understanding of how deeply the two men hated each other.

Nick was surprised, yet he wasn't. He had known there was a child somewhere, but until now he could only guess the gender. A daughter. He was both pleased and afraid to pick up the phone. Helen watched him. The moment seemed to last an hour.

"Hello…"

The voice he heard was rich and had a pleasant sound. "Nicholas Winterstein?" she asked.

"Yes."

"My name is Nicole. Do you remember Janice Dean?"

"Yes, I knew her in law school."

"She was my mother. I have reason to believe you are my father."

"You said *was* your mother."

"She passed away."

Nick tried to think of her, but the only image he had was a nineteen-year-old girl with dark hair and a tender way. He remembered the look on her face when he had denied the child was his. It was a moment that never could be undone.

"I'd like to meet you," she said. "Is that possible?"

"Yes, Nicole. It certainly is." He felt an instant need to somehow protect her, which seemed odd since he didn't know her or anything about her. Yet an ethereal connection had formed even before this phone call.

"Are you in the Detroit area?" he asked.

"No, I'm in Maryland, outside Baltimore."

"I could be there—"

"No," she said. "I'll come to Detroit. I'll drive."

"Are you sure? I have an airplane."

"Thank you," she said. "But I'll leave tomorrow. I'll call you when I arrive."

Nick agreed, while at the same time feeling at a loss for words. As he hung up the phone, he felt something had changed in his life, while something else was still missing. He looked up at Helen. She seemed at a loss.

He turned in his chair and stared out at the river. Returning to work—to his thoughts before the phone call—seemed impossible. Nicole's voice was so rich, so pleasant to the ear. How had she gotten her name? Who had named her? Was she named after him? It was such a selfish thought that he pushed it from his mind. He saw Janice in memory, the look on her face when he'd said, "Maybe it belongs to the math guy." He squirmed with shame.

He turned back to his desk. He rearranged a few papers, placed a manila folder in the front drawer, then stared into space. He knew virtually nothing about Janice. He had the memory of a face from more than forty years ago and nothing else. He looked up to see Helen still in the doorway. He shook his head as if to admit the moment had overwhelmed him.

"Go home," she said. "Go for a run. I'll clean up around here."

He nodded, staring at her with nothing to say. He pulled open his desk drawer and took out the pistol he'd taken from the would-be carjacker. He gave it to her.

"It can't be traced," he said. "Nine millimeter. It replaces the other one."

He spent the remainder of the day at home, trying to keep busy. He went for another run and cleaned up around the house, but he always kept things in such a neat, orderly fashion that there was little to do.

The next morning he called Helen and said he was taking the day off. There was an understanding tone to her voice. He then called Sandy and asked whether she'd like to meet him for lunch.

"What a wonderful idea," she said, "and a bit of a surprise."

He agreed to meet her at a café in Birmingham. During the drive from Grosse Pointe, he worried where Nicole might spend the night— certainly not Detroit. If she left early in the morning, she might arrive in the late afternoon.

Nick was at the café before Sandy arrived and sat at an outside table beneath an umbrella. Cars were parked diagonally to the curb. The shops and specialty boutiques were busy with shoppers, some stopping in front of the display windows, while others strolled along the sidewalks. Across the street Starbucks appeared busy. Folks were lined up inside.

A young waitress stopped at Nick's table and asked whether he wished to order anything. "Yes," he said. "White wine." As she left to fill his order, he wondered what Nicole did for a living. He felt the need to tell Sandy about her, to relieve the pressure of the coming evening, but he knew in his heart that he wouldn't mention Nicole. He saw Sandy from a distance as she stepped from her car. Her silver hair stood out. He watched her approach the table; he found her deeply attractive and very sexual.

She reached out to cover his hand with hers as she sat down. "I can spot you a mile away," she said. "That smile—the silver hair." She ordered a glass of wine then turned to him again. "So how are you, handsome?"

Suddenly Nick had nothing to say and wondered whether it had been a mistake to ask her to lunch.

"Thank your lucky stars," she said, "that you don't have children. Young Edward is threatening to take me to court again. Something to do with proxy votes. You should represent me, Nicky—you really should. But I know how you feel about that."

This wasn't what Nick wanted to hear. He had hoped for something light and flirty—not the problems of parenthood.

"His sister isn't much better," Sandy said. "Why can't they wait 'til I'm dead and gone then do whatever they want? I'm really sick of it. I am." She sipped her wine. "How about a few holes of golf?"

This was unexpected. He looked for a way out. "I can't," he said. "The Marshall case. I have a meeting."

"How's that going? The Marshall case."

"Not good. I have a meeting with the SEC." That part was true, and if he could link it to the lie he'd just told, he might not trip himself up down the road. "It seems Carthage got greedy, and it's going to take Marshall down too."

"Jessup Carthage," she said. "I can't stand the sight of him. I hope he goes to jail."

"He might. But there's a strong political shield around him. The media has his back."

"The media! They're no better."

"We know that, but they make the rules."

"Rules." She reached for her wineglass. "Don't you ever get tired of that crap? The rule makers deciding how *we* should live?"

"Rules change with the culture, like the clothes we wear. What's taboo today is protected tomorrow."

With the wineglass to her lips, Sandy seemed to suddenly notice something on the sidewalk. "Did you *see* that?"

"See what?"

"My daughter," she said. "She looked straight at me and turned away! Do you think she followed me?"

"She's still living with you, isn't she?"

"Yes, it's part of her probation."

"She could be here for any number of reasons."

The waitress arrived to take their orders, and Nick was thankful. He didn't want to listen to Sandy lament her role as a mother while *he* felt so full of guilt. He looked for ways to change the subject until finally he kissed her at the end of lunch and apologized for having such a full afternoon ahead of him.

"You're leaving?" she asked.

"I must. I have an engagement this afternoon. Very important. Sorry...I really am."

He saw her disappointment. But his thoughts were of Nicole, and his chest was full of butterflies. He kissed her again and promised to call later.

On the drive back to Grosse Pointe, he tried to imagine how Nicole might look to him. The memory of her mother was barely distinguishable. The surrounding countryside sped by. Where there once had been open fields and farmland there were now strip malls, office buildings, and expressways. Whoever said change is good? They're crazy. It's full of pain.

He arrived home by midafternoon. He was at a loss as to how to occupy his time until he heard from Nicole. He poured a cup of coffee and sat in his office to listen to music. By four o'clock his cell phone rang. He looked at the area code. "Hello?"

He heard the pleasant voice. "I'm in the area and checked into a motel."

"Where are you staying?"

"An area called Troy."

"I can be there shortly."

"I'd prefer to meet in your neighborhood," she said. "I'm curious, I guess."

"Do you have a GPS?"

"Yes, a portable."

He gave her the address of a restaurant in the village on Kercheval. "See you at five."

He was more nervous than he'd ever been in a courtroom.

At the start of football season, Nick was surprised when he made the starting lineup. He was in the seventh grade and the smallest member of the team. The coach praised his speed and his running instincts. His father never missed a game. He was always on the sidelines or in the stands. The day Nick was carried from the field on a stretcher, his father looked down and squeezed his hand as he walked alongside him. Cheryl was in tears.

His left knee took many weeks to heal. He sat near the woodstove in his father's shop with his leg in a cast. He arranged a writing desk with a notepad and pen near the stove. He felt his father's pride when he looked at him. His love was more comforting than a blanket.

By spring it seemed he never had been injured. At baseball practice the other boys refused to catch the ball when Nick threw it. They complained he threw too hard. The coach gave Nick the ball and went behind the plate with the catcher's mitt. He told him to throw it straight. The way he threw the ball impressed the coach. The speed was unexpected from someone so small. He made him a starting pitcher and told him not to throw curveballs. His arm was too young, he explained, but Nick did it anyway.

Through the school season and all through the summer league, Nick was on the pitcher's mound. The curveball was his favorite toy. It was fascinating to see the batter jump out of the way only to see the ball curve over the plate. His father was always there behind the backstop. He watched every pitch, every play.

This was the time Nick also learned about golf. On a midsummer evening, he showed his father the money he had made that day. He and his cousin had carried golf clubs and gotten paid for doing it. The country club grounds were beautiful, and the people wore such nice clothes. The grass looked so smooth, with pools of white sand along the fairway and greens. One of the men showed Nick how to hit the ball then gave him a few clubs to keep. He was going to throw them away, the man said, so why not put them to use? Nick carried them home across the handlebars of his bike.

Golf was alien to his father. It was something the executives at GM and Ford did. He didn't share Nick's interest in this game played by the wealthy. Football and baseball had the potential of a scholarship. Those had worth.

The 3-wood was too long for Nick. He showed it to Grandpa Reichmann and explained the problem. His grandfather looked the club over, held it for balance, then cut two inches from the length. He rewrapped the grip with friction tape, followed by layers of gauze then another layer of friction tape.

Nick dropped a ball on the grass and hit it out past the long garden. He looked back at his grandfather with a big smile. Nick liked Grandpa Reichmann; he could do almost anything, and he was fun to be around.

Nick parked behind a blue Toyota on Kercheval. It was an older-model Corolla with Maryland plates. The car was in remarkably good shape. The paint was still clear and bright, and the tires appeared new. The inside was clean and without clutter.

Nick pulled open the restaurant door and stepped inside. A few tables in from the door, a woman, perhaps forty-years-old, with dark hair, was watching the entrance. Their eyes met. The resemblance to Cheryl Winterstein was striking; it was as if he were looking at his mother. He walked to her table. "Nicole?"

"Yes. Please sit down," she said. She wore a pink V neck with a black necklace.

For a long moment they stared at each other. She had the deep-set eyes of Winterstein and the high cheekbones of Reichmann. "Your eyes are very blue," he said.

"So are yours," she answered

"You have your grandmother's nose, her cheekbones."

"So…I guess you can't deny me."

He said nothing.

"I'm sorry," she said. "That wasn't fair."

"I don't even remember your mother's last name, Nicole. We were together only a few times."

"I understand," she said. "I have a daughter, but I never married. I have no idea where her father is."

He had a granddaughter! "What's her name?"

"Bridget. She just turned nineteen. Are you married?" she asked.

"No," he said. "No, I'm not."

"When I was a girl, I wondered about you. All I had was a name. Mom never talked about you. Not much anyway—sometimes when she was drinking. I guess she never knew much about you."

"How did you find me?"

"I searched the records at Detroit Mercy. After that it was easy."

"You said your mother passed away?"

"A drug overdose. Prescription drugs. That was over a year ago," she said. "It wasn't until then that I started looking for you. Before that it was just a daydream I'd ever see you."

"I'm glad you did."

"Did you ever think of finding me?" she asked.

"I was afraid to," he said.

"Hope I'm not too scary."

"No." He smiled. "Somehow you seem familiar."

"I feel comfortable too," she said. "Maybe it's just blood."

Nick ordered a club sandwich to split between them and two glasses of wine. For a moment they fell silent, but it wasn't awkward. He looked up to find her staring at him.

"Sorry," she said. "It's just catching up with me."

"I understand," he said. "I feel it too."

"My grandparents...I mean *your* parents—are they still alive?"

"No," he said. "They're both gone."

"What were they like?"

"Your grandfather could lose his temper at the drop of a hat. It was like waiting for a volcano to erupt, and your grandmother could do algebra in her head."

"What a combination. How'd they ever get along?"

"Tragically."

When they had finished lunch, Nick paid the check in cash. He left a ten-dollar tip beneath his wineglass. Nicole glanced at the tip then at him again.

"What do you do for a living?" Nick asked. "If you don't mind."

"No, it's a normal question," she said. "At the moment nothing. I spent two years in a community college, but I was never trained for anything. My last job was as a waitress. Fortunately I manage money well."

"Would you like to see the area? I can show you around."

"I'd like to see where you live."

"We can start there." They got up to leave. She was trim and no more than five feet tall. Another resemblance to the Reichmanns and the Wintersteins, but he knew nothing of the Deans, the in-laws he'd never known.

He suggested she leave her car in his garage. Her smile was happy, yet she wasn't telling him something. He watched her get into her car before he pulled out in front of her so she could follow him to the house.

The garage doors opened, and Nick parked in front of the first bay. He motioned her toward the end bay and met her in the breeze-way. They entered through the kitchen.

"It's big enough for a restaurant," she said. He led her through the dining room, his study, the library, and the living room. She stopped in front of each painting then looked at the furnishings, the thick Persian carpets. Then she looked at Nick and said nothing. He led her to the second-floor sitting room with its stone fireplace and through the four bedrooms, each with a separate bath.

At the end of the tour, with her hands in her back pockets, as if she were nervous, Nicole looked at him. "You have wonderful taste."

Nick was unsure what she was feeling. Maybe this was too much all at once. He knew nothing about her background. Had she grown up in poverty? Had there been a father figure, the love of grandparents? Were there happy memories? He suggested he show her where he'd grown up. It wasn't far away. It might help fill in a few blanks.

"Yes," she said. "That would be nice." Now her smile appeared sad.

They drove just three miles from Detroit to where the Gratiot Airport once had stood; it was now a strip mall. Then they went a mile west to the land Arthur Reichmann had owned. The property had been an acre wide and ten acres deep, covered with gardens and orchards. Great-aunts and great-uncles had lived just doors away, but now apartment buildings and crime covered the area.

The land and the house where Nick had grown up, however, were still there. He showed her the back, where the garden once had been. Now it was overgrown with weeds. He also showed her the garage, the doors boarded over, where his father had made handcrafted cabinets. Nicole walked to the side of the house and pulled at the oversize padlock on the door, then walked to the front of the house. Nick watched her. She read the notice taped to the front window: UNFIT FOR HUMAN HABITATION.

He realized nothing he had shown her explained much of anything. Without the memories there was nothing to see but decay.

His father was in a foul mood. He'd cut an expensive piece of wood to the wrong length. It was ruined! He hurled it across the shop, and it smashed through the window. Glass flew out the other side. Nick slipped out the side door. This was no place to be, not now.

His sister stood near the corner of the house and motioned to him. She'd heard the cursing and the sound of breaking glass. "Did he hit you?"

"No," Nick explained. "He was mad at the wood."

Kathleena held out her hand and opened it. There was a fifty-cent piece and some quarters, dimes, nickels, and pennies. They'd fallen from Dad's pocket near the bed, and she'd picked them up from the floor. The carnival was at the corner of Gratiot and Ten Mile, and she wanted to go. The carnival had gotten there yesterday, Linda had said; her mom had taken her. Nick was reluctant to go. What if his father wanted him to help again? But his sister said, "Please and double please."

He rolled his bike across the backyard to Firwood Road. His sister jumped up on the crossbar. Nick looked back at the garage as they rode away. On Ten Mile Road, they passed Brown's Dairy, and Kathleena wanted to stop for ice cream. But that would take too much of their money, Nick said. He had the coins in his pocket, and they kept riding toward Gratiot.

Once there Nick leaned his bike against a willow tree, and they walked across the empty lot to the carnival. There were few people around; almost everyone came at night. Kathleena bought a cotton candy. It was blue and sticky on her fingers. She wiped them on her dress. Nick wanted to try the shooting gallery, but he worried about how he would explain himself at home if he won anything. He got five shots for fifteen cents and missed everything. He was disappointed.

He looked around and didn't see his sister. He walked past the cart of red candy apples and saw her near the Ferris wheel. It was twenty-five cents a ride. They got in the swinging seat, and a man in bib overalls put the safety bar in place. It was a little like flying but much slower. At the top of the wheel, he saw all of Gratiot and the other side of Ten Mile toward the lake. They went around three times.

Once back on the ground, Kathleena said the man in bib overalls wanted her to go in the trailer with him, but she didn't like him. His teeth were missing, and he didn't smell good, and she was afraid he might do what Grandpa Reichmann had done. She made Nick promise to keep it a secret; she didn't want to get in trouble. Grandpa Reichmann had unbuttoned his pants, taken his thing out, and wanted her to lick it, but she was afraid to. Nick made her promise never to tell anyone. "Promise?" She nodded.

The next day Nick told his mother what Kathleena had shared with him. She covered her mouth. Oh, no, not his granddaughter too! She told Nick never to mention this to his father, ever. He agreed not to say anything as they heard a loud noise from the shop.

A piece of wood flew out the door.

They drove back to Grosse Pointe in silence. It was early evening, and the light was soft and pleasant. They drove along Gratiot Avenue, down Nine Mile, and along Lake Shore Drive. Nick worried Nicole had little money, but there was no room to ask about her finances; maybe in time he may offer help, but now wasn't the time. He glanced at her. She seemed far off in thought.

He pulled into the driveway but didn't activate the garage doors. He parked in front of the first bay. Nicole came back from her thoughts. She cleared her throat. "I'll call in the morning, OK?"

"That's fine," he said. "I'm up early."

"So am I." Her smile was sad but not uncomfortable. He opened the garage doors with the remote. She got out of the car and walked toward the end bay.

He called after her, "Nicole, if you need anything—"

"I'm fine," she said, "but thank you."

Nick watched her enter an address into the GPS and back out of the driveway.

Inside he poured a glass of wine and made a light salad. He carried his wine into the study and turned on the news. The Detroit chief of police had been asked to step down, and a new chief was to be named. He was the third chief to leave in six months. One had been caught stealing narcotics from the evidence room; another had been arrested for trying to board an airliner with a loaded weapon. And now this one had been caught in an affair with the wife of the city prosecutor. It was a carousel of fools. If you're going to live by your own set of rules, first understand how others live. Nick switched the channel.

It was after nine, and he was ready for bed. He had showered and was now sitting in the armchair in the bedroom, sipping a cup of hot broth, when his cell phone rang. It was Nicole. "Hope I didn't disturb you," she said, "but I was wondering what time I should—"

"You didn't disturb me," he said, "not at all. Why don't you bring your things with you in the morning? You can stay here. There's plenty of room."

"I'd like that," she said. The unspoken thought had been expressed; there was now an ease between them. "I'm glad you showed me where you grew up. It's a lot like my old neighborhood outside Baltimore. We didn't have much money. Mom never passed the bar exam. She tried once, but then she just stopped trying. She worked as a paralegal here and there, but she had a problem with pain pills. It got in the way. I don't think she ever forgot you."

Nick felt the shame of a youthful act.

"Bridget is a lot like her," Nicole said. "It's funny how you can be more like a grandparent than your parents." She fell silent for a moment. "Well...thank you. I'll see you in the morning."

Nicole had a quiet wisdom, an old soul in a young body. He realized she saw him more clearly than he might ever have imagined.

She arrived early the next morning. As he finished his run, he saw her car parked in front of the garage door at the end bay. She was walking the grounds. She noticed him and walked toward the garage.

Her smile was warm. She opened the trunk of her car, and there were three suitcases. "They're not all mine," she said. "One is Bridget's. I packed it for her."

"Bridget's?"

"I think she's here, in Detroit."

"Detroit?"

"I guess that will take some explaining." Nicole took one of the bags, and Nick took the other two. They went in through the breeze-way and up to the second floor.

"Which room would you like?" he asked. He was still thinking about Bridget, but he wasn't going to ask questions. Nicole wasn't a client; she was his daughter. When she was ready, when she was com-fortable, she would tell him.

"This one," she said. "I can see the lake from here."

"What would you like to do today?" he said. "It's up to you."

"I can't think of anything special."

"I have a few things to do at the office."

"May I go with you?"

"Of course."

"It might help me fill in a few more blanks," she said, "although I feel like I already know you."

On the drive into the city, he still thought about Bridget. Who was she? What did she look like? The need to protect both mother and daughter swept over him.

On her way into the office, Helen stopped at Starbucks for croissants and fresh coffee to brew. She and Nick hadn't spoken since the phone call from Nicole, but Helen knew in her heart they would arrive to-gether this morning at the office. Her thoughts went beyond curios-ity. Her loyalty and affections for Nick also reached to his daughter. She and Nicole were the same age. There was no reason for Helen to hide who she was. She remembered the richness of her voice over the phone; the tender, almost vulnerable tone. This was a soul who didn't judge.

Helen saw Nick's car pull into the parking lot down below. The car doors opened, and they got out. Helen watched on the security-camera monitor as they entered the building. A moment later the elevator doors opened on the fifth floor. The two women looked at each other through the glass door to the office. Nick pushed open the door, and Nicole stepped inside. Helen reached forward with her hand. "Hello, Nicole. I'm Helen."

"Hello, Helen. I'm glad to meet you." Nicole glanced at Nick, and Helen realized he never before had mentioned Helen's name. The moment passed, and Helen offered coffee and a croissant. Nicole offered to help.

Their eyes met, and Helen felt at ease.

Nick watched from the front yard. There were men with trucks and long boards and shovels, and they were digging trenches in the corner lot next to their house. The workers were preparing to pour a concrete foundation, his father explained, for a new house to rest on. He followed his father to the empty lot where the men were working. A man holding a thermos and a rolled-up drawing said he was the general contractor. His father asked how many square feet, and as the man answered, they walked around the perimeter of the trench. The man pointed to something with the rolled-up drawing, and his father nodded.

At dinner his mother asked what was going on next door. There was roasted chicken at the center of the table. Grandpa Reichmann had chopped its head off in the chicken yard the day before as Nick watched. His father pretended he didn't know where the chicken had come from. They would have new neighbors soon, his father said. "Klinebocker is building it, and he already has a buyer—eighteen thousand dollars."

"How much?" his mother said in disbelief. "That's a lot!"

His father took the second drumstick. Nick hated white meat, but there it was, right in front of him on his plate. His father bit into the drumstick.

A few days later, Nick stood on the side of the road with his sister, watching the men raise the frame walls to the house. His Daisy air rifle was slung over his shoulder by the strap. Kathleena asked whether any kids were going to live there, and Nick shrugged and said he didn't know. She asked whether he had shot any birds today, and he said no; shooting things made him sad.

It was the end of summer, and school would start the day after the holiday weekend, but Nick never could remember the name of the holiday. He stopped asking which holiday it was because his father got mad that he never could remember the name, no matter how many times he told him. So Nick didn't say anything and just pretended he knew.

Each year he got a few school supplies to start school: notepads and pencils, a new fountain pen, and a new coat for the coming winter. But most of his clothes came from two older cousins. His mother cut the seams with a razor and took everything in to make it fit. Grandma Reichmann made dresses for his sister. His father didn't like Grandma Reichmann either. He said she talked behind his back.

A week before the holiday with the name Nick couldn't remember, the new family moved in next door. A gray Pontiac was parked on the gravel drive, and a pickup truck made several trips to the house with furniture tied down in the back. Two men unloaded the truck and took the furniture into the house. The front door was propped open as they carried stuff inside. There were a boy and a girl who looked to be near the same age as Nick and Kathleena, and their father's name was Joseph too. He made a lot of noise and cussed a lot. "Goddamn it, the son of a bitch is in my goddamn way. Move the bastard, goddamn it—no-good, rotten bastard." But for all the noise he made, there was nothing serious about it. It wasn't like the fury Joseph Winterstein released. When that happened, you got out of the way.

The mother had dark hair and dark eyes, and she smiled a lot at Nick's dad, and when she did, he was always in a better mood. Kathleena didn't like the mother. She said her smile was like listening to someone tell a lie.

A few days after the new family moved in, the woman next door came over to visit and have coffee with Nick's mother. Her name was Melina Kopecny. They sat in the kitchen and added evaporated milk to their coffee, while Melina smoked cigarettes then crushed the butts out in the ashtray. She often looked at the side door that led out to the garage. When Joseph came in from the shop, Melina sat differently in her chair, smiled, and offered him a cigarette. Cheryl Winterstein watched as this woman struck her lighter and held it out to light her husband's cigarette.

Nick was standing at the window, talking on his cell phone, and looking toward the river. "I understand," he said, as if his nod were in agreement. "You have no choice." He looked over his shoulder as the two women entered his office. Helen carried a tray with three cups and a pot of coffee; she placed it on the corner of the desk. Nicole set a plate of croissants next to it. There was a natural ease between the two women.

Nick turned back to the phone. "If you like, I can be there," he said, "to discuss something before you answer. I can wait in the hall."

Helen seemed to know what was going on; Nicole didn't. "OK," Nick said. He folded his phone and slipped it into his pocket.

"Was that Marshall?" Helen asked.

"Yes, he's been called to testify in front of the grand jury."

"What will happen?"

"I don't know. If he's smart, he'll make a deal and give them Carthage. Either way it'll make national news."

Nick noticed the look on Nicole's face. "You've heard of Jessup Carthage?" he asked.

"Of course," she said. "Who hasn't?"

"He and Goodwin Marshall have made a living at pressuring white businesses to hire more blacks," he explained, "while ensconcing themselves in the management structure, all in the name of civil rights. Now the US Attorney's Office has them on insider trading."

"Your father's been hired by Judge Marshall," Helen said. It was the first time Nick had been referred to as Nicole's father. The words hung in the air for a moment.

"What does it all mean?" Nicole asked.

"I don't think they're after Marshall," Nick said. In his mind he still heard Helen's words: *your father.* "I think they want Carthage. He has friends in the attorney general's office, but I don't think they can help him. Or maybe I'm wrong."

Nicole set her cup and saucer on the corner of the desk. "I have something to tell you," she said to Nick. "I should have mentioned it earlier."

Helen got up. "I have something to finish in the other room."

"No," Nicole said, "please stay." She turned toward Nick. "Bridget is here in Detroit somewhere." She looked back at Helen. "Bridget is my daughter." She turned back to Nick. "I think she came looking for you. I told her about you and where I thought you were. She's never had a father figure in her life. Her grandfather died so young—she never knew him. And I never married; I'm not even sure who her father is. He's just an alcoholic memory."

"When did you last see her?" Nick asked.

"Couple of months ago. She's always had a problem with drugs. So did my mother, but Bridget was using the hard stuff, snorting it and using a needle."

Helen looked toward Nick; their eyes met.

"I don't know for certain that she's here," Nicole said. "But I feel it. I talked about you, and she knew I was looking for you." Her eyes welled up with tears. "I'm sorry. I show up out of the blue, and I bring my crappy life to your doorstep."

Helen took her hand and held her in her arms as she cried. "I'm so sorry," Nicole sobbed. Nick didn't think it was possible to feel any worse than he did at that moment. A lump had formed in his throat, and tears fell down his face. All this had been set in motion many years ago, when he had denied Nicole was his.

"We'll find her," he said. "I promise."

Later in the afternoon, near the end of the day, Nicole received a phone call on her cell. She was in the office with Helen. She wanted to help and had asked for things to do. She said she was good at math and could do almost anything with an Excel spreadsheet. Sometimes she created complex formulas with embedded graphs just for fun. Helen thought for a moment; she did have something Nicole could do. She opened Excel to accounts receivable, expenses, potential income versus actual, investments, and taxes for city, state, and federal. Within moments, as if doing algebra in her head, Nicole said she saw a pattern. "I can do something here," she said. "With a little work, we can turn this into one statement, a single equation…make it all work together."

That was when her cell phone rang. In an absent-minded manner, Nicole reached for it. "Hello?" Her eyes opened wide. "Bridget! Where are you?"

Nick appeared from his office. He and Helen watched Nicole.

"Honey, slow down. Tell me where you are." Nicole looked up with fear. "Bridget, tell me where you are." The line went silent. "Bridget!"

"What happened?" Nick said.

"She's gone. It sounded like someone took the phone from her."

Nick took the phone; the line was disconnected. "What did she say?"

"That he wouldn't let her go. She didn't use a name—just *he*. Then…I'm not sure…but it sounded like someone hit her." Worry and pain covered her face. "Call back," she said.

"Not yet. Whoever it was will know and won't answer."

"How long then?"

"An hour," Nick said. "Maybe more."

"But that could be too late!"

"I know, but we've got to be patient. We'll have a better chance. Please trust me."

Nicole nodded. "I do. I do trust you."

"What did she say exactly?"

"I couldn't understand her. She tried to hurry, but it didn't make any sense. Like she was drunk yet wasn't."

Nick returned to his office, placed the cell phone on his desk, and stared at it for a moment. He turned the news on. Nicole and Helen were still in the outer office. He stared out at the river, looked back at the phone, then turned again toward the river. The sky was overcast, with rolling gray clouds moving in from the west. Drops of rain hit the window.

An hour later he opened the cell phone and pushed "redial" on the last incoming number. Helen and Nicole stood in the doorway to his office. The phone rang seven times. A male voice answered.

"Is this Rico?" Nick said.

"Rico?" the voice said. "Who are you?"

"I'm looking to score; I heard Rico can help."

"Ain't no Rico here." In the background someone asked who was on the phone.

"It's *her* phone," the second voice said.

"I was told five grand," Nick said.

The second voice came on the phone. "Who is this?"

"A customer."

"How'd you get the number?"

"From Bridget. Look, maybe I called the wrong number."

"Maybe you didn't." There was a short silence. "Tell me again what you want."

"I was told I could score. Five grand would do it."

"Maybe...You be at Hurlbut and Kercheval," he said, "at ten o'clock."

"Look for a white Lincoln Navigator," Nick said.

"You bring five grand," the voice said, and the call disconnected. Nick closed the phone and looked at Nicole.

"I'm going to keep this," he said, slipping the phone into his pocket. "He might call back. We don't know."

Nicole nodded.

"We don't even know if Bridget is with him," Helen said, "or if he's holding her against her will."

"I know…" Nicole said. "Drugs control her. It's so painful to watch. The things she'll do…It's so hard to understand."

"You wait at the house tonight," Nick said. "Helen and I will go."

Nicole nodded again. "Call me on the landline when you know anything."

Later that night Nick picked Helen up at her apartment in St. Clair Shores. He drove the black Volkswagen. Helen was waiting outside when he arrived. She was in the headlights as he pulled up. She wore snug-fitting jeans, an old sweatshirt, and a fanny pack around her waist. He knew by the way the fanny pack was centered over her hip that there was a gun inside.

They drove south on Lake Shore Drive to East Jefferson, past the water works, and turned right on Cadillac. There was a boarded-up building at the corner of Kercheval and Hurlbut. Nick came to a stop a few hundred feet short of the intersection.

"Is that him?" Helen said. A man in a baggy shirt stood at the intersection. He looked in one direction, then the other.

"You know him, don't you?" Helen said. "I can see it in your face."

"It's Michael Carthage," he said. A dark Cadillac cruised past Carthage, but Carthage paid little attention to it. "He's looking for a white Lincoln."

B arbara Thompson had frizzy red hair and red nails. She wore her hair pinned back on one side with a rhinestone barrette, while the top was full of frizzy curls. She wore ruffled blouses that revealed her shoulders, like a gypsy. Her daughter was Nick's age; her name was Bonny, and she already played with lipstick and wore her hair frizzy on top. When she looked from one side to the other, she moved her head and shoulders at the same time so as not to mess up her hair. The only thing missing was the cigarette.

The Thompsons lived on the back side of Cheryl's garden. Their property lines touched. Although Cheryl didn't share Barbara's sense of fashion, they were good friends. They drank coffee together in Barbara's kitchen and listened to Hank Williams and Patsy Cline.

Barbara's husband, Julius, was a machinist at General Motors, and in the summer, he planted a small garden in the back to provide kitchen vegetables. Crossing Barbara's backyard, Cheryl noticed their garden was torn up. The small tomato plants had been ripped from the ground, and the furrows had been trampled and kicked into a mess. Barbara said the Lassider kid had done it. He was mean for no other reason than to be mean, just like his father, she said.

The Lassiders lived next to the Thompsons on a three-acre lot with tall maple trees and a stable out back for the horses. Old Man Lassider used to beat the horses while they were in the stall and couldn't get away. He cursed and beat them across the back with a whip, and the horses neighed and stamped and tried to break free, but they couldn't. Hearing the horses smash about inside the stable when Lassider beat them gave Nick a sick feeling.

Nick rode his bike down Firwood Road before the oil trucks sprayed oil on the gravel to keep the dust down. He rode as fast as he could then looked back to watch the dust rise up like a long plume of smoke following him. He jammed on the brakes, and the back tire skidded in a half circle, into the Thompsons' driveway. He dropped his bike on the grass and looked back. The dust still hung in the air.

He started for Barbara's back door then stopped. He heard screaming at the Lassider house next door, then a door slamming, then more screaming. The Lassider boy was in the front yard, scream-ing that he hated his father and wished him dead. His father came out the side door, dragging his wife by the hair. She was on her knees, and he hit her with his hand until blood appeared above her eye, and she was crying and sobbing. Lassider looked down at his wife and tightened his belt, as if it were a job well done. The boy was still screaming at his father that he hated him. Lassider looked at his son and laughed out loud then got in his truck.

Nick never had seen anything like this before. The woman was still on her knees, crying, with blood on her face. And the boy was crying too and throwing stones at the truck as it backed out of the drive and drove down the dusty road. He still was screaming, "I want you dead! I hate you!"

Nick and Helen watched from the car with the lights out and the engine still running. There was little traffic along the street where Michael Carthage waited. The streetlights at the corner and in front of the house were out. There was one light at the center of the block, and that was all. A woman approached Carthage; she held her arms as though she were cold. He motioned with his head over his shoulder toward the house. She went up the steps, still holding her arms, and kicked the bottom of the door. Someone opened the door, and she went inside. Carthage walked to the corner and looked in all directions, but it didn't seem as if he had noticed the black Volkswagen parked at the center of the block.

Nicole's cell phone rang, and Nick reached for it in his pocket. The caller ID read, "Unknown." He answered, "Hello?"

There was a pause then a female voice. "Who's this?"

"Nicholas Winterstein."

"Where's my mother?"

"Bridget?"

"Yes…Who's this?"

He had no idea how to answer her. It all sounded so complicated in his mind. "I'm Nicole's father."

"Winterstein?" she asked.

"Yes…Where are you?"

"Police station," she said.

"Were you arrested?"

"I don't know."

"Let me talk to one of the officers."

There was a long silence; then someone came on the phone. Nick identified himself as Bridget's attorney and learned she was at the ninth precinct station. He put the car in drive, turned the head-lights on, and made a U-turn onto Cadillac, driving north to Gratiot. Helen unzipped her fanny pack and placed her pistol in the glove box. There was another gun in there, a nickel-plated revolver. She'd never seen it before.

Bridget wasn't in a holding cell. She sat in an open office area on a wooden bench. Several were officers in the area, but no one seemed to be in charge; there was a sense of vacancy here, a lack of purpose. Bridget looked up as Nick approached her. She was blond and petite in a gray sweatshirt stained with blood and dirt. Her hair was greasy and matted, and her left eye was black and blue. There was a scab over her eyebrow, and her lower lip was swollen and cracked open. Nick asked her what had happened.

She shook her head. "I don't know."

An officer appeared from a back room. His hair was reddish blond, his eyes gray. "I found her in the middle of Gratiot Avenue," he said.

"Shouldn't you have taken her to the hospital?" Helen said.

"She's safer here," he answered. The irony had no humor to it.

Nick explained who he was and offered his hand to the officer. "Thanks for getting her off the street."

Helen helped her to her feet and put her arm around her. "Your mother's waiting to see you."

"How did you end up on Gratiot?" Nick asked.

"I ran away," she said. "He kept me locked in that room." She sounded coherent, but something wasn't right. In the middle of an unrelated sentence, she started to cry; tears streamed down her cheeks. The tears came from nowhere; then her voice cracked. It was the beginning of withdrawal.

Helen led Bridget out to the car. Nick opened the backdoor, and she slid in. As he closed the door, she stared up at him. Once in the front seat, he caught Bridget's eyes in the mirror. "Where are we going?" she said.

"To the house," he said. "Your mother is there. And there's a room for you as well, with everything you'll need."

"You're my mother's father?"

"Yes," he said, still looking at her in the mirror.

"She's been looking for you," Helen said.

"Who are you?" Bridget asked.

"I'm Helen. I work for your grandfather."

"Are you a lawyer?"

"No, I'm his paralegal."

Nick looked at Bridget in the mirror.

"My mother's been looking for you a long time," Bridget said. "But she was afraid to call." She looked out the side window. "I wonder if she likes you." Her speech was slow, as though every word came through an opiate fog. She looked at Helen. "Did you know my grandmother?"

"No, I didn't."

"She's dead, you know. She died from too many pills. She was depressed." Looking out the side window, she added, "I think it was on purpose. It would be easy, you know. Swallow a handful of pills and go to sleep."

Helen looked at Nick then turned back to Bridget. "We'll get you home, sweetheart."

"Home," Bridget said. "I wish I had one."

Nick started the car and thought quickly for the safest way to Grosse Pointe from where they were. He put the car in gear and pulled out from the curb. He wondered what kind of drugs Bridget had taken. What was still in her system? Was there any permanent damage?

It was near midnight when they arrived in Grosse Pointe. Bridget sat with her head against the window. The moon was reflected like a bowl of crystal on the lake. "This is pretty," she said. "You live here?"

They pulled into the drive, and a single garage door opened, but Nick didn't pull into the open bay; he parked in front of the door. Helen got out to open the back door and reached her hand in for Bridget. They entered through the breezeway.

Nicole stood at the entryway to the living room. "Bridget!" She took her in her arms and squeezed her, kissing the side of her head, then held her at arm's length. "What happened to you?"

"You found him," Bridget said. "I wanted to find him first."

Nicole started to cry. She wiped her eyes. "Yes, I found him." She looked at Nick.

He fought against the lump in his throat.

Nicole held Bridget close. "You're shivering."

"I'm cold," she said.

"We'll get you in a hot shower and give you something warm to sleep in."

"Can I have a drink?" Bridget said. "Please?"

"A brandy?" Helen said, looking at Nick.

He nodded. "In the morning we'll get you in to see a doctor."

Nicole led Bridget up to her room, and Helen went to the living room to pour the brandy. As she started up the stairs with the drink, Nick said to her, "Look for needle marks."

Nick saw the handlebars sticking above the clear water in the county ditch. The ditch was five feet wide with willows growing along the banks. It stretched for several acres back to a swamp, but where Nick stood, it ran under the road through a culvert. The polliwogs were the size of dimes. They swam around the handlebars and the seat of the motor scooter. Nick stepped down the bank to the edge of the ditch. Frogs jumped into the water. He couldn't reach the handlebars. He needed something to lasso them.

Back at home he searched the garage for a length of rope. His father asked what he was doing, and Nick told him about the motor scooter he'd found in the ditch. From the road, standing over the culvert, he showed his father the handlebars sticking above the water. At the water's edge, his father reached forward and, with the power of a bulldozer, pulled the motor scooter onto the bank with one arm. He set it upright and pushed it up the bank and onto the road. It was an Allstate, he said. Sears and Roebuck sold them.

Near the garage the motor scooter now rested on its kickstand. Nick removed the cover from around the engine and rinsed it clean with the garden hose. He had no idea how to make it run. His father didn't care for engines because they were covered with grease and oil and could ruin a good piece of wood. Nick started to take things apart, but once he had a part removed, he was stumped.

Melina was in the shop, visiting with his father. Her company always put Joseph in a good mood; they laughed and shared the same cigarette. But Nick wasn't about to test the limits of his father's mood by pushing the motor scooter down the road to his grandfather's to ask for help—not while his dad was home anyway. He found time the next morning.

His grandfather didn't talk much, and it may have been hard to know what he was thinking, but you could tell when he was listening. When Nick finished explaining how he had found the scooter, his grandfather looked at the engine and wiped it with a rag.

He removed the carburetor, fuel line, spark plug, magneto, and cylinder head. He cleaned everything in solvent, cut a new gasket for the cylinder head, and replaced the spark plug with one he took from a drawer. He oiled the kick starter and the throttle cable, then raised the kick starter and pushed down with his foot. The engine started on the third try. At first blue smoke came from the muffler, but then it turned clear. Nick was sure the only reason the Chrysler plant on Lynch Road made cars was because his grandfather was there to show them how.

His grandfather told him to go slow on the concrete walk and test the brakes. They worked fine. Grandpa Reichmann added air to both tires, and Nick started home. His grandmother watched him ride down the crushed-cinder drive and onto the street.

As he neared the house, Nick looked for his father's red pickup truck. His father would know Grandpa Reichmann had fixed the motor scooter, but he hadn't thought of that beforehand, and now it gave him butterflies of worry. But the truck wasn't there; his father was gone.

Nick parked the motor scooter on the other side of the garage, under the window his father had smashed out when he had thrown the piece of wood he'd cut wrong. Nick looked back at the scooter with pride. From the house next door, he heard Joe Kopecny yell, "Every goddamn time I turn around, you're over there. You're screwing the bastard, aren't you? You are, goddamn it. I know it!"

Nick's mother stood on the front porch with a white handkerchief in her hand. She squeezed it as she listened to Kopecny yell.

Nick received an early morning call from Marshall; he wanted to meet with Nick today but not at the office. Nick suggested they meet at the house in the afternoon, because his morning was tied up. He'd just finished making an appointment for Bridget to see Dr. Rotheim.

Marshall agreed. "Two this afternoon."

Nick started to give his address, but Marshall said, "I know where it is."

"You sound agitated," Nick told him. "What is it?"

"I'll explain later."

Nicole came into the upstairs office adjacent to Nick's room. She was having a hard time getting Bridget out of bed; she said she was sluggish and not making much sense. "I've seen this before," Nicole said. "She's going through withdrawal. I know it. She'll go from this to being nasty and mean."

"Can you get her into the shower? Use mine," he said. "It's big enough for both of you. You can help her."

Nick heard Nicole coax Bridget out of bed and toward the shower. A few moments later, he heard the water running in his bathroom.

In the kitchen he made scrambled eggs and toast. He kept everything warm on the stove until the girls came down. But Bridget said she wasn't hungry and asked for a drink, just a little one.

"You have an appointment this morning," Nick said, "with Dr. Rotheim. I'm sure he'll draw blood to run tests. Save the drink for later, OK?"

The bruises around her eye and the scab above the eyebrow looked worse in the morning light. Her lip was still swollen and split open. "I can't eat." Her voice cracked. She put her hand to her throat and tried again. "Maybe later." Nicole had a pained look on her face. She smoothed Bridget's hair back from her forehead and kissed the top of her head.

There were no patients at Allen Rotheim's office. While Bridget was in the examining room, Nick and Nicole waited in the private office. Near the window was a large desk of African bloodwood, polished and trimmed with blackwood. Through the window was a sun-filled yard with lavender and pink flowers.

When Allen Rotheim returned to the office, he took a seat at his desk and wrote out a prescription. "This will help her get through the hard part," he said. He handed it to Nicole. "She's been down this road before, hasn't she?"

Nicole nodded.

"I'll have test results by this afternoon," he said. "Other than that…I don't know what to say. I'm sure you've heard it all before."

Dr. Rotheim's nurse led Bridget into the office from the examining room. "We've put something on that lip," she said. "It should heal faster."

Nick thanked them both, and Rotheim repeated that he'd call later that afternoon with the test results. On the way home, they stopped at the pharmacy. Bridget sat with her head against the headrest, her eyes closed, as Nick went inside to fill the prescription.

As Nick pulled into the driveway at home, he saw Marshall's white Escalade in front of the garage. He hadn't expected him this soon. The appointment wasn't until two in the afternoon; it was now eleven o'clock. He pulled in and parked next to the Escalade. Nicole looked through her window at Marshall then turned to Nick. "I'll take Bridget in."

Nick offered Marshall a seat on the patio and asked whether he would like something to drink—coffee maybe? Marshall waved it off. He looked ill at ease; his usual confidence, if not cockiness, was gone. "They're going to indict," he said. "Their chief witness is Carthage. I've seen this so many times before, one witness turning against the other. Now it's happening to me."

Nick saw the anxiety on Marshall's face; the judge was truly puzzled as to how or why this was happening to him. Years ago Marshall had watched the Young Socialists of Michigan exact petty extortion on local merchants to fill their campaign coffers, but he saw no connection to his own behavior. His crimes had been committed in the name of civil rights. His cause was noble, as shown through the NAACP and the media. To pressure businesses for a seat on the board of directors was to keep watch on them, to watch *their* behavior. Robin Hood served the underprivileged, but Robin Hood was a thief, pure and simple. He lived by his own rules.

"Have you had contact with Carthage since your testimony?" Nick asked.

Marshall shook his head. "No, but he talked to Purcell since he was last in front of the grand jury."

"Purcell?"

"The lead prosecutor," Marshall said. He looked up at Nick. "Maybe a small brandy?"

"Of course." Nick stood and entered the house through the kitchen. He stopped at the stairway and looked toward Bridget's room. It was quiet upstairs. He poured a brandy and returned to the patio.

"The name 'Purcell,'" he said, as he handed the drink to Marshall, "doesn't ring a bell."

"He's young. I'm not sure how he got there or where he's from, but he's in charge."

Somehow the pieces didn't seem to fit. The US Attorney's Office wanted Marshall, and that was it, while Carthage went his merry way? The rules of the grand jury were the rules by which the public must play, but the US Attorney's Office did as it pleased, and it seemed that was the way it was now.

"Did you trade any stocks directly?"

"No, but Carthage did."

"Did he act on your behalf?" Nick waited for Marshall to answer.

"I signed my shares over to the CCLC."

Nick watched him take a sip of brandy. How could a man of his intelligence not see the blatant stupidity of what he'd done? "Where's the money?" Nick asked.

Marshall didn't answer.

"How many shares in all?" Again Nick waited.

Marshall finished the brandy. "A hundred thousand." Before the announcement of the merger, Marshall had purchased the stock at a mere fraction of its present value. He must have seen a return of several million. But where was he hiding it? Carthage knew. He knew a great deal. It was time for Nick to meet him.

Marshall set the empty glass down and said he had to leave. He had arrived early and now departed early. His behavior had become abrupt and erratic.

It was late afternoon when Nick received a call from Allen Rotheim. He had poured a second glass of wine and refilled Nicole's glass. They were on the stone patio facing the backyard. The grass was a rich green with lavender and purple irises along the wooden fence.

"Wish I had a garden," Nicole said. "I'd love to plant something and watch it grow."

"Plant it here," Nick said. He motioned with an open hand. "There's plenty of sunlight."

"You mean it?" she said.

"Yes, I mean it." To his mind this was her home.

His cell phone rang, and he reached for his pocket.

"Hello?" He listened for a moment then said, "Nicole is here with me. Do you mind if I put you on speakerphone?" He pressed the speaker button and set the phone on the patio end table.

"The test results are back," Rotheim said. "I wish I had better news."

Nick looked at Nicole as he asked Rotheim, "What did you find?"

"It appears she's diabetic. Her glucose is very high. We can start with an oral medication; if that doesn't work, we'll go to insulin shots."

"But that's treatable," Nicole said. "Right?"

"Yes, it's manageable. But there's something more serious," he added.

"What?" Nick asked. "Something from the drugs?"

"I don't know—maybe."

"Allen, please get to the point."

"Bridget's HIV positive."

H is mother was bent over the garden hoe. Once the weeds were free from the soil, she scraped them into a pile. The dirt was soft and black with moisture where she hoed, and the furrows were straight and long. The tomato plants were tied to stakes with white string. The corn was already a foot tall.

She stood up straight and looked toward Nick. He glanced over his shoulder to see what had caught her attention. Melina had come across the yard to visit his father in the shop. They would drink coffee together and share the same cigarette. The only time she visited his mother was when his father wasn't there, and she usually stayed until he came home. Her smile looked bigger and happier when she saw him. Nick knew the best time to ask his father for something was when Melina was there. His moods were good then; he never yelled or got mad or said no.

His mother turned back to the hoe and continued until she had gathered all the weeds into piles. Nick helped her collect them into the wagon then into one large pile near the toolshed. She sprayed water on the pile and covered it with canvas. In the fall she would spread the mixture over the garden and work it back into the soil.

She removed her gloves and placed them in the toolshed. The hoe, rake, shovel, spade, pickax, and pitchfork were hung on the wall. Everything was orderly and easily found. Her seed corn was on a shelf and protected, as were a hundred or so canning jars with their lids.

On her way to the house, she stopped at the shop and said she was going to visit her mother for a while. Melina didn't acknowledge her or even say hello. Joseph looked as though he'd been interrupted.

Nick was in the shop with them when Joe Kopecny appeared. The garage door was open, and when Nick looked up from the wood lathe, he saw him there. Nick was trying to make an arrow from a piece of pine, but the wood was too soft, and as the shaft narrowed, it split into pieces. A piece flew over his shoulder and hit his father, but his father was looking at Joe Kopecny in the doorway. Kopecny told Melina there was stuff on the goddamn stove, boiling. When the hell was she going to take care of it? Melina told him to turn it off himself; he was standing right there. Kopecny got angrier and told her it was *her* goddamn job. Then he turned and walked off, throwing in another "goddamn it."

Nick watched him through the window above the lathe as he crossed the front yard. He always had liked Kopecny. He made a lot of noise and cussed, but he used adult words to explain his thoughts to Nick. His favorite topic was "those goddamn politicians"; although Nick didn't understand the subject, he liked being treated as an adult.

Although Bridget was given medication to ease the pain of withdrawal, her symptoms were still visible. She was unable to sleep, and she lay in sweaty clothes while wrapped in a blanket to keep warm. Her voice was shaky, and she now refused to talk at all. She'd been given oral medications to treat her high glucose levels, but they had little effect. Nicole managed her insulin injections. She coaxed Bridget into at least trying a spoonful of broth. Nick looked in a few times, but it was too difficult to watch.

Nick and Helen were in the upstairs study. Helen had just made a pot of coffee and filled Nick's cup. She sat on the sofa with her cup and saucer in hand. Nick explained that Bridget was on a combination of antiviral medications to hopefully control HIV-related infections, but the state of her general health didn't help.

Nicole entered the study through Nick's room. She saw Helen on the sofa. "You're so pretty, Helen. You truly are. Your features are so perfect."

"Thank you, Nicole. That's very kind of you." She reached to take Nicole's hand. "Would you like some coffee?"

"Thank you." Nicole sat on the sofa with Helen. "This is the worst I've ever seen her. She's shivering and sweating at the same time." The subject was painful, but there was a need to discuss it. She looked at Nick as she spoke. "The drinking started when she was thirteen or fourteen. I should've known, but I didn't see it. Mom was always taking pills, and I was too concerned with *me*. I used sex the way Mom used pills. Then she died, followed by both grandparents. I didn't know what to do." She caught the look on Nick's face. "I know what you're thinking," she said, "but don't. Everything happened as it did. It wasn't you; it wasn't your fault."

His thoughts of the past were incomplete images of embarrassment and pain for the behavior of a young man. He wanted now to simply fix things.

"I'm so ashamed of the way I behaved," Nicole said. She stared at her coffee then looked up. "I used to bring men into the apartment while Bridget was there. There were times when I didn't even know their names. More than once Bridget walked in on us. She was no more than six or seven."

"God knows I'm no one to judge," Helen said. She glanced at Nick.

"If I had given her a normal home life," Nicole said, "none of this would've happened."

"What's a normal home life?" Nick said. "Don't beat yourself up, Nicole. Nothing good will come of it."

Nicole wiped her eyes.

"By today's standards your great-grandfather was a pedophile," Nick said. "He had a penchant for little girls. But we grew up in one piece. We all survived. Those who don't are marked in some other way—usually by being told they're *supposed* to be marked."

"Your grandfather," Nicole said. "A pedophile?"

He nodded. "Arthur Reichmann."

"Didn't you once defend a pedophile?" Helen asked.

"Yes, a long time ago. He was guilty, but I convinced the jury to acquit. After that I had clients lined up at the door. They shared no sense of what was moral or immoral. There was only self-interest. It motivates us all."

"Morality is just another means of control," he continued, "and if morality doesn't work, we invent laws, and we enforce them at gunpoint. But in the end, neither morality nor the law can change the human heart; and if the human heart is the only constant, where does that leave morality?"

He refilled his coffee cup. Nicole and Helen were quiet. They watched him as he stood near the coffee tray. "I loved my father dearly," he said. "I don't judge him, and I certainly don't judge my grandfather."

"That view alone," Nicole said, "is a judgment against you. We're expected to know right from wrong."

"Yes, but what's wrong today might be right tomorrow; it depends on who controls public opinion. It all changes with time. Right and wrong can even switch places. There's no math involved."

"It's depressing," Helen said, "to know the least capable make the rules for the rest of us."

"First understand *their* rules," Nick said, "and how they use them. Then make your own."

Nicole looked toward the window, as if off in thought. "Whose phone did she use?" She looked at Nick. He looked confused. "I'm sorry," she said. "I mean Bridget, when she called."

"The phone belonged to Michael Carthage. I know him, or at least I met him. He was outside what looked to be a crack house on Hurlbut."

"Bridget spoke of a Michael. He wouldn't let her go. He's the one who hit her. He forced her to the streets. Is that how she became infected?"

"I don't know," he said. "Sex, needles, both." The look on his face was pained.

"How did she know him?" Helen said. "How did they meet? And what are the chances?"

"The drug culture is its own world," Nick said. "Users, sellers—they find each other."

Nicole set her coffee cup on the desk. "I'm going to check on her."

She was gone only moments when they heard breaking glass from Bridget's bathroom. Helen was there first to see what had happened. Bridget was at the sink. Broken glass was scattered on the tile floor at her feet. Nicole stood next to her. Nick appeared at the bedroom door.

"She tried to take these." Nicole held out her hand. "It's Valium." The capsules lay in her open palm.

"That might have killed her," Helen said.

It was a family tradition to gather at the Reichmanns' for the Fourth of July. Cheryl was in the kitchen, preparing potato salad for the picnic, when she noticed Melina cross the front yard on her way to the shop. She didn't bother to disguise her intentions by stopping to say hello to Cheryl. She went straight to the shop to greet Joseph with a smile for the world to see.

Cheryl added diced onions, celery, and hard-boiled eggs to the salad. The relatives were from the Reichmann and Lewis side of the family, and Cheryl hoped her husband would conceal his contempt for them or at best not make a scene. Joseph's affair with Melina had become family knowledge. Cheryl was prepared for the whispers and glances of sympathy as they discussed the topic among themselves, but not for her husband's reaction, should he notice.

Cheryl wanted to bring more to the picnic, but her mother insisted the potato salad was enough. Food was always abundant at the Reichmanns', especially for family gatherings. Long picnic tables had been pushed together end to end and covered with white cloth. Cold chicken was served, sliced cucumbers and tomatoes in sweet vinegar with onion, potato salad, fruit and cheese, deviled eggs, green salad, fresh-baked pies, and pitchers of home-brewed beer.

At all Reichmann gatherings, Joseph wore a sullen expression amid all the laughter and conversation. Mary Reichmann's laughter was infectious and could be heard above all the rest. The adults stuck croquet wickets in the grass and argued and laughed over who was cheating and who wasn't while driving the wooden ball. The grand-kids and cousins played softball out back, while Joseph sat at a table, drank coffee, and smoked a cigarette by himself. Cheryl noticed him sitting there, as if, in some perverse way, he were feeling sorry for himself. *Why can't he for once forget his anger and join in?* she wondered. Cheryl watched him walk toward the long cinder drive and get into his truck. He turned the key, but the truck didn't start; he tried again and again until the battery was nearly exhausted. He got out of the truck and raised the hood to look inside, but the cables, wires, spark plugs, and engine were a strange world to him. Cheryl saw his frustra-tion, but at least he wasn't angry.

Hearing the engine laboring to start, Arthur Reichmann watched from a distance near the picnic tables. Joseph saw him, and with an effort, as if to overcome his dislike of Reichmann, he called to him. He asked whether he would take a look. Maybe he'd know what was wrong. Without a word Reichmann came forward to check the en-gine. The two men didn't look at each other, but Cheryl hoped this might be the beginning of a peace between them.

Reichmann looked under the hood. A spark plug wire was frayed, its copper threads exposed. He pulled the dipstick from the oil well; the oil barely registered. He removed a needle valve from the carbu-retor and saw it was clogged with dirt. It was a wonder the engine *ever* had run.

Joseph asked whether he could fix it, but Reichmann didn't an-swer. He pulled at a loose battery cable and stared at the mess in front of him. Joseph lost patience while waiting for an answer. At the top of his voice, he demanded to know what the hell was wrong with it.

The commotion got everyone's attention. Joseph's booming voice and childish outburst, however, did not intimidate Mary Reichmann. She told him to keep his britches on and not to go screaming at an old man with a heart condition.

Reichmann went back to his shop, and Cheryl came forward and looped her arm around her husband. She asked him to be patient. A few minutes later, Reichmann returned with electrical tape, a cleaning rag, and motor oil in a metal container with a spout. When he was finished, he started the engine from under the hood and reset the idle. He listened to the engine for a moment then closed the hood and returned his tools to the workshop without a word.

Cheryl asked her husband to please come back and have a seat with her. Joseph reached in through the truck window and turned off the ignition. A car passed in front of the driveway on the street. The horn sounded, and Melina waved her arm from the window. Joseph looked up. Cheryl gently tugged at his arm. She wasn't ready to admit she was losing her husband.

Nick stood at the office window and looked out at the river. Tall, white clouds rose against a blue sky and drifted east. He had plenty to do, but since the arrival of Nicole, and now Bridget, he was being pulled in another direction. The thought of Nicole warmed his heart, but with Bridget there was pain. Was he seeing what his life might have been like with Janice?

He heard Helen ask something. He turned. She stood in the doorway to his office. "I'm sorry," he said. "I didn't hear...I wasn't listening."

She smiled. "Why don't you take the day off? Do something with Nicole. I can handle things here."

He looked toward the river then up at the sky. "It's a beautiful day, isn't it?" He turned back toward Helen. "I think I will. Just call if you need me."

"I will."

At first he left his notes, open folders, and loose papers on his desk as they were. He didn't bother to put them in order or arrange them in anyway. But as he left his office, he glanced back. The desk looked like a mess. He returned and arranged his papers. He placed his notes in one pile and clipped the loose papers together before returning them to the correct folders. He then placed everything in one pile with the notes on top. He rinsed his coffee cup and set it in the drying rack in the kitchen.

Helen was at her desk. She looked up as he passed. "Give Nicole my love."

"I will." Nick stopped at the door and looked back. "You're a sweetheart, Helen. You truly are."

In the parking lot, he started his car, put it in reverse, backed out, and turned onto the street. At the intersection he pulled up behind a police cruiser. The engine was running, and the front window was down, but there was no one inside. He looked to the right and to the left, and in the mirror, but there was no one in sight. He waited for a moment, then a moment longer—still no one. He pulled around the cruiser and drove ahead. As he drove on, he looked in the mirror at the empty cruiser receding in the distance.

When he arrived home, the garage doors were open. Nicole's car was in the end bay next to the black Volkswagen, but in the first bay, where he usually parked the Lincoln, there was a wheelbarrow set at an angle. He got out and walked to the expanse of yard to the left of the garage. Nicole didn't notice him. She had a large rectangle of lawn staked and marked with white twine. It was several yards in length, and the sod had been peeled back and piled along the edges to form a retaining wall a few inches high. The exposed soil appeared black and rich.

Nicole looked up. "Hi." She wore a T-shirt, cutoff jeans, and tennis shoes with no socks. She was all smiles. "I can't tell you how good this feels," she said.

"You have a great start."

"I'm going to keep it simple," she said. "Tomatoes, cucumbers, peppers, string beans, lettuce, and carrots. Oh, yes, radishes too. I love radishes."

"So do I."

"I found these tools in the garage."

"They're your grandmother's," he said. "The rake, the hoe, shovel, and spade. She used them."

"I thought they looked pretty old." She looked at the shovel in her hands. "That's a neat thought: this belonged to Grandma Cheryl."

She'd called his mother *Grandma* Cheryl. He liked the sound of it.

"Let me change, and I'll give you a hand," he said.

"You have a lot of old tools in the garage. All those saws—were they your father's?"

"Yes," he said. "Every tool your grandfather owned is in there."

"Do you know how to use them? There are so many. I don't even know the names of half of them."

"I grew up using them," he said. "I can't remember *not* using them."

Nick went in to change, and on his way out, he stopped at Bridget's door and listened. He heard the TV, but he was reluctant to knock. Her condition was too painful to see; the thought of her living with HIV was at times more than he could bear. He knew he had to somehow resolve the thought, but for now he didn't knock. On his way downstairs, he thought himself a coward.

Nicole had a good start on removing the sod. Nick started on the opposite end. He used a square-edged shovel and cut along the white twine, peeling the sod back in long sections and piling it along the edge the way Nicole had started. Once all the sod had been removed, they loosened the dirt and raked it smooth. Nicole took a notepad from her back pocket and opened it to the diagram on the second page. She had figured which vegetable would go where and the size and dimension of each section. Down the center of the garden, she left two walkways for easy access to weed and water around individual plants.

"We need something around the perimeter," Nick said. "A six-inch board to hold the sod back and dress it up. What do you think?"

They measured the perimeter with a yellow tape measure then looked through several bins of used boards in the garage. Nick pulled a bundle of one-by-six-by-ten boards from the rack and looked at it. "There's enough here," he said. He cut the bundle free and separated the boards. He measured them to the right length, marked them with a pencil, and switched on the saw. The screech of the saw blade cutting through the wood was a familiar sound to him. Each time he heard it, his father's image came to mind; he was a boy again.

He cut a dozen stakes and collected a box of wood screws and his portable drill with a screwdriver bit. They set the boards against the sod to hold it in place and drove stakes into the ground. Then Nick attached them to the boards with the wood screws. They were all but finished, and he was applying pressure to the last screw, when the drill slipped and the bit cut into his finger.

"Goddamn it!" Blood dripped from the end of his finger as he grabbed the drill by the handle and threw it several feet against the fence.

"Well"—Nicole laughed—"we have quite a temper."

Nick looked at Nicole and laughed too, but in his heart, he was convinced he didn't have a temper. It had merely been a passing moment of frustration.

Later in the afternoon, they drove north of Mount Clemens to a plant nursery. Nicole coaxed Bridget into going with them. The ride, the fresh air, the change of scenery would do her good. Bridget was reluctant to go, but it seemed she didn't have the energy to resist. She sat listlessly in the backseat and stared out the window.

At the nursery Bridget remained in the car. Nick and Nicole picked out tomato plants, peppers, and packages of seeds. Nicole wanted to create a border of zinnias around her garden to attract butterflies. Her smile was radiant, and Nick thought of what her life might have been had he been there throughout her childhood.

On the way back, they stopped for ice cream. Bridget refused any, but again Nicole coaxed her into trying it. She ate a spoonful then threw the container out the window in the parking lot. Nick waited until they were ready to leave then picked up the container of melting ice cream and dropped it into a trash receptacle. He was careful not to imply anything by doing so; he could only imagine the inner torment Bridget was enduring.

At home Bridget went back up to her room and closed the door. Nicole asked through the closed door whether she was hungry, but there was no answer.

Nick took several ibuprofen tablets and rinsed his finger under cold water. It was swollen and sore. Nicole asked to see it. She dried his finger with a clean towel, applied an antibiotic salve, and bandaged it.

"So Daddy has a temper," she said, applying a fresh bandage. "There."

His first rifle was a .22-caliber single shot, bolt action, with a shortened stock to fit his arm length. His father had a high-caliber hunting rifle, several shotguns, and a .38 revolver. The revolver was fun to shoot, but it was hard to hit the tin can hanging from a string off the tree branch. His father hit the can almost every time, even when it was still swinging from the last shot. Nick took so long to aim that his arm started to shake, and when he squeezed the trigger, the gun jumped.

The twelve-gauge, double-barrel shotgun was heavy and hard for Nick to hold. The twenty-gauge was a bolt action with a clip and seemed complicated to use. The .410 was his favorite, and he considered it to be his. The chamber opened to eject the spent shell and to reload. The shotgun was lightweight, simple, and sleek.

His father bought the hunting license at the same hardware store where he bought the shotgun shells. He inserted the license in a clear plastic envelope and pinned it to the back of his hunting jacket. Because of his age, Nick was exempt, his father explained. Nick could hunt with his father's license.

Nick had seen ring-necked pheasants in his mother's garden in the fall, when the corn stubble turned brown and there were still a few kernels of corn on the ground. But he and his father were going north to hunt, up to New Haven, Michigan. His mother made egg-salad sandwiches, wrapped in wax paper, and a thermos of coffee flavored with cream. His father wrapped the shotguns in burlap and placed them in the back of the truck.

As they backed out of the gravel drive, Melina was getting into her car. His father watched her in the mirror as she backed onto the street. Nick turned to look back. She was right behind them.

They followed Gratiot north of Mount Clemens. His father said they were going to hunt on private land. He'd done some work for the man who owned the farm. From Gratiot they turned onto a gravel road and drove past acres of corn stubble and a twisting line of brush that followed the creek. Gravel stones hit the underside of the truck as they sped along.

They came to an entrance gate alongside the road. His father unfastened the chain, pushed the gate open, and parked the truck on the other side. Out over the corn stubble, the morning fog was thin and wispy. In the distance a car appeared along the road. It slowed down, came through the gate, and parked behind the truck. It was Melina. Her smile was white and pretty. Nick knew his father would be in a good mood today.

Nick breeched the .410, inserted a shell, closed it, and set the safety. Melina and his father walked together, with Nick thirty yards to their right. His father said, "If anything flies or runs to the left, don't shoot; let it go. Anything straight ahead or to the right, lead the target by several feet."

Nick saw what he thought was a clump of dirt move then noticed it was a rabbit. He shouldered the .410 and pulled the trigger. Dirt flew into the air where the rabbit used to be as it ran into the brush. Melina called to him, "Good try! You almost got it!" But her words didn't sound real, like she was trying too hard to be nice.

They crossed the creek into a field of dried weeds. A few yards into the field, several pheasants took to the air all at once. For a moment Nick was startled; then he shouldered the shotgun, aimed at the fancy-colored one, and pulled the trigger. The gun bucked hard into his shoulder, but the pheasants kept flying into the distance. His father said with a smile, "You have to lead the target. They're moving faster than you think."

When they stopped for lunch, Melina and his father shared the same sandwich, coffee, and cigarette. Nick ate the other sandwich and drank the sweet coffee. He was soon finished and ready to start again, but his father and Melina continued to talk to and stare at each other.

By late afternoon Nick had taken a half dozen shots, but he didn't have a pheasant or rabbit to show for it. His father carried the twelve-gauge in the crook of his arm with the breech open. He didn't fire it or even close the breech all day. Now his father placed the shotguns in the back of the truck. Across the road a pheasant entered a long, sloping glide and disappeared behind the weed-covered field. "Go ahead," his father said. "One last try." He handed Nick the .410 and a shell.

Nick crossed the road into the field of short weeds. Suddenly the pheasant took to the air. Nick aimed and fired. The gun bucked into his shoulder, and as he lowered it, the pheasant continued to climb at a steep angle. It flew several feet higher; then its wings folded, and it fell straight to the ground. Nick yelled to his father, "I got it! I got it!"

Nick knelt beside the pheasant and placed his shotgun on the ground. The pheasant was so beautiful. It was greenish purple and chestnut brown and beige, and so soft and smooth. He stroked the silky features. The pheasant was still warm. A lump came to his throat. His tears fell to the pheasant's beautiful feathers. He heard his father come up from behind and kneel next to him. He felt his father's arm around him as he kissed the top of Nick's head.

"I know," he said.

The grand jury indicted Judge Goodwin Marshall on six counts of securities fraud, conspiracy to commit wire fraud, and tax evasion. The charge of conspiracy implied an accomplice or accomplices, but there was no mention of Jessup Carthage. The force behind the indictment was Robert Purcell of the US Attorney's Office in Detroit.

Nick called Purcell's office to arrange a meeting, but he wasn't in, so he left a voice mail with his cell number. This was early morning, and by noon he still hadn't heard back. Near one o'clock he called Sandy. He hadn't seen her since Nicole had arrived, more than a week, but she certainly had been in his thoughts.

"Didn't think I'd ever hear from you," she said. "I left you a message at the house."

Nick hadn't thought to check for messages on the landline. He had taken for granted that she would call his cell. "Let's get together," he said. "How about golf?"

"I'd love to," she said. "Play here?"

"I'm on my way," he said. "See you in about an hour."

"I'll call for a tee time."

As he was about to leave, Helen asked him to take a look at something; she had a printed page in her hand, an e-mail Nick had forwarded to her without having opened it. He read the first paragraph. It concerned a wrongful-death suit. "You've done quite well with these," she said.

He had done very well with such cases, but he wasn't as interested in the practice of law anymore. The law had become more of an entertainment to him, a seat in a movie theater—not a way to earn a living.

"I don't think so," he said, as he handed it back to her. He saw the look on her face. "But I'll tell you what—if you put it together, and there's a lot of work involved in something like this, we'll pursue it. If we win, you keep any percentage of the settlement we receive."

Her expression changed. "You mean that, don't you?"

"Yes." He smiled. "I do."

As he left the office, he felt Helen's energy fill the room.

His golf clubs and golf clothes were in the trunk of the car. As he pulled out of the parking lot, he heard his cell phone. The caller ID read, "Unknown." He guessed it was Purcell and let it go to voice mail. A few minutes later, he checked his messages. It *was* Purcell; he'd acknowledged Nick's message and suggested they meet at the earliest convenience. Nick folded the phone and placed it on the car seat.

He left the parking lot and drove east toward the Chrysler Freeway. A few blocks from the freeway entrance, a Detroit police car was parked at the side of the road. The rear tire was flat; the driver's-side door was open; and steam rose from under the hood. But there was no driver. As Nick drove onto the freeway entrance, he looked back in the mirror at the abandoned police car. If left unattended for too long, it would be stripped of its parts.

He exited the freeway in Troy and drove along Big Beaver Road to Birmingham. For Nick, Birmingham was a nice area, but it lacked the romance of Grosse Pointe and the history of the Ford name.

As he approached the back door, Sandy was there waiting for him. It was a pleasure to see her again. He held her in his arms, squeezed her. Her perfume was delicious. "What a welcome," she said. "I need more of that."

Nick changed into his golf clothes and poured a small glass of wine from the fridge. Sandy came back into the kitchen while attaching an earring. "Mellissa is being a real bitch," she said. "You know what she's doing?"

Nick shook his head. It was the last thing he wanted to hear. But he also heard the concern in Sandy's voice.

"I mentioned she was relying too much on sleeping pills. And she is. Now she won't talk to me." She went into the dining room to check her earrings in the mirror. "You'd think I called her a drug addict!" She looked at Nick in the mirror. There was more to the issue than she was admitting; Nick saw it in her face.

"Kids grow up, but they never go away. You don't know how lucky you are, Nicky." She turned to face him. She took his wineglass and finished what was left. "We're going to be late."

At the clubhouse a young man loaded their golf clubs onto the cart and asked whether there was anything more he could do. Nick thanked him, said everything was fine, and handed him a tip. As they started for the first tee, Sandy said, "You overtipped him. You always do."

"A tip is more than just money," he said. They pulled up to the first tee box. "As an undergraduate," he said, "I drove a cab at night. I once took a fare from the airport to a hotel. He was a young guy, thirties maybe, from England. He gave me a twenty-dollar bill and said, 'Keep it.' The fare was only a couple bucks. He looked at me and said, 'You'll remember me, even years from now.'" He looked at Sandy. "And forty years later, I'm telling you the story."

"He certainly knew what he was doing."

"He was a barrister."

"That fits."

Nick teed off with a four iron; he and the driver were not on speaking terms. Sandy didn't tee off from the ladies' tee box but played from the white marker with Nick. He watched her bend over to place the ball on the tee then straighten up.

"I felt that," she said.

"My pleasure," he told her.

She looked over her shoulder and smiled.

By the time they finished the fifth hole, the score was tied and remained tied at the end of nine. Several times in between, she had completely missed the ball. "What's bothering you?" he asked. "Your game is way off."

"It's Mellissa," she said. "It's more than just sleeping pills." Nick didn't ask any questions. He waited for her to tell him what was bothering her.

At the end of nine holes, they called it a day, dropped off the cart, and drove back to Sandy's house. She opened a fresh bottle of wine, and they sat in the living room on the sofa. Nick knew that what she needed was for someone to simply listen.

"It started with prescriptions of some kind," she said, "and then it went to pain-killers. She's not herself anymore. She's been lying and not just about little stuff. She denies going into Detroit, but I'm sure she has. I've found these little plastic baggies, some with capsules in them."

"Have you talked to her about it?"

"She gets so defensive. And now she won't even talk to me. What if she *is* going to Detroit? A white woman looking for drugs—she could end up dead. On top of that, she's still on probation."

Nick wanted to tell her about Bridget, but he didn't. It seemed too complicated to explain, too painful.

"I can't tell you, Nicky, how it feels—to watch your child self-destruct.

Melina was in the shop with his father. They drank coffee from the same cup and smiled at each other. His father never got angry or threw anything when she was there. His moods were always good then.

Nick was across the yard, watching Kopecny make a sign. His father ridiculed Kopecny anytime he used a hammer or saw. Kopecny had built a toolshed with a wooden floor inside and an electrical outlet near the workbench. His father scoffed and made fun of the shed, but Nick thought it looked pretty good.

The sign Kopecny had made was nearly the size of a whole sheet of plywood and painted white on each side. He said he was going to attach it to the utility pole at the corner of the road so people could see it from all directions. At each corner of the sign he painted several red stars. The lettering was blue: JOE KOPECNY FOR CITY COUNCIL. He said it was time to get rid of those goddamn politicians and let ordinary folks run things for a change. He said Nick could work for the campaign as a volunteer and gave him a stack of flyers to distribute throughout the neighborhood on his bike. Nick rode all the way up to the city boundary at Hayes Road, dropping off a flyer at everyone's front door. He worked almost the whole afternoon for the campaign, except for the time he stopped at the empty lot next to Elmer's house to play baseball with Ronnie and Elmer and some kids from Roseville.

In the late afternoon, he stopped at his grandparents' place on his way home. Grandpa Reichmann took one of the flyers from the basket on the front of his bike and read it. He nodded and said Kopecny was a "good union man." From the cinder driveway, Nick saw his mother in the kitchen with his grandmother. He laid his bike down and went inside. His mother had been crying. She wiped her eyes with a white hankie and tried to smile when she saw Nick. When Nick asked what was wrong, his grandmother gently pushed him out the door and told him not to bother his mother right now. Nick looked back through the screen door. His mother was still wiping her eyes.

Nick finished delivering the flyers, and when he returned home, Melina was still in the shop with his father. Nick told his father he'd been working for the campaign. Joe Kopecny was going to be elected to the city council; maybe he would even become mayor. Melina and his father looked at each other and laughed.

Nick arranged a meeting with Robert Purcell. At first Purcell insisted on meeting in his office, but Nick suggested a lunch meeting. He had learned that to meet on someone else's turf gave that person an advantage; on neutral ground, and especially while sharing a meal, it was easier to manage things. Before Purcell had time to object to an off-site meeting, Nick asked, "What's your favorite food?"

Purcell hesitated, and Nick suggested, "Tom's Oyster Bar. Is one o'clock good?"

Purcell agreed. "That'll work."

Helen had looked into the Purcells' backgrounds, but most of what she had learned she referred to as rumor or Internet gossip—but Nick wasn't so sure. He sat at his desk and read through the file Helen had put together. Purcell had been married and was thirty-five years old. His ex-wife was much older, fifty-one, and was a law-school graduate. She'd come to the marriage with a great deal of money, and although it was suggested that she had insisted on a prenuptial agreement, no such agreement existed. After four years of marriage, she had filed for divorce, accusing him of infidelity. Eventually their dirty laundry became public. They each had hired a private investigator to follow and photograph the other. The photographs ended up on her Facebook page. Although benign in appearance, the message was clear. Each had something on the other.

"How's Bridget?" Helen asked, standing in the doorway to Nick's office.

"Oh…" He was looking at a black-and-white picture of Purcell. "Nicole is going to show her my old neighborhood today…where I grew up."

"That area has changed," she said. "It's a shame."

"It's like watching something die right before your eyes," he said, placing the picture on his desk, "and you're helpless to do anything."

⟝⟞ ⟝⟞

Nick arrived at the oyster bar early. He took a seat where he could watch the door and ordered a glass of wine. He ordered a sweet dessert wine; his taste was changing.

He saw Purcell approach along the sidewalk. As Purcell came abreast of the building, he looked toward the roof. Nick was well aware of the surveillance cameras in front and at each corner of the building. It seemed Purcell was taking in the position of each camera.

As Purcell came through the door, Nick rose to his feet. Purcell noticed him and came toward the table. He had blondish hair, disheveled and thinning in the front, and gray eyes. His necktie was askew, and the button on the left corner of his button-down collar was missing. Nick offered his hand; Purcell wore a Rolex.

"Nicholas Winterstein," Nick said.

"Yes," Purcell said, "I've heard of you." As he took a seat, he added, "Aren't you a little out of your element—securities law?"

"That could be," Nick said.

"Maybe we can work something out," Purcell said without looking at Nick.

The waitress came to their table. "BLT?" she asked Nick. "Just a half?"

"Yes, thank you," he answered. She wrote his order on her pad then looked at Purcell. He ordered a hamburger with everything on it and a glass of beer. When she left to put the order in, Purcell looked at Nick. "You come here often?"

"Not really."

"She seems to know you...A little something on the side?"

"No," Nick said. He didn't like the question. "I did her a favor once."

"A favor?"

"Someone smashed into her car while it was parked. The insurance company offered only book value. The car was fifteen years old but in excellent condition. I convinced them to replace it with one of equal life value."

"How'd you convince them?"

"Maintenance records, photos. Anyway, we got her a much newer car."

"And you did this as a *favor*?"

"Yes," Nick said. "Why not?"

"The anarchist helping the little guy," Purcell said. "Amusing."

"Anarchist." Nick laughed. "I wouldn't put it that way."

"What is it you believe, Winterstein? From what I've heard, you think everyone should be allowed to do as they goddamn well please. No laws, just anarchy."

"No laws? Why not?" Nick said. "Let individuals settle things."

"Without laws you'd have chaos."

"You don't know that."

"Well, what would you call it? Harmony?"

"You'd have a system without laws, as opposed to a system with laws. Each is a system. Which is better? Only one has been tried."

Purcell laughed. "You must be crazy, Winterstein."

"I've been called worse."

"So you think murder is OK?"

"But that's not why we're here, is it?"

"I think you're putting me on. You can't believe that shit."

Nick looked at him. "There's an intersection," he said, "in Shelby Township. At the corner some guy put up a sign that was perhaps two feet by two feet. It said, DO NOT LITTER MY NEIGHBORHOOD. The guy fastened aluminum cans, Styrofoam cups—odd pieces of trash—to the sign. Passing cars, the would-be litterers, used the sign as a target. They threw bottles and cans at it. The trash piled up, and every so often, the guy would clean it up. But a few days later, the area was trashed out again. After about a year, the guy took the sign down. Perhaps he felt disheartened, defeated. But you drive by that intersection now, and the corner is clean. No sign and not a single piece of trash."

"So what's your point?" Purcell said.

Nick thought to explain it further but changed his mind. The explanation would receive no more understanding than the story had.

"What's the stupid point?"

Nick shook his head. "Nothing, Robert...nothing at all."

The young waitress brought their orders and set them on the table. She asked Nick whether he wanted another glass of wine, and he said no. Purcell asked for another beer.

"So what do you want?" Nick asked Purcell.

"I want Carthage, and I want Marshall to help. He'd save his own ass if he did."

"So why not go after Carthage?"

"I don't think I can win in court. But with Marshall's help," he said, "I have a better chance."

"What's in it for Marshall?"

"Marshall agrees to retire, permanently. That includes politics and all business activities."

"So he pleads to a lesser charge?"

"No. He pleads no contest, and he gets a slap on the wrist."

"What's a slap on the wrist?"

"Three to six months. Of course the judge will have the final say. If he doesn't cooperate"—he took a bite of the hamburger—"he's looking at a possible twenty years," he said while still chewing. A piece of onion hung from the corner of his mouth.

There was no guarantee, but Nick felt he could beat Purcell in court. Purcell's sloppy and crude demeanor wasn't a clever diversion. Purcell might have thought so, and it might have served him well in the past, but Nick saw a naked actor.

Nick opened the BLT, ate the bacon, and left the rest. When Purcell had finished, he asked, "What's her name?"

"The waitress?" Nick asked.

Purcell nodded while taking a drink of beer.

"Karen."

Purcell called to her by name then motioned for the check. Karen set two checks at the center of the table, and Nick picked both of them up. Purcell nodded his thanks and excused himself for the restroom. Nick stood and placed a twenty-dollar tip beneath his wineglass then went to the register to pay the checks.

In the mirror at the end of the bar, he saw Purcell emerge from the restroom and pass their table. Purcell noticed the tip, and with a sleight of hand, he pocketed it as he passed the table.

The winters were long and cold and the days short. Through the front window, Cheryl watched the snow blow sideways through the bare trees. Nick and Kathleena were in school, and her husband worked in the shop. There was a new order for cabinets, and they were grateful to have the work. She put on a heavy cardigan to go out to the shop to help her husband anyway she could, but as she opened the side door, she saw Melina walking, with her head down against the blowing snow, toward the shop. Cheryl stepped back inside. She leaned against the door as tears fell down her cheeks.

On rare occasions the gray clouds of February gave way to the sun. In a short jacket, scarf, and fuzzy mittens, Cheryl rolled Nick's bike out of the toolshed and rode to Sy's Lebanon Market two miles away. The center of the road was dry and clear of snow.

Sy's had a butcher's counter, canned goods, produce, a wine shelf, and a standing cooler for beer and soft drinks. Cheryl collected a pound of bacon, two pounds of dried beans, and several onions; she took them to the register at the front counter. Sy called from the back that he'd be there in a moment. His daughter usually worked the cash register, but she was sick. He thought it was the flu. He needed someone to fill in—someone good with numbers.

"I am," Cheryl said. "I'm good with numbers. It comes easy for me." She started work the next day. Sy would teach her what to do: how to pay the vendors from the cash register, deposit the invoices in the cash drawer, and keep a record of expenses.

The job was more rewarding than she'd imagined—the pleasure of making all the numbers balance at the end of the day, the pleasure of everyone's company and the men who made small talk and flirted with her—it was heart lifting.

The Stroh's deliveryman came twice a week. He parked in front, loaded several cases of beer on his hand truck, and wheeled them inside. He was young and handsome. Curls of black hair hung over his forehead, and his smile was white. After filling the cooler with beer, he handed the invoice to Cheryl. She felt giddy as he stood there and smiled at her. She noticed the ring on his left hand, and she too was married, but the thrill of his smile was all she needed.

In time he asked her whether she liked hockey. The company handed out complimentary tickets to their customers. He had two tickets and urged her to take them. "Take your husband," he said. The Montreal Canadians were in town to play the Red Wings. She loved hockey! It was so fast and exciting.

Her husband said he wasn't interested in going and questioned the man's motives behind the free tickets. In that case she would take her son to the game. The look from her husband was that of mere tolerance.

Nick wanted to take his hockey stick, but Cheryl convinced him it wasn't a good idea. He asked whether they would see Maurice "the Rocket" Richard, Gordie Howe, and Terry Sawchuk. Joseph appeared sullen that his son could somehow replace him.

The Detroit Olympia was a magic show of color and ice and sound. The French-Canadian fans wore sweaters with a *C* on the front, and many of the girls wore matching plaid skirts of red and green. The voice from the overhead speaker system was in both English and French, and when the Canadians scored a goal, their fans jumped to their feet and screamed and shouted, "*Les Canadiens!*" The night was full of romance. Cheryl felt as free and happy as the young French-Canadian girls waving their colorful pennants.

The exhilaration of the night lasted into the frigid drive home over snowy streets. Oh, if only she could be young again and know what she knew now.

As she turned into the drive, the headlights fell across the snow-covered yard. She saw Melina leave the house from the side door and step into the headlights. Melina looked up, her hand raised to shield her eyes against the light.

Nick was at the computer in his study when Nicole asked to speak to him. It was early morning, and she was in cutoff denim shorts and canvas sneakers without socks. There was garden soil on her knees. She looked toward the balcony then back at Nick. At that moment he again saw the striking resemblance to his mother.

"What is it?" he asked.

She sat down. "I want to change my name," she said, "legally."

"Your name?"

"Yes, my last name," she said, "to Winterstein."

For a moment Nick said nothing. His daughter had just asked to be known by her rightful surname. A sense of pride welled inside him. "Yes, we can do that," he said. "And for Bridget too, if she wishes."

Nicole's apprehension turned to a smile. Without a word she got to her feet. She turned to go, but she stopped at the door. "Do you like hockey?"

"Yes, although I haven't been to a game in years."

"I saw those hockey sticks in the garage. They look pretty old. One has your name on it."

"I did that with a woodburning tool. I was just eight or nine. My father made an ice pond in the backyard."

"Bridget said she's been to that house. The one you grew up in."

"My old house?" he asked. "In the old neighborhood?"

"The lock was torn off. That black guy, Michael, took her there. She met him at the bus station. She went from Baltimore to someplace in Philly to here."

"It was Carthage," he said. "It had to be. How'd she get hooked up with him?"

Nicole shook her head. "I don't know. Drugs...She was looking for you."

"Did she talk about Carthage, say anything about him?"

"She said he was nice to her, gave her something to eat, a place to stay. She said she fell in love with him."

"Love?"

"Then he got mean toward her. He passed her around to his friends, made her work the streets. That's when she ran off. He started hitting her." Tears filled her eyes. "What kind of mother am I?"

"At least you were there, Nicole."

"What good did it do? Look at her now. She used to be such a sweet thing. And then the drugs. I don't recognize her anymore."

The next day Nick asked Helen to collect the necessary forms to begin the process to change Nicole's surname to Winterstein, while he arranged to meet with Judge Marshall to discuss the deal Purcell had suggested. He spoke to Marshall over the phone. He asked to meet with him the following day. Marshall was slow to agree. "Where?" he asked.

"I think my office is best."

The next day Marshall arrived in the morning. They had agreed on ten o'clock, but Marshall didn't arrive until after eleven. For Marshall the inevitable was hard to confront. He had been exposed to the law all his adult life, either on the bench or while arguing before it, but now that he was subject to its penalties, his demeanor was cautious. They met not in Nick's office but in the conference room at an empty table with a yellow notepad in front of Nick. He offered Marshall a cup of coffee and spoke politely, but the seriousness of the issue was in his tone.

The US Attorney's Office, with stipulations, was willing to make a deal for his testimony in the prosecution of Jessup Carthage. Marshall listened; he wasn't at all surprised at what he heard. He easily could agree to retire from the law and all business activities, but he wanted a guarantee of no prison time whatsoever.

"Going to court is risky," Nick said.

"What do you think of Purcell? I've never seen him in a courtroom."

"He's sloppy, and I don't think it's an affectation. I think it would be easy to dismantle any debate he put forth. But he also has hard evidence. You'd need a carefully selected jury."

"I've got to think about it, Winterstein."

"Taking the deal is the safest choice."

"Carthage and I go back a long ways."

"He was willing to sacrifice you," Nick said.

"It comes down to self-preservation, doesn't it?"

"Yes, it does."

"But there's no guarantee. I could still end up in prison." He looked at Nick. "What would you do…if it was your freedom at stake?"

"I don't know, Judge. But I'd put a great deal of thought into it."

After and during their meeting, Nick still thought of Michael Carthage and Bridget. He couldn't let the thought go. The irony was compelling and painful. He let Helen know he was leaving early and would see her Sunday at the house for the picnic. Yes, she too was looking forward to it. As he left the office, he looked back through the glass door. Helen was busy putting together her wrongful-death case.

He drove north on Gratiot Avenue toward the old neighborhood. The streets he'd known as a boy were basically the same but older. The empty lots of open field were gone, and the people he now saw were strangers to him. At the corner of Frazho Road and Gratiot Avenue, there used to be a pool hall. As a young man, he'd once thought he could earn a living playing pool. The thought now made him smile.

He continued down Frazho to the old house. He stopped in front of it then pulled into the drive. From the driveway he saw the side door. It looked to be open. As he walked toward it, he saw the padlock had been ripped from the doorjamb. Wooden splinters hung from the door.

Inside, the floor was littered with hypodermic needles, cellophane wrappers, and plastic baggies no larger than a coin. A blood-stained mattress lay on the floor in the bedroom. In the living room, a stairway without a railing led to the attic bedroom where Nick and his sisters used to sleep. He went upstairs. The glass was broken in the window, and trash covered the floor. He returned to the living room and checked the front door. There was a closet in the entryway. He opened it. The tile his father had laid in 1955 was still in place. He stared at it for a moment then closed the door. On his way out, he stopped at the side door and looked back at the interior. How had Bridget ended up here?

He returned to the driveway and opened the car door. An elderly woman watched him through her kitchen window next door. Melina once had lived there. He got into the car and looked toward the old woman. Their eyes met.

Blowing snow collected in the corner of the shop window. Near the window the draft was strong and cold, and the light was dim. In the winter months, the garage door was closed, and Joseph worked beneath the fluorescent lights that hung from the ceiling joist. He put his hands together and warmed them with his breath. When his son was here, he kept a fire in the woodstove and the coffeepot at the edge of the stove to keep it warm, but Nick was in school now. He missed his son during these winter afternoons in the shop. He might go for hours without talking to him, but to look up and see Nick puttering in the shop was pleasant company.

He tapped on the front window to shake the snow free to see across the yard. Joe Kopecny was at work, and the children were at school. Melina was alone. The window steamed over from his breath, and he wiped it clean again. He caught a glimpse of Melina as she switched on the kitchen light.

He rekindled the fire and filled the coffeepot with water from the house then added fresh grounds to the basket and placed it on the stove in the shop. His wife was at Sy's Market. Her job gave them time away from each other. Since Melina and her husband had moved in next door, he'd been confronted with the mistake of his marriage. While he was in the service, he'd received her letter that she was pregnant; the news had taken him by surprise. Before he had gotten his thoughts together, she had arrived at the Greyhound station in Rapid City, and they were married. Much later he thought about the timeline between her pregnancy and the birth of their son, and he grew suspicious that she hadn't been pregnant at the time of their marriage. As the years went by, he felt he'd been duped into a marriage he'd never wanted.

He stoked the fire, and the flames went from blue to yellow. The coffee started to perk. He could smell it.

The side door opened, and Melina stepped in from the snow. Her smile was white and beautiful, her complexion almost olive, her eyes a deep hazel, her hair dark and wavy with flakes of snow in it. Her presence changed the cold to warmth. She was everything that ever had attracted him in a woman. She stepped closer to kiss him. He never could see enough of her. She assured him that when the children were older, she would divorce Kopecny, and then they could be together. He held her close, but in his heart, he knew he never could initiate a divorce while his children were still under his roof. A divorce had to come from Cheryl, but he didn't admit this to Melina.

For the next few hours, they sat near the fire and drank coffee from the same cup. They shared dreams and memories and their plans for the future, but in their young hearts, there was only the moment, and in the moment, there was no thought of the pain they created for others.

The afternoon grew short, and the time for Melina to leave was near. Pulling away from each other was difficult, but they might find reason to meet again this evening. Not realizing they were in the open door, he kissed her good-bye. A snowflake stuck to her eyelash as she pulled away. Moments later he stood alone in the shop. He heard the wind blow against the garage.

Back at home, Melina stepped through the back entry into the vestibule and closed the door behind her. She stamped the snow from her shoes, and then she leaned against the door as if in thought. A moment later she removed her woolen coat, hung it on a hook, and went into the kitchen. She looked across the yard to the garage she'd just left. The blowing snow again covered the garage windows; the light inside appeared soft through the snow.

She sat down at the kitchen table. The house was quiet and still. Everything outside was covered in white, and even the sound of a passing car was silenced in the fluffy snow. Melina always had taken silent pride in her inner strength, her ability to conceal her emotions. Her anger might burst forward, sometimes with fury, but she saw that as a minor flare of temper. She didn't consider it an emotion. She thought of Joseph, her lover across the yard—now *he* had a temper. The thought made her smile. They were alike in many ways. But she would never allow another person to see her inner pain. That was weakness. In the solitude of her house, now covered with snow, the protection of privacy, tears welled in her eyes and trailed down her cheeks.

She had married too young—a girl of seventeen from a small town in north-central Michigan. Joe Kopecny had been in his twenties; he appeared worldly and wise, flamboyant, boisterous, with money to spend, and stories of city life in Detroit. He'd boasted that he knew Henry Ford, even called him "Henry." His chin held with pride, he'd talked of his job at the Ford plant, his position as supervisor, a foreman of importance. The night she had met him beneath the lights of a country carnival, Melina saw a chance to leave the dull country behind and find a place in the city. Far above the Ferris wheel, deep into the velvet night, she saw a shooting star and wished upon it.

But once she was married to Kopecny, with the noise of the city and the smoke of factories forever in the background, his stories fell apart. Although his job was dependable and it supported them, he wasn't a supervisor or a foreman but a machinist, one among many other machinists. Kopecny seemed unaware of the stories he told. After a year of marriage, Melina found herself standing next to him while he retold the same stories—flamboyant lies—to a new listener. She realized he did not hear himself, was unaware…He was like a blind man describing a color he never had seen. The color was his fantasy world. At first she was angry, hostile—having been duped by his lies. Then her anger turned to sympathy and then indifference.

Now, sitting at the kitchen table, wiping tears from her face with her hands, she saw Kopecny pull into the driveway. She looked up at the wall clock. It was already four! She went to the bathroom to rinse her eyes and face. She wouldn't return to the kitchen to begin dinner until her eyes were clear. Not a single tear.

Not a trace.

A picnic table covered with a white tablecloth had been set on the patio. Nicole placed cushions on the chairs and set the table with dinner plates trimmed in gold. There was a wineglass along with silverware on a cloth napkin with each setting. Next to her father, she set a place for Sandy. She looked forward to meeting the woman Helen referred to as her father's girlfriend.

Nick pushed croquet wickets into the lawn. At the other end was Nicole's garden. There were tomatoes and zucchini, bell peppers, carrots, radishes, and scallions. Pink and lavender zinnias grew along the perimeter of the garden. Butterflies floated above the flowers.

Nicole went upstairs to coax Bridget into the shower. She spent all her time in front of the TV. It didn't seem that she paid it any attention; she simply stared at the screen. When asked why she didn't do anything, try to participate in something, she said she was depressed and didn't care about anything. "What's the use?" she said. "I'm going to die. I have AIDS."

"You don't have AIDS," Nicole said, "and don't think that way. You have the virus that could lead to it. But if you take your medication, you can prevent it."

While Bridget was in the shower, Nicole opened the shower door and handed her a bottle of shampoo.

"I don't need it," Bridget said.

Nicole looked for patience. "Please, honey, do it for me." Through the shower door, she saw Bridget lift the bottle to her head, squeeze it, then let it drop to the floor. Nicole waited a moment longer to see the shampoo lather, then went back to the bedroom. She picked up from the floor Bridget's jeans, a pair of shorts, a blouse, soiled underwear, and an empty soda can. She then looked through Bridget's closet. They recently had been shopping, but most of the new items were on the closet floor.

Wrapped in a towel, Bridget appeared in the bedroom with her hair dripping wet. "I don't want to go," she said. "I can't. I don't want to see anybody."

"Please, Bridget…The sunshine will do you good."

Bridget sat down on the sofa. "I can't."

Nicole got a towel from the bathroom and started drying her daughter's hair. "Would you like your hair done this week? Maybe a little shorter? I can make an appointment."

"I don't care."

Nicole took her by the hand and led her to the bathroom to use the hair dryer. "Why is he doing all this?" Bridget asked.

"Because he's your grandfather."

"He doesn't feel like it. He doesn't feel like anything to me."

"We're family, Bridget."

"But how? He doesn't know us. How can you care for someone you don't even know?"

Nicole turned off the hair dryer and looked at Bridget in the mirror. "If you came into my life just a week ago, I would still love you."

Nicole finished drying her daughter's hair then picked out something for her to wear, but Bridget didn't like her choice. "I'll wear these," she said.

"The jeans? They're torn."

"They're clean."

"But they have holes in the front."

"I like them."

Nicole said no more about it. On her way down through the kitchen, she stopped for a bottle of Chardonnay and a corkscrew. Once on the patio, she found that Helen already had opened a bottle of Riesling and handed a glass to Nick. "Sandy doesn't know, does she?" Helen said.

"No," he said, "but she will after today."

"It might come as a shock. How will she take it?"

"I don't know. But what was I supposed to do? She's not a witness to be prepared beforehand. It all feels so complicated."

At the moment the exchange between Nick and Helen meant nothing to Nicole. She paid little attention to it; not until later did the pieces fit together.

Helen looked at Nicole. "How's Bridget?"

"She'll be down soon, I hope."

Nicole watched her father for a moment. With a pair of lawn scissors, he cut fresh flowers and arranged them in a bouquet at the center of the table. His movements were smooth and fluid, while the man inside was hidden. He looked up and winked at her as though he knew she had been watching him.

Nicole poured a glass of wine and sampled a piece of cheese she'd gotten at Whole Foods. Her father had taken her there; she complained it was too expensive, but she could see he wasn't interested in prices. It made her smile and feel even closer to him.

Helen came from the kitchen with a plate of hors d'oeuvres and set it on the table. They heard a car pull into the drive, but nothing appeared in front of the garage. Her father walked toward the drive. A moment later Nicole heard voices.

A woman with graying hair appeared with her father, her arm looped through his. She was dressed casually, but the jewelry she wore appeared expensive. Her necklace caught the sunlight. Nicole was eager to meet her father's friend. She stepped forward with her hand out. "Hello. I'm Nicole."

"Hello. I'm Sandy...Nicole?"

"Yes, Nicole Winterstein."

"Winterstein? Are you a cousin?" She looked toward Nick then back at Nicole.

"No," Nicole said, "father and daughter."

From the look on Sandy's face and the silence that followed, Nicole realized Sandy had no idea Nick had a daughter. The moment was awkward.

Helen broke the silence. "Sandy, I'm Helen Wincraft." She offered her hand. "I'm no relation," she said in a light manner. "I work for Nick...his paralegal."

"Oh, yes. Nick mentioned you. But he didn't tell me how beautiful you are."

"Thank you," Helen said.

Sandy looked at Helen for a moment longer, but she said nothing more. Bridget came onto the patio with a glass in her hand. Nicole worried it was brandy. Sandy turned to look at Bridget then back at Nick.

"My granddaughter," Nick said.

"My," Sandy said, "the surprise that keeps on giving. May I have a glass of wine?" She glanced at Nick in an unkind manner.

Nicole suggested a seat on the patio, while Helen poured Sandy a glass of wine. Bridget sat opposite them. Nicole noticed Bridget's glass was nearly empty.

Helen handed Sandy the wineglass. "I think you'll like this," she said. "It's Nick's favorite, a Riesling."

"It might be the one I gave him." She looked at Helen over the top of her glass. "You look familiar," she said. "I can't place it, but I've seen you someplace before."

Nicole glanced at Helen then at her father. She realized Sandy knew nothing of Helen's background.

"Do you have kids?" Bridget asked, looking at Sandy. Her glass was empty.

"Yes," Sandy said. "I have a daughter, Mellissa." She looked at Nick then back at Bridget. "And a son, Edward Jr. He was going to come with me today, but something came up, and he couldn't. He's really a sweet boy. He'd do anything for me."

Nicole thought her words sounded shallow, if not untrue. As they sat down to lunch, it seemed to her that Sandy was a bit removed, if not distant, from Nick. She couldn't read her father.

"What's your daughter like?" Bridget said. "I'm all fucked up. I have AIDS."

Sandy's eyes opened wide.

"Bridget, stop!" Nicole said.

When Sandy found her voice, she said, "Mellissa's quite a young lady. She won a 4-H ribbon when she was fourteen and was homecoming queen at Seaholm High. I'm very proud of her."

"Homecoming queen." Bridget rolled her eyes. "I fucked a nigger and got beat up."

Nicole stood up. "Bridget, that's enough!"

"You mean, I can go now? Thank God." She left the table and walked toward the house.

"I'm sorry," Nicole said. "It's been difficult."

"Sounds like an understatement," Sandy said.

Nick had stopped eating his salad but said nothing. Sandy looked irritated over his silence.

"Maybe we should all take a breath," Helen said. "Change the subject...have another glass of wine."

Sandy's expression changed. "Oh, my God, now I remember! You went to prison for having sex with children."

Without looking at her, Nick said, "Sandy, please!"

Sandy got up from the table. Her napkin fell to the ground. She took her purse and turned to go but stopped. "A secret family, a pedophile...I thought I knew you, Nicky!"

She got into her car and slammed the door closed. Through the windshield she looked at Nick, but he didn't come forward to stop her. This wasn't the time. He should have handled the situation differently; he should have warned her, should have given her some indication of what lay ahead, but he hadn't. He couldn't undo it.

Sandy backed out of the driveway.

It snowed for three days. On the north side of the house, the snow drifted to the top of the window. Nick helped his father shovel snow from the front door to the drive and from the side door to the shop. His father said there was no work in the shop, and there might not be any until early spring. His mother said they would be fine. There were canned goods in the pantry, and she earned a few dollars at Sy's Market. Things were nice when they got along.

In the early weeks of winter, his father had made an ice rink in the backyard. He rolled logs into place and packed sod along the bottom of the logs to form a seal. It was twenty yards long and ten yards wide. The fire department ran a hose from the hydrant on Firwood Road and flooded the rink. Nick and his friends replayed the final game of the Stanley Cup over and over, and the Red Wings always won.

It stopped snowing as the weekend came. The sun was blinding off the new snow, but in the late afternoon, the light was soft. As the sun grew closer to the horizon and the shadows longer, the days grew lonely.

Monday was the first day of winter camp, and this year his father was a counselor. Everyone met at the school and packed their gear into the yellow buses to drive north to Cedar Lake. There were six boys to a group, and they shared bunk beds in a single cabin. The cabin next to them was all girls, and the boys were told it was off-limits. Nick's father was the counselor for a different group of boys, and Nick saw him only at mealtimes. Nick's counselor was Linda Matlock's father. Nick had a crush on Linda, but she'd never liked him because he had freckles. She'd never said that, but Nick guessed that was what it was—the freckles.

Breakfast was served in a large log-cabin cafeteria with long wooden tables. Nick's father sat at a table with all the teachers and the other counselors. The school superintendent, Mr. Tower, was there. He never smiled, and everyone was afraid of him. He smoked a pipe and sat next to Nick's father. They talked for a long time. Mr. Tower jabbed the air with the stem of his pipe while he talked, and his father nodded as he listened. They sat together in the evenings too, and sometimes a teacher would join them, and they would all laugh together.

At night the boys lay in their bunk beds and talked to one another in the dark. Charles Anderson wanted to knock on the window of the girls' cabin to scare them, but no one wanted to go out in the snow in his pajamas. Later in the week, the girls crossed the open snow between the cabins in the dark and threw snowballs at the boys' windows. The boys ran out in their bare feet to chase after the girls, but they already had run back in their cabin, and the boys were left standing there, barefoot in the snow.

The days were spent in workshops learning how to walk in snowshoes and use cross country skis and how to tell when the ice was too dangerous to hold your weight. Charles Anderson said they would know when they fell through the ice, and the teacher raised an eyebrow at him. Toward the end of the week, everyone made a logbook with a wooden cover to record all the events and lessons learned.

Nick carved his name and the date on the front cover with a wood-burning tool.

On the last day of camp, Mr. Tower walked toward Nick. He removed his pipe and said, "Your father is a fine man, Nick." Mr. Silvisky, the math teacher, had said the same thing earlier in the morning, and he'd heard the same from Linda Matlock's father. Everyone liked his father. Nick felt proud.

That night at home, with the house half buried in snow, his father pulled the blanket up around Nick and kissed him on the forehead. He said good night to Nick's sisters too. He called them Princess One and Princess Two.

It was late evening. Nick, Nicole, and Helen were in the living room. Helen and Nicole each poured a brandy and sat on the sofa. Nick had a cup of hot broth in a coffee mug. For years he'd had several drinks before he went to bed, until he noticed the ritual had gotten out of hand, and then he never went back to it.

"I feel so bad about what happened," Nicole said.

Helen squeezed her hand.

"I'll let Sandy have a few days," Nick said, "and then I'll call her. We have a special history together. It'll be fine."

"She was more hurt than anything else," Helen said.

"And betrayed that I hadn't mentioned it," Nick said. "I really should have. But how? I'm just learning what to do myself. It was my fault."

"There was no reason for Bridget to be so nasty," Nicole said.

"Bridget isn't to blame," Nick said. "Look at what she's living with—HIV, the confused anger she must feel, the inevitable 'Why me?'"

Helen finished her brandy and poured another one. "I'm beginning to feel this," she said after taking a sip.

"Spend the night here," Nick offered. "Don't drive home. It's late."

"Thanks. I think I will."

"Your room is made up," Nicole said. She added more brandy to her own glass. "How did you meet Sandy?" she asked Nick. "Have you known her a long time?"

"Since high school," he said. "She was dumped by her boyfriend—whom she later married and then divorced—and I had just been dumped by Betty."

"Betty?"

"Betty Kleinhower," he said. "She broke my heart. I was sixteen, and she was my first love."

"The first love," Helen said. "That's something we never forget."

"I met Sandy that summer at a baseball game. I saw her a few times while she was married too. Then I didn't see her again until after her divorce. I ran into her on the golf course."

"It doesn't sound like there's any real connection there," Nicole said.

"I like spending time with her," he said. "But there's another side to her—you saw it this afternoon—and her daughter isn't what she made her out to be. She's on probation for shoplifting and has a drug problem. Sandy sees it as her fault—failure as a mother, failed marriage."

In the silence that followed, Nicole stood. "How do you know what to do, what's right?" She set her drink on the coffee table. "I'm going to check on Bridget." She walked toward the stairway in the hall.

"You got a phone call yesterday," Helen told Nick. "I didn't want to say anything earlier."

"Marshall?"

"No, Jessup Carthage."

"Carthage? I can't represent him, if that's what he wants."

"He wants to meet with you. He said Monday at your office."

Nick thought for a moment. "It could prove interesting. Did he mention a time?"

"Ten a.m.," she said. "I checked your calendar. There's nothing."

He raised his mug to sip the broth, but it had gotten cold. He went to the kitchen to warm it in the microwave. He noticed the bottle of cooking brandy was empty. It was the one Bridget had gotten into that afternoon.

When he returned to the living room, Nicole was there. She was upset. "Bridget passed out."

"The cooking brandy is gone," Nick said. "She drank the whole thing!"

"It's not that. There's a needle mark on her arm—it's all bruised."

"Needle mark," Helen said. "How'd she get it? She hasn't left the house."

"I don't know." Nicole was near tears.

"Rotheim has a nurse practitioner. She makes house calls."

"Shouldn't we call 9-1-1?" Nicole said."

"No," Helen said. "They're dysfunctional."

"Then it goes public," Nick added. He searched his pockets. "Where's my cell phone?"

"Is it on the charger?"

Nick found his phone on the end table in the hallway. He unplugged it from the charger and made the call. It rang a half dozen times, and he was afraid it would go to voice mail, but then a man answered. It was Rotheim. He and his wife were separated but not yet divorced. He had since become romantically involved with Adele, his nurse practitioner.

"Allen?"

"Yes."

"Is Adele there? Bridget has passed out. I think it's a drug overdose. I'm not sure."

"Is she breathing regularly?"

"I don't know."

He heard Allen say something to Adele. Then he said to Nick, "We'll be right there."

Nick went upstairs to Bridget's room. Nicole and Helen were there. Bridget lay on the sofa in front of the TV. Her arm dangled to the floor. He took her hand and placed two fingers on the inside of her wrist.

"Her pulse is slow," he said, "her breathing shallow." He looked at the bruise on her forearm. "I'll wait downstairs for Allen."

Nick waited at the front window where he could see the head-lights turn into the drive. He checked his watch and then again. He saw a car in the distance; it slowed and turned into the drive.

Adele was much younger than Allen. She could have been his granddaughter. Her red hair was long and full of natural curls worn in a loose bun. Her eyes were ocean green. She had freckles on her forehead and across her nose. There was a studious silence in her face, patience without judgment. Nick led them upstairs.

Allen knelt next to Bridget, who lay on the sofa. He put the stetho-scope to her heart and her lungs then lifted her eyelids back. "Her pupils are just a pinpoint," he said. "Her lips are turning blue. Has she been drinking?"

"She's been drinking brandy," Nick said, "and she's concealed Valium in the past."

Allen turned to Adele. "Naloxone, ten milligrams."

Adele looked at him without moving, as if questioning his request. A moment passed. Allen stared at her; he appeared confused for an instant. "No," he said. "Five milligrams."

Adele's hand went swiftly to the medical bag. She prepared the injection and handed it to Allen. As he accepted the injection, the correct dose, their eyes met for an instant, and then he turned to Bridget and injected the naloxone into her vein.

Several minutes passed after the injection. "One more," he said, looking at Adele, their eyes in agreement. "Three milligrams."

Adele handed him another injection. Moments later Bridget be-gan to respond.

"Bridget," Allen said, "can you hear me?"

She nodded.

"Do you know who I am?" he asked.

She nodded again.

"Take a deep breath, through your nose. Can you do that?"

She inhaled slowly then exhaled. "I'm tired," she said, "sleepy."

Allen stood up. He looked down at her for a moment then knelt again next to her. He put the stethoscope to her chest. Several moments went by...long moments. He stood up again.

"Let her rest," he said, "but keep an eye on her." He looked at Nick. "And don't hesitate to call—if there's any change at all."

Adele touched Nicole's hand. "She'll be OK." In Adele's tone, her touch, the softness in her eyes was the quiet wisdom of a woman well beyond her years. Nicole sensed this; Nick sensed it; and Helen's attention was captured by it.

"Thank you," Nicole said, as if in another voice she were saying, *I'd like to know you better.*

Nick walked Allen and Adele downstairs. Allen descended first, and from where Nick stood in back of him, he saw Allen's profile. He saw the young boy he'd grown up with, gone to school with—the young man he'd warned against the foolish marriage Allen had fallen into headlong without thought at nineteen.

At the front door, Nick said, "Allen, I can't thank you enough."

Allen placed his hand on Nick's shoulder and smiled. Adele looked at Allen. "We go back a long way," Allen said to her. "Actually we're related. Second or third cousins?"

"Second," Nick said. "It goes back through the Spanglers' side."

Nick waited at the door until the car backed out of the drive and turned onto the street; then he returned upstairs.

Helen met him at the bedroom door. "You aren't going to believe this," she said.

"What?"

They returned to the sofa and stood next to Bridget. "Bridget, honey," Nicole said, "tell me again. Where did you get the drugs?"

She answered in a sleepy, opiate-induced voice, "Michael. He loves me."

"Michael," Nick repeated. "Michael Carthage?"

Nicole nodded.

"Carthage." He looked at Helen then back at Bridget. "How, Bridget? Did you meet him somewhere?"

She shook her head. "He came here."

Nick turned red. "He was in my house?"

The snow melted by early spring, but the mornings were still cold. Nick could see his breath in the air, and the county ditch was covered with clear ice. Melina's son, Dale, was a few years older than Nick, and he dared Nick to cross the ice. Nick placed one foot on the ice, but the sound of it beginning to crack made him draw his foot back. Dale wasn't a bully, but in his old neighborhood, in the inner city, the other boys were tough. Dale told stories of having been beaten up after school and having his bike taken. He now stood with his thumbs hooked in his front pockets and dared Nick a second time to cross the ice, but Nick refused.

That summer Melina bought Dale a Red Ryder BB gun, and when Dale shot out the windows of a neighbor's toolshed, Joe Kopecny threatened to "beat his ass" and "take that goddamn BB gun away," but Melina told her husband to shut up because she was sick of listening to him. Soon after that Dale hid in the shrubs in front of his house and shot at passing cars in the street. A neighbor from across the street complained about the gun, and Kopecny took "that goddamn BB gun" and threatened to "break the son of a bitch in half," but Melina told him he wasn't going to break anything.

The following year Dale turned fourteen and got his driver's license for motor scooters less than five horsepower. With his thumbs hooked in his front pockets, he told everyone he was going to get a Cushman Eagle, but Joe Kopecny said he wasn't getting a goddamn Cushman because they cost too goddamn much. Soon after that Melina enrolled in night school to learn typing and shorthand, and in less than six weeks, she had a secretarial job. Each paycheck was set aside to buy Dale a Cushman Eagle motor scooter.

The motor scooter was shiny black with chrome trim. Resting on the kickstand on the gravel drive, it looked like a real motorcycle. Boys from the neighborhood gathered around to look it over and dream. Nick asked whether he could sit on it, and Dale said no, not 'til he was older.

Soon after Melina finished paying for the motor scooter, she quit her job and again spent most of her time in the shop with Nick's father. She sometimes visited Nick's mother, although his mother never looked pleased to see her. Kopecny still complained that she spent too goddamn much time over there, but nothing changed. He wandered into the yard one night to tell Nick's father Melina was just a whore—always had been and always would be. Pointing and waving his finger, he said he'd caught her screwing a nigger—caught her in the goddamn house with him. Nick's father walked away. He wouldn't listen to it. Kopecny turned to Nick, the only one left standing there. "In the goddamn house," he said, "with that nigger."

The phone on Nick's desk rang, and he saw the call was on line one. He waited for Helen to pick it up. He heard her voice but couldn't make out who was on the other end. A moment later Helen appeared in the doorway.

"It's Jessup Carthage," she said.

Nick reached for the phone. "Hello."

"Winterstein, this is Jessup Carthage. I arranged to meet with you this morning, but something came up. I have to ask a favor."

Nick never had before spoken to Carthage, but the halting cadence of his speech, as if great thought had been given to each word, had the sound of a news clip rehearsed and delivered before an audience.

"A favor?" Nick said.

"Yes, my daughter, ah, would like to meet with you."

"What seems to be the issue?"

"Well…I'll let her explain. And, ah, I'd like to thank you for helping my grandson…though your bill did seem a little high."

"Is your daughter aware of this call?"

"She spoke to Marshall." He paused. "He mentioned your name."

Something was going on between Marshall and Carthage. To become further involved with Carthage had the appearance of an oncoming collision, but Nick agreed to talk to his daughter. What happened to Monica Carthage meant nothing to him. Her son was the motivation.

"I'll call her," Nick said. "Does she have a private number?" He wrote the number on a yellow pad.

Stories of an investigation into Monica Carthage and the misuse of campaign funds had first surfaced more than a year ago. When reporters had confronted her about it, she gave "no comment" rather than an outright denial. She already looked guilty.

From the very beginning of her career, Monica Carthage had campaigned on race and race alone. She traveled the campaign trail in her trademark red Lincoln Navigator. Reporters and camera crews followed her around the city as she stoked the crowd. "Slavery and lynching ain't dead in America; it's right here, in your state, right now!"

She was in her final term as a state senator, and as word surfaced that she was going to run for a vacant seat in the US House of Representatives, stories of shopping trips to New York and Caribbean vacations, rumored to have been paid for with campaign funds, began to appear.

The Chicago Christian Leadership Conference owned Monica's Rosedale Park home and the Lincoln Navigator. Meeting on someone else's turf for an initial interview was against Nick's policy, but he wasn't interested in helping Monica Carthage. He was curious to see this side of Michael Carthage. With the advantages that surrounded him, why did he prefer the streets and the image of an outlaw, the Black Panther motif? From all accounts women found him charming and charismatic. They were drawn to him. But there was a darker side too; Nick had had a glimpse of it.

When Nick arrived at the Rosedale house, Monica Carthage answered the door. He had expected a staff member or an aide to answer the door, but she was by herself.

"Thank you for coming, Mr. Winterstein." She led him into the living room. "Judge Marshall speaks highly of you." She was less portly than the camera had portrayed her, and on the surface, her manner was cordial. There was no evidence of the strident campaigner. "May I get you something to drink?" she offered. "Coffee? Glass of wine?"

"White wine sounds fine."

When she left the room, Nick looked around. There were several pieces of African art—paintings on the wall and sculptures on an end table. Above the mantel there was a pair of diamond-and-leaf-pattern crystal bowls, one of which was exclusive to Tiffany's. Around the corner to an adjoining room, Nick saw a zebra-striped chair.

"I hope you like this." She reentered the room with two glasses of wine. "You might think it a little sweet."

Nick tasted it, paused, and managed to say, "It's fine."

She sat on the sofa and Nick in a chair opposite her. "I want to thank you for helping my son," she said. "It's so difficult raising a child on your own. His father and I never married, and he died so young. It was tragic."

"Tragic?" Nick asked. Although he knew the story, he was surprised she would bring this up. If someone doesn't ask to see your dirty laundry, don't wave it in the air.

"He was murdered," she said. "They never found who did it."

"I'm curious," Nick said. "It's been rumored he was the son of Huey Newton. Is there any truth to that?"

"That's been talked about for years. And I don't really know. There was a resemblance," she said, "and he did come from California."

"California?"

"Yes, Oakland. But I don't know what's true and what isn't. James *did* tell stories. He enjoyed having people think he was Huey Newton's son. In the end it may have been the reason he was killed."

"What were the circumstances behind his death?"

"Personally I think it was drugs." She shook her head. "But who knows? Drugs. The Black Panthers. He was young." She was quiet for a moment, as if deep in thought. "Now Michael's going in that direction. His grandfather has offered guidance, but he won't listen."

Nick no longer was sure of her motives. Did she want help for herself or for her son? Or were Jessup Carthage and Goodwin Marshall somehow the issue?

"Does your son live with you?" Nick asked.

"Sometimes," she said. "You know how kids are."

Nick nodded.

"Maybe you could offer him advice," she said. "He speaks nicely of you. He said you had him to your house for dinner."

Nick looked at her in silence. "Well…I'll see what I can do," he managed to say.

"But we've gotten off track," she said. "That's not what I want to talk about. Judge Marshall and my father said you might help or offer advice."

"What's the issue?" Nick asked. "What are we talking about?"

"I'm sure you've heard. I may have a problem with campaign funds. Some money got mixed together. And if that's the case, it was definitely a mistake."

Nick nodded as if he were paying close attention, but his thoughts were of Michael Carthage.

"I'd like to know I can come to you for advice," she said. "And, if necessary, turn everything over to you. My father will take care of any legal fees."

"Is your father in contact with Judge Marshall?"

"Oh, yes," she said. "They talk most every day."

"And your son…Where is he now?"

"With a friend," she said, "somewhere on the east side."

"Wouldn't be on Hurlbut Street, would it?"

"Now that you mention it," she said. "Do you know the area?"

"My great-grandparents lived on Hurlbut," he said, "when they first arrived in this country."

Nick heard a sound toward the back of the house, as if a door had closed, and then there were footsteps on the hardwood floors. Nick looked up. Michael Carthage stood in the doorway.

"Michael," his mother said. "We were just talking about you."

"Yes," Nick said with a faint smile at the corners of his eyes; the rest of his face was without emotion. "I mentioned how I enjoyed your company at dinner. When was it? Three nights ago?"

Carthage stared back, smiling, as if to say, *Yes, I'll come and go as I please.*

In July Nick's father bought a boat with an outboard engine. The engine was by Mercury, and the hull by Chris Craft was eighteen feet long. His father repaired and treated the lower half of the hull with a red marine paint then built a cabin with two bunk beds inside and attached a canvas canopy to the upper-deck windshield. His mother said there wasn't enough money to buy and maintain a boat, but she didn't argue the point. She mentioned this to Nick. His parents seldom spoke to each other anymore.

Melina and his father worked on the boat together. She made curtains for the inside of the cabin and sewed the canopy into a single piece that fit the metal brackets like an umbrella. She also helped with the painting. Nick didn't care much for the boat. He asked his father whether they could go flying again, but he never answered. Melina was there.

The Gratiot Airport had been closed for almost a year now, and new construction had started on the grounds. They were building a shopping center and a new Federal Department Store. His father's airplane had been moved to Big Beaver Airport. Nick often rode to the airport on his motor scooter. He was too young for a driver's license, and the motor scooter didn't have a real license plate on the back, but his grandfather had made one with white numbers painted on a red background. It looked so real that no one said anything. Nick was beginning to see that there was no such thing as right and wrong if no one noticed.

He kept the airplane clean and all the weeds cut around the tie-down spot. His grandfather had given him a set of tools, which Nick wrapped in a heavy rag and stored in the airplane. He waited until he was alone before he taxied onto the grass runway. He sat on a rolled-up blanket and a cushion to make the seat higher. He pushed the throttle forward, and the airplane started down the runway, gaining speed, as he pulled back on the stick and the airplane lifted off the ground.

Through mistakes in the air, he learned how to use the flight instruments to keep the airplane safe. He flew into a cloud, and suddenly everything was white all around him. He didn't know whether he was up or down or sideways until the airplane came through the bottom of the cloud and he saw the ground coming at him. He pulled back on the stick, and the airplane leveled off. Being lost in the clouds had scared him, and his heart beat fast, but as he thought about what had happened, he grew confident. The flight instruments made sense to him now, and he understood their importance. Each time he took the airplane up, he looked for ways to test his new knowledge.

Before returning home he purchased gasoline in a can to refuel the plane. He did this each time he flew it. He poured it into the wing tank with a funnel and returned the can to the gas station. By the time he got home, the sun was going down. The soft colors of sunset were over his mother's garden, and the shop lights were on. He pushed the motor scooter quietly past the shop. He worried that his father somehow might know he'd had the airplane out.

He parked the motor scooter in the toolshed and went toward the side door of the house. Lined up on the grass were bushels of corn and cucumbers and zucchini next to large red tomatoes spread on a piece of burlap. Through the screen door, he saw his mother washing something at the kitchen sink.

Melina was in the shop with his father.

Robert Purcell made it clear the deal was good for another day, and then it would be off the table. Nick was on the phone with him. Helen was in the doorway, her arms folded, leaning against the doorframe.

"Let me know by tomorrow," Purcell said.

"I'll try to get in touch with him."

"If you don't, it's over," Purcell said. "Meet me at the oyster bar, same time." He hung up.

Nick looked at Helen, the phone still in his hand.

"How do you see this playing out?" she asked.

"I don't know," he said. "Monica Carthage said Marshall and her father are talking. Marshall says they're not. Something's going on."

Nick phoned Marshall and left a voice mail. Minutes later Marshall returned the call. "Not on the phone," he said. "I'll meet with you. We'll discuss it then."

Nick arrived early for their meeting at Starbucks. He ordered a croissant and black coffee and took a seat in a leather armchair near the window. Across the street a police cruiser had pulled a car over.

The officer got out and walked toward the car. He was overweight, and his shirttail was out in the back. He motioned for the woman to roll down her window. At first she refused, but then she rolled it down. The argument continued until he reached inside the car and grabbed her; she rolled the window back up, trapping his arm. She started to drive off with his arm still stuck in the window. As he ran to keep up with the car, he stumbled, and she rolled the window down. He fell to the road then got to his knees and started shooting at the car as it sped away.

Marshall pulled into the parking lot while the officer was still shooting at the car. He glanced at the scene and walked into Starbucks.

He didn't stop at the counter to buy coffee. He came toward Nick, stopped to read something from his cell phone, then closed the phone and put it in his pocket.

"What are you going to do?" Nick asked. "Purcell wants an answer by tomorrow, or the deal's off."

"I've thought about it," Marshall said, and fell silent.

"I'm surprised he hasn't charged you both."

Marshall looked at Nick.

"It's not as if you're innocent," Nick said. "Take the deal. It'll keep you out of prison."

The word *prison* changed Marshall's expression. "It's not all that black-and-white," he said. "It's more complicated."

"Since you're not going to fill in the gray, take the deal."

Marshall nodded his consent.

"You'll have to sign off on it," Nick said, "but you know that."

The irony of Marshall's position was painful to watch. Nick liked him and wished he could do more. In his heart he knew a man's choices were not his own.

"I'll call when there's something to sign," Nick said. "I'd say the day after tomorrow." He stood up. "I hope you're ready for this."

"It's not easy," he said. "I like him; we go back a long way."

"It'll keep you out of prison, Judge."

"I know."

Nick left him to his thoughts. From outside he looked back through the window. The judge still sat there, by himself.

Nick crossed the street to his car. There was another police cruiser in back of the first one. The officer who had shot at the fleeing car stood there listening, his shirttail hanging out the back. The incident never would see a police report.

Nick did not go back to the office. He was headed home. He called Helen and said he would see her in the morning before the meeting with Purcell.

He pulled into the drive and parked in front of the open garage. Nicole was around the corner in her garden. She was spraying the plants with a homemade insecticide of jalapeño peppers mixed with garlic and water. The metal spray can once had belonged to Arthur Reichmann.

She looked up as Nick approached. Her smile was warm. "Catch any bad guys today?"

"There aren't any," he said, "just folks being themselves."

"Look at this," she said. "It's really exciting. I crossed a yellow zucchini with an acorn squash." The teardrop fruit was green with yellow flames. She pulled it from the plant. "Let's have it tonight," she said. "We'll bake it in brown sugar and butter."

Nick kissed the top of her head. "With fish?" They started toward the house. "How's Bridget?"

"Much better," she said. "That medication really helps."

"Where is she? Upstairs?"

"No, she's in the library."

He looked at her. "Really?"

Nick poured a glass of ice water with a wedge of lemon and went to the library. Bridget was in his reading chair next to the open window. The lake breeze was pleasant. "What are you reading?" he asked

She looked up from her book. "I don't know. Just something I found."

"Let's see the cover," he said. "*The Great Gatsby*."

She closed the book. "I don't know what to call you. Mom's started calling you 'Dad.' That seems so odd. You're just a stranger."

"I don't know how to answer that," he said. "But I'd like to ask you something. How did Michael Carthage get in the house?"

"I let him in."

"Why was he here?"

"I called him. I needed something."

"And he just came?"

She didn't answer.

"Doesn't the medication help?" he asked.

"It's not the same."

He earned his living by asking questions, pushing for answers, but this was his granddaughter, not someone on the witness stand. He decided to let it go.

That evening the three of them had dinner together on the patio. Serving the hybrid squash gave Nicole great pleasure. She watched her father take the first bite. His smile was her praise, and her presence was now part of his life.

In the morning Helen arranged the notes of Nick's last meeting with Purcell and set them out for his review. There was also another page of background on Purcell. It seemed there was a budding relationship between the first-assistant US attorney, Melanie MacArthur, and Purcell. If this were true and became public, his removal from the Marshall case was assured.

Nick arrived at the oyster bar a half hour before Purcell. He sat at the same table with a view of the sidewalk and the street leading to the intersection. He made himself comfortable and ordered a glass of wine.

Fifteen or twenty minutes later, he noticed Purcell at the intersection. Purcell waited for traffic to clear and stepped from the curb. He again paid close attention to the position of the security cameras atop the oyster bar, while across the street, the driver of a blue Toyota was interested in him. The driver photographed him through a long lens, right up to the door of the oyster bar and after he entered. He continued to take pictures as Nick watched. Nick mentioned none of this to Purcell. He greeted him with a handshake. Once seated, Purcell looked around. "Where's your friend?"

"Friend?"

"The waitress," he said. "She get fired?"

"I don't think so. Might be her day off."

A young Mexican man came to their table with menus. Purcell opened the menu and, without looking up, said to Nick, "Bet you anything he's illegal."

Nick couldn't have cared less but said nothing.

A moment passed. "You think you're better than me, don't you, Winterstein?"

Nick closed his menu and looked at Purcell. "I may find humanity repugnant, Robert, but that doesn't mean I don't like you."

"What's that supposed to mean?"

Looking at the menu, Nick said, "The BLT sounds good."

"It's the way you carry yourself," Purcell added, "the way you dress and act."

"I'm being baited for some reason," Nick said, putting the menu down. "What is it?"

"You sue insurance companies," Purcell said. "OK, I get it. But you put doctors out of business, good people who provide something. How do you live with yourself?"

"I follow the law, Robert, as it's written. And who writes the law? You, Robert, and people like you—people with dirty laundry and secrets to hide."

Purcell returned to his menu. "I see you've got a pedophile in your office," he said without looking up. "You're quite the zoo keeper."

It seemed Purcell had been doing his homework.

"You have a short fuse too," he added. "Does it get you in trouble?"

Nick shook his head, as if bored.

Purcell ordered a cheeseburger and a glass of beer, while Nick ordered the BLT. Nick ate only the bacon and tomato and refused the waiter's offer to pour a second glass of wine.

"Marshall has agreed to the deal," Nick said. "He'll sign the agreement tomorrow. At the district office."

Purcell held the cheeseburger with both hands and took a bite. "Good," he said while chewing. "Maybe it'll keep him out of prison."

"Maybe?"

Purcell shrugged. "We'll see."

"If we don't like what we read, there's no deal. The man's not stupid."

"Then why's he in this position?"

The blue Toyota was still across the street. It seemed odd that the driver remained so obvious, his camera still pointed toward the window, toward Purcell's smug profile as he chewed.

When Purcell had finished eating, he left for the restroom. Nick picked up the check to pay at the front register. He signaled to the young waiter and put a rolled-up twenty-dollar bill in his hand. The young man gave a slight bow. "*Muchas gracias*, senor."

At the front register, Nick watched Purcell leave the restroom. He hesitated near their table, as if looking for something.

There was no tip...

At first Nick didn't like the boat, but then he grew fond of it. It was docked at the mouth of the inlet to Black Creek. The first time he backed out of the slip and pushed the throttle forward, it all seemed so natural to him. His father stood with his head above the windshield as the bow rose and the boat planed across the open water. A half mile from shore, Nick throttled back, and the boat came to a slow drift. He threw the anchor overboard, and once it hit bottom, he secured the rope to the bow.

He took two fishing rods from the cabin. His father's mood was quiet. Since the remodeling of the boat, he had seemed distracted, and of late Melina wasn't around. His father found a warm bottle of beer in the cabin and a tube of lipstick. He threw the lipstick overboard. He didn't bother to bait a hook or pick up a fishing rod. He tied the bottle of beer to a rope and let it over the side of the boat to the bottom of the lake to chill.

Nick caught a fish, and his father said it was big enough to keep, but after freeing it from the hook, Nick threw it back. His father seemed not to notice; he stared out at the water and drank the beer.

He offered Nick a swallow, and Nick felt honored and grown up to be offered beer. The taste was warm and slightly bitter.

Nick didn't catch another fish. The sun was at a low angle now, and the air was humid and still, the water calm. As they returned to the mouth of the inlet, Nick pulled the throttle back. He used forward and reverse to maneuver the boat into the slip.

They returned home with the car windows down. His father was quiet for the whole trip. Nick told his mother he'd caught a fish, but he could see she wasn't listening. His father was sitting on the front porch. Melina was on her front porch. His father looked over there, but Melina didn't look back.

His father showed little interest in the boat anymore. Nick rode his motor scooter to the inlet to take the boat out by himself. He'd heard talk of Strawberry Island. The man at the marina said it was five miles east, at forty-four degrees. Nick checked the fuel tank. It was full. He started the engine and backed the boat out of the slip, heading for the open lake. He positioned the boat to forty-four degrees on the compass and pushed the throttle forward. As the hull slapped against the whitecaps, water sprayed over the boat and speckled the windshield.

In the distance Strawberry Island came into view. Several boats were anchored off the beach. Nick circled the island, but there was really nothing to see. It looked the same all the way around. He circled until the compass read 224 degrees then pushed the throttle forward. The ride was choppy and rough. It was like flying in the middle of the afternoon when the air was hot and bumpy with rising currents.

He throttled back as he came to the mouth of the inlet. The bow eased down, and the boat moved slowly through the inlet. As the dock appeared, he saw a police car parked near the slip. The officer was looking at the motor scooter then at Nick as the boat came around to line up with the slip. He pushed the throttle forward then reversed the engine to slow it down. The officer took hold of the bow and fastened it with a rope to the dock.

It was a Mount Clemens police officer. He said he liked the motor scooter. He asked what year it was and said he liked the color. Nick didn't answer the question but said his grandfather had mixed the color and painted it. The officer walked around the scooter again, looking it over, and said that now with that new law passed, he was thinking of getting one for his son. He looked back at Nick and asked how old he was. "You look pretty young to have a license."

"Everyone says that," Nick answered.

The officer walked back to the boat and asked whether he'd gotten any fish. Nick said he didn't like fishing, not really; he didn't like seeing the fish jump around at the end of the line when he lifted them into the boat.

The officer laughed and said he'd better get over that. "Or life will eat you alive, son." The officer got back into the police car and rolled the window down. He looked again at the motor scooter, and Nick worried that he was looking at the homemade license plate. The officer waved, and Nick watched him drive off.

On his way home, the traffic on Gratiot Avenue was light. Everyone was home from work already. Nick was concerned his father might know he'd had the boat out and had been on the highway with the motor scooter.

It was nearly eight o'clock and still light out when he pulled into the drive. His father was in the shop by himself. He stood near the table saw with a coffee mug in his hand and stared out at the road. Nick pushed the motor scooter past the shop door. His father said nothing.

He parked the scooter in the toolshed and went up to the house. Inside, the kitchen light was on, but his mother wasn't home.

Nick was in his study, adjacent to the bedroom, when the desk phone rang. He stood near the balcony with a book in his hand. It was Sunday evening. The air was close and humid, the trees still. He looked over his shoulder at the ringing phone. He was hesitant to answer it, but then he changed his mind.

"Hello."

"Nicky, I don't know what to do! It's Mellissa. She's been kidnapped."

"Kidnapped?"

"She called. He won't let her go."

"Sandy, slow down. Start from the beginning."

"She left yesterday," she said. "I found the address on her desk. It's in Detroit. She went to buy drugs—I just know it—and now they won't let her go. They'll make her a prostitute, Nicky. I know it."

"Yesterday? When?"

"The afternoon."

"Did she use her cell phone?"

"Yes. Her name showed up."

"What's the number...and the address?"

Nick wrote the number and the address on a notepad. "What did she say when she called?"

"They have her car keys, and they locked her in a house. Are you going to call the police?"

"No, not at this point."

"Is there *anything* you can do?"

"Yes, there is. Can you drive? Do you feel you can come here to the house?"

"Yes," Sandy said. "I can."

"Good. You can stay here with Nicole."

She agreed, and Nick reassured her he would do everything he could—without giving her false hope.

He pulled the address up on Google Maps. It was an abandoned apartment building in Highland Park. From the satellite view, he studied the neighborhood, the streets, the alleys, and the building itself. He counted the number of windows, entrances, exits, and fire escapes. He printed several pictures, from the general to the detailed view, then called Helen. He briefly explained what had happened, and Helen said she could be ready in ten minutes.

He told Nicole he was leaving for a few hours, and Sandy would arrive at the house soon. He gave few details but said Helen was going with him. Sandy's emotional state would provide detail enough. When Sandy's car pulled into the drive, Nick went to the garage to meet her. Nicole was with him. Sandy looked pale and shaken. Nicole suggested she come inside; perhaps a drink would help. Nick left the two women to discover their shared misfortunes.

Helen was in the car's headlights as Nick pulled up to her building. She wore jeans and a black sweatshirt. Her fanny pack was over her right hip. She opened the side door and got in. The photographs Nick had printed were on the dash. She studied them under an LED light.

Nick dialed Mellissa's cell phone. At the first ring, he set his phone to speaker. A man answered and asked who it was. They listened for any noise in the background. There was nothing at first, and then a door opened—and there was another voice: male. The man again asked who it was, and then the line went dead.

They had no choice but to try the address. Something told him he wasn't dealing with kids but someone more experienced. The risk wasn't worth another phone call.

They took the freeway to McNichols. Once they turned off Six Mile, there were no streetlights. The abandoned houses and vacant lots were in the dark. On a side street, he stopped the car and got out. He took a hand-painted license plate from the trunk and clipped it over the back plate.

As they drew near the apartment building, Nick turned off the headlights. Across the street and a hundred feet from the address, he parked and again looked at the photographs. They agreed that Helen would enter first. The sight of a woman would be less threatening. They got out of the car and quietly closed the doors.

The apartment building door was open. Inside, a small foyer opened to a hallway, and to the right, a stairway led to the second floor. Newspapers, soda cans, and beer cans littered the floor. Along the hallway some apartment doors were missing, while others were closed. The smell of human feces and urine was strong. Helen unzipped her fanny pack, withdrew a 9mm pistol, clicked the safety off, and activated the laser sight. Nick carried a revolver in his left hand.

He signaled Helen to wait for a moment. He pressed "redial" on his cell phone, and they listened. The sound of a ringing phone came from the second floor. They heard a voice upstairs. Nick ended the call. Helen started quietly up the stairs. The red laser sight on her pistol was pointed down. Nick was opposite her on the stairs.

At the top of the stairs, there was a light under the door and voices on the other side. Helen slowly turned the doorknob and raised her right foot to the door, pushing it open with her weight as both hands returned to her pistol. Within a split second, she was out of Nick's view, and he heard two shots in succession.

Nick came through the doorway with his revolver raised. One man lay facedown, blood pooling from his head, while the other was on his knees, holding his chest, a shocked look on his face. Blood dribbled from his mouth as he tried to speak. He fell forward on his face.

Mellissa was tied to a chair. Her face was bruised, and there was dried blood beneath her nostrils. Helen untied her and held her close. "Everything's OK," she said. "You're safe now. It's OK."

"Hurry," Nick said. "We've got to get out of here."

The two women followed Nick down the stairs. He paused at the door, looked in each direction, then hurried across the street. Helen got into the backseat with Mellissa to comfort her. Nick drove to the end of the block before he turned on the headlights; then he turned toward Six Mile. He looked in the rearview mirror and met Helen's eyes.

They arrived back in Grosse Pointe, and as Nick entered his drive, the garage doors opened. He drove the black Volkswagen into the open bay.

When Sandy saw Mellissa, she gasped. "Oh, my God!" In the light Mellissa's face was puffy and bruised. Helen cleaned the dried blood away with a wet cloth. Sandy placed her hand on Helen's arm. "Thank you."

Mellissa looked at Helen. "Who are you?"

"I'm Helen."

"Look at that face," Mellissa said. "Helen of Troy."

"Hardly," Helen said.

The following day the bodies at the apartment building were discovered. The incident received only brief mention on the evening news until a witness came forward and said she'd seen two white women leaving the apartment building at the time of the shooting. The story then received the coverage of a world event. Reporters and camera crews were sent to the apartment building to do follow-ups, while the story ran morning, noon, and night in their search for the two white women now accused of the "brutal murders."

Jessup Carthage soon became involved and took to the streets. When some suggested that drugs were the cause of most killings in the city, he paused and, in his familiar cadence, replied, "Drugs come from white people. They produce them; they have the wealth... They turn our women into prostitutes, our young men to murder." Looking out at the crowd, waving his finger back and forth, he continued, "Let there be no mistake." He paused. "Without whites there are no drugs." Monica Carthage stood next to him, applauding, as the crowd cheered him.

Nick set the TV to mute. Helen stood next to his desk, a cup of coffee in her hand. "Is that Michael Carthage," she said, "in back of his mother?"

Beneath the silent images, a ticker streamed across the bottom of the screen: WITNESSES HAVE FURTHER IDENTIFIED A BLUE FORD WITH TWO BROKEN HEADLIGHTS LEAVING THE MURDER SCENE.

"Did you read that?" Nick said.

"Where the hell did that come from?" she said. "A blue Ford?"

"*That*," he said, "is the reliability of an eyewitness."

The summer was hot, and there were many weeks left before Nick went back to school. His mother worked in her garden in the early morning and at Sy's Market in the afternoon or sometimes into the night. On Friday evenings Nick worked at the market, bagging groceries, shelving cans, and watering the produce.

Sy was very friendly. His hair was wavy black and his smile white. He liked Nick's mother a lot. She now kept the books for him, and he said he couldn't get along without her. He smiled and touched her arm and put his hand to the small of her back as he praised her.

Sy had a summer home on the shores of Lake Huron near Caseville. Nick and his mother spent a weekend there before his father said she had to quit her job. Trees surrounded the house, and the beach came right up to the backyard. A channel had been dredged to the boathouse where Sy kept his cabin cruiser, but when Nick and his mother got to the house, the boat wasn't there. His mother said Sy was in Canada.

The house was made of logs, painted brown with yellow trim, and there were flower boxes under the windows. The flowers were pink and lavender and hung over the boxes. There was a stone fireplace inside, and from the kitchen window, he saw the lake and the boat-house off to the side.

Nick was eager to go swimming. He changed into his swimsuit and ran for the beach. His mother called after him to be careful and not to go near the channel. From the beach Nick walked from one sand-bar to another, and still the water was only to his waist. To the right the water was dark blue where the channel led to the boathouse. He walked toward the channel until the bottom went away, and then he swam into the boathouse and pulled himself onto the wooden dock.

That evening a boat appeared out on the lake at the far end of the channel. The hull was white and the cabin varnished. As it got closer, Nick saw Sy standing at the helm, guiding the boat through the water. The engines made a deep rumble, and then he cut the engines and the boat glided into the boathouse. Sy quickly jumped from the bow and secured the boat with ropes.

He slapped Nick on the back and said he looked fine. When he saw Nick's mother, he forgot Nick was there and started toward the house. She smiled and held her hand out to him. They spoke for a while, and she continued to hold his hand.

When they got inside, the table was set for three, and there were tall, white candles at the center. Nick's mother held up a green whis-key bottle and asked whether she had gotten the right kind. Sy smiled, said yes, and thanked her. His mother looked very happy, and then Sy said something about his wife, and her smile went away. Sy whispered something to her in the kitchen, and she nodded and said it was OK.

The steaks his mother prepared were wrapped in butcher's paper from Sy's Market. She created a large salad with vegetables from her garden and steamed asparagus from Sy's produce. He poured whis-key in a glass over ice and poured one for Nick's mother too. She said she never had tasted Scotch before. Sy laughed and said it was about time she did.

The dinner was pleasant. Nick didn't have to worry about his father getting angry and throwing his plate out the side door because the food gave him heartburn. Sy smiled a lot, and when he tasted his steak, he said something in Arabic to show his pleasure. His mother looked happy.

After dinner they roasted marshmallows over the open fire pit in the backyard. The night was full of stars, and the lake shimmered like crystal in the moonlight. Sy roasted marshmallows and handed them to Nick's mother at the end of a sharpened willow branch. Nick pulled them from his own willow stick. The marshmallows were sweet and sticky, the color of roasted honey, and stuck to his fingers.

His mother said Sy was staying the night because the weather was too bad to cross the lake. From his bedroom window, Nick looked up at the night. He never had seen so many stars. In the morning Sy was gone, and his mother was sitting on the back deck with her coffee, staring out at the lake.

The water was calm and seemed to go on forever.

Mellissa and Nicole were the same age, but Mellissa was far more connected to Bridget. Helen listened as Mellissa and Bridget gave comfort to each other through stories of pain and isolation from those who didn't understand the world of addiction. Nick and Sandy were held at a distance. Helen was accepted; she had crimes to her name. She was trusted.

Seated on the patio, Mellissa smoked cigarettes as she revealed her past and what had happened the night she was taken. Bridget listened with a sense of love and understanding as her new friend spoke of things she too had endured.

"I'd been there one other time," Mellissa said, "but these guys were different. I'd never seen them before. They said to come upstairs, and when I got up there, they forced me to bend over and raped me."

"When did you call your mother?" Helen asked.

"After they raped me, he pushed me in a chair. That's when I called. When he saw my phone, they took it and tied me up."

She lit another cigarette with a plastic lighter and exhaled. "That shit's been happening so long," she said. "I had to give a blow job to a store detective once. I was already on probation. There're times when you'll do almost anything. My mother acts like it's just sleeping pills and aspirin—or maybe she really *doesn't* know." She drew on her cigarette. "I used to get money from my brother. I had to fuck him for it. But then his wife got suspicious, and that ended. I can't stand her, Miss Prim Shit…If she only knew."

From the garage there was the sound of the table saw cutting through wood. "Maybe they're making my coffin," Mellissa said. "I think about it sometimes…just ending it."

"I know," Bridget said. "People get all concerned and tell you not to think that way. But they don't live with it. They don't know."

Mellissa squeezed Helen's hand. "Have we depressed you? I hope not."

"I don't think so," Bridget said. "I admire you, Helen. Nothing bothers you."

"I wouldn't go that far," Helen said.

"But you're so strong."

"On the outside maybe."

There was hammering in the garage, and then Nick shouted, "Goddamn it!"

"I'd say your grandfather hit his finger again," Helen said. She got up from the lawn chair and went to the garage. Nick was holding his hand, and Nicole was trying not to laugh.

"He hit the same finger twice," she said.

Nick threw in another "goddamn it" and looked ready to throw his hammer across the garage, but he checked his temper, and when he looked at Nicole, smiling, he smiled too. "Sorry," he said. "Sometimes my father shows up."

Nick set sections of the arbor upright on the floor and fastened them with screws. Nicole had decided to paint it white and set it at the entrance to her garden for the roses to entwine.

"I like it," Helen said. "You guys are good."

Sandy's Jaguar pulled into the driveway. She parked behind Helen's red Ford and walked toward Mellissa. She kissed the top of her head and asked her if she could please stop smoking. Mellissa looked toward Bridget and rolled her eyes as Sandy started for the garage.

Sandy reached for Helen's hand and squeezed it. "It's so good to see you."

"What do you think?" Nicole said. "I'm going to paint it white."

"I like it," Sandy said. "Nicky, is there anything you can't do?"

"Yes," Helen said. "Control his temper."

Nicole and Sandy gathered fresh vegetables from the garden for a salad. They placed tomatoes, cucumbers, snow peas, scallions, and red leaf lettuce in a basket to take into the house and wash under cold water. Helen rubbed seasoning on the steaks, arranged them on a platter, and carried them out to the grill. Nicole asked Bridget to please cover the patio table with a white tablecloth and set out the silverware and plates. Nick opened three bottles of wine and carried a plate of cheese and olives to the table.

Seated at the table, Nick raised his glass. "Here's to Helen's first case."

"Really?" Sandy said, looking at Helen. "Are you going to court?"

"That's up to Nick," she said.

"I believe they'll make an offer to settle," he said. "And whatever it is, we'll take it."

"Good for you, Helen!"

"And she deserves it," Nick said. "She's put a lot of work into it."

Mellissa and Bridget shared stories and seemed unaware of the others at the table. Mellissa's cigarette burned in an ashtray on an end table while she ate. Bridget ate the snow peas from her salad with her fingers.

"I'll paint it tomorrow," Nicole said. "I saw some white paint in the shop."

"I never thought of the garage as a shop," Sandy said.

"The way the tools are set up," Nicole said, "the table saw and… What's the other one called?"

"Cutoff saw," Nick said.

"It's like a shop. I like the smell of wood and the feel of sawdust on the floor."

"You're quite industrious," Sandy said. "Wish it would rub off on Mellissa."

Mellissa looked up.

"Have you heard anything?" Helen asked Nick.

He shook his head. "Nothing. It might as well have happened in a void."

"I did a search," Helen said. "The traffic cameras don't even work—none of them." She noticed Bridget looking at her and realized Mellissa had told her about the shooting. Helen looked away.

The afternoon turned to evening with a night chill. The sky was clear and full of stars. In the living room, Sandy said she was tired and was going upstairs to take a shower. Mellissa was in the guest bedroom; Bridget was with her. Nicole asked Helen whether she would spend the night.

"Not tonight," Helen said. She sat on the sofa and sipped a brandy. Nicole sat with her. "There's something I should tell you," Helen said to Nick. "It concerns Mellissa."

She told him about the rape before they had arrived for Mellissa and about how deeply she was involved with hard drugs. "She was getting the money from her brother. He paid her for sex. It seems it went on for a long time."

"Has it stopped?"

"Yes. The wife got suspicious."

"Does Sandy know?" Nicole asked.

"I don't think so," Helen said. "No, I'm sure she doesn't."

"She'll never hear it from me," Nick said.

Nick went upstairs to take a shower and get ready for bed. He stood for several minutes under the hot water, and then from the medicine cabinet, he took an anti-inflammatory. He put on clean underwear and a T-shirt.

He got into bed with Sandy. She turned off the light on the night-stand, leaned over, and kissed him on the temple. She laid her head on the pillow and whispered, "I love you deeply."

Melina had been gone from the shop for days on end, and then one day Nick came into the shop, and there she was; whatever disagreement she'd had with his dad was resolved, and they were talking again, sharing cigarettes, and drinking coffee from the same mug. It seemed as if she'd never been gone. Joe Kopecny called across the yard that the goddamn coffee was boiling, and she still ignored him.

His mother never came out to the shop anymore. She worked longer hours at Sy's Market, and Nick was given an added day to work in the produce department. His mother's vegetables were now sold at Sy's Market, and Nick kept them sprayed with water and shiny.

Kevin was older than Nick, and he'd worked at Sy's Market longer than any of the other stock boys. He smoked Lucky Strikes and kept them in his shirt pocket for anyone to see. His hair was long, and he carried a comb in his shirt pocket with the cigarettes. He was thin and had an Adam's apple that showed, and the girls really liked him, but he was never fancy about his popularity. Kevin used words Nick never had before heard. His vocabulary had Nick's attention and admiration, and Nick started looking up words in the dictionary so he could sound like Kevin. He looked for words at random, and for a long time, it seemed nothing made sense, until suddenly new words popped into a sentence while he was talking. He told his father that one side of the cabinet looked "antithetical" to the other side, and his father looked at him and said, "What?"

Nick asked his mother whether he could always work the same days as Kevin, and she said she would talk to Sy. When his mother posted the next schedule, Nick worked Friday afternoon and Saturdays with Kevin. Although Nick never carried cigarettes, he now carried a comb in his shirt pocket and stopped to comb his hair back on the sides the way Kevin did.

As the summer grew to a close, Nick was eager to start school in September. By then the days were still hot, and the classroom windows were open, but there was little breeze. This year everyone had to write a paper on what he or she would do when he or she grew up. Mr. Sinkewitz called it "choosing a career."

Nick asked Kevin what he thought about choosing a career, and Kevin said he was going to go to law school. "But what is law school?" Nick asked. "And what do you do?"

"You become a lawyer, a master of litigation, an attorney. You learn how to make your own rules, like Sy does for everyone at the store."

The idea of making his own rules was a comfortable thought. Although difficult to explain, it was easy to understand. During an open discussion in social studies, Nick asked Mr. Sinkewitz why it was so wrong to have sex before you were married. Married people did it, and they didn't look any different; they weren't disfigured from it. So why were kids always told they couldn't do stuff?

Mr. Sinkewitz didn't answer. He turned to the chalkboard, wrote out a history assignment for the following week, and said they would break early for recess. On his way out the door, Nick stopped at the chalkboard and told Mr. Sinkewitz he was going to be a lawyer.

Mr. Sinkewitz turned. "Somehow that doesn't surprise me," he said, then turned back to erasing the blackboard.

Nick was at his desk when he heard the office door open and a man talk to Helen. He looked out the office window to the parking lot below. A delivery van from a courier service was parked at the door.

Helen came into the office. "Look at this," she said. She had several black-and-white photographs in her hand and a large brown envelope. She spread the photographs on his desk. From the profile it was Melanie MacArthur. She was in the back of an SUV, her skirt pulled up to her waist, on top of Robert Purcell.

"It's broad daylight," Helen said. "How stupid can they be?"

Nick looked inside the brown envelope.

"That's it," she said. "Just the photographs. Who do you think sent them?"

"Could be someone on our side. Or maybe it's Purcell's wife. Who knows?"

That afternoon Nick accompanied Marshall to the US Attorney's Office. They sat in the parking lot in the cream-colored Lincoln. Marshall was somber and reluctant to move when they arrived. "We go back a long way," he said. "I know the man. He believes in what he does. It's hard for you to understand, Winterstein…growing up in the South in the forties and fifties. He told me about the time he saw his brother clubbed to death by police—white police. That doesn't go away. It stays with a man."

There was nothing Nick could say; he listened with a sense of respect.

"Once I do this, my life is over," Marshall said. "There'll be no place I can show my face…I'll become 'the man who gave up Jessup Carthage' to save his own skin."

"You don't have to do it, Judge. We can leave now, put together a defense."

"I can't, Winterstein. I can't face the thought of going to prison. I'm a coward."

"We could win, Judge. I've won some pretty tough ones."

"We both know that wouldn't happen."

They locked the car and walked toward the district office building on Fort Street, and once inside they were escorted to a conference room on the second floor.

Purcell stood with hands in his pockets, his suit coat unbuttoned, and his necktie undone. He stood near a window that overlooked the sidewalk below. Sylvia Blackwell was seated at the conference table. Her arms and legs were crossed, and she wore a bright-red dress. She stared at Marshall as he entered. Blackwell dealt with antigang initiatives, drug trafficking, and community outreach. It seemed odd that she was there. Melanie MacArthur entered through a door at the far end of the room. She offered her hand to Judge Marshall and thanked him for coming. She said she looked forward to working with him.

Seated at the table, Marshall read through the agreement he was to sign. Nick opened his briefcase and removed a notepad and the brown envelope with the black-and-white photographs. He had no intention of revealing its contents. It was in view for Purcell's speculation.

Judge Marshall accepted the agreement as written. It granted immunity in exchange for his cooperation in the prosecution of Jessup Carthage. He signed his name with a fountain pen.

MacArthur stood. "Thank you, Judge. We look forward to your help."

"Nothing less than a detailed road map," Purcell said.

MacArthur looked at Purcell, and he shut up.

Blackwell slid the agreement to her side of the table and leafed through it, stopping to read here and there. It wasn't the first time she had seen it; Nick was sure of it. She looked at Marshall. He avoided her eyes.

Nick drove Marshall back to his residence. Marshall didn't mention the agreement or anything that indicated a future. He spoke of his childhood.

"My mother did cleaning for the Whitmore family in Grosse Pointe. They were an elderly couple. At least I remember them that way. Of course I was very young. During the summer months, my mother took me with her. It was safer; it kept me off the streets." His tone was melancholy.

"They had lost their only child from rheumatic fever. I was a kind of substitute, I guess. Anyway, they took me to their summer home on the shores of Lake Huron...just outside of Caseville. The neighborhood boys never treated me any different. I guess we were too young to know and too removed from the city. We played baseball in an open area with the lake in view. Anything hit into the water was an automatic home run." The judge smiled. "Those are very fond memories, Winterstein."

Nick stopped at an intersection and waited for the light to change. The judge looked forward. "There was a general store, or maybe it was a coffee shop, in Caseville. It was walking distance from the house, or it seemed that way. It was the first time I'd ever seen a woman play a pinball machine. She had a pile of nickels on the glass top of the machine. I'd say she was in her late twenties or early thirties. I stood there and watched her play. She had shorts on, and she showed me the crease along her thigh where she pressed against the machine to jiggle the ball. It's funny how some things never leave you. They remain so clear...or at least you think they do."

Nick turned onto a side street then into the drive in front of the judge's house. He put the car in park, the engine running. There was a white Dodge SUV in front of them near the garage. Nick had seen that car before; it had been parked outside the house on Hurlbut Street the day he had dropped off Michael Carthage.

"There was a boy," Marshall continued, "a white boy everyone made fun of. His ears stuck out, and his face was an odd shape. He was thought to be slow-witted...because of the way he looked, I suppose. Years later that boy won some money in the lottery—not a lot but enough to buy a broaching machine. He set it up in his basement." He looked at Nick. "It later became McQuade Manufacturing."

"I've heard of them," Nick said.

Marshall offered his hand. "Thank you, Winterstein."

"I didn't do anything, Judge. I wish I had."

"You did enough," he said. "You didn't judge me."

"Judge, whose car is that? Have you seen it before?"

"Yes," Marshall said. He opened the car door and got out. He walked to his front door without looking back. Nick sat there for a moment, even after the front door had closed, then put the car in reverse. He glanced again at the white Dodge in the driveway.

He drove back to the office along Woodward Avenue. Near the downtown section, he passed a police car stopped at the side of the road with the hood raised. Steam rose from the engine. The officer was inside the squad car, talking on his cell phone. Nick looked in his rearview mirror. A cloud of steam still rose from the engine; it mushroomed against the half-raised hood.

When Nick arrived at the office, Nicole was there. She and Helen had set up a second computer for Nicole. An Excel spreadsheet was open on the screen.

"How did it go?" Helen asked.

"It was depressing," he said. "But it was what he wanted."

In less than an hour, the phone rang. He heard Nicole answer it. "Winterstein and Associates…Yes, just a moment, please."

Nicole stepped around the corner to Nick's office. "It's for you. Monica Carthage."

J oe Kopecny lost the election to city council. Melina said he was more hurt than disappointed. Nick's father said it was scary that anyone voted for him at all. Kopecny said the goddamn election had been rigged. Why else did he get only five hundred votes? "Those bastards rigged it."

Kopecny collected all his campaign signs and stacked them in back of the shed. The one really large sign he cut into pieces and made into a storage box. He said it was for old car and engine parts, but he never filled it. He left it empty behind the shed. Sometime in late spring, a stray dog used it for a den and gave birth to three puppies. Two of the puppies died, but the third one was healthy. Kopecny fed the mother table scraps from the house and lined the box with burlap bags.

Before and after work, he checked on the dog. In the evenings he sat on the grass and played with the puppy. Nick asked him whether it had a name, and Kopecny said he didn't have time for a goddamn dog, let alone time to name it. The puppy tugged at his pant leg, and Kopecny said, "See that? The little shit likes me." As time went on, the puppy spent more and more time with him. He and Melina argued over its staying in the house. "See that?" she'd scream. "You're going to clean it up." Nick heard the arguments from outside.

One summer afternoon when Melina was in the shop with Nick's father, Kopecny backed out of the gravel drive. The puppy was resting in the shade under the back tire of the car, and Kopecny ran over it. Noticing he'd hit something, he got out and looked. He got to his knees and picked up the puppy. Its neck had been broken. He held the dead puppy and cried that he didn't know. Nick never had seen a grown man cry before. Kopecny held the limp puppy to his chest as tears came down his face.

Days later the mother dog was gone, and Kopecny took the storage box apart with a hammer and burned it for scrap. Melina said, "Good riddance to that dog."

Kopecny was even more alone without the mother dog. His wife was constantly next door. "How much can a man put up with? Right under my nose!"

It was a warm summer night when Kopecny came across the lawn and called Winterstein out. He stood in the opening of the garage door and told him he'd had enough. Melina was in the shop. She watched in surprise. Cheryl came out of the house when she heard Kopecny shouting. Nick had no idea what was happening until he saw Kopecny strike the pose of a boxer, his fists up. His father had no pose. He ducked under the first punch and threw a roundhouse blow to Kopecny's left side. Kopecny buckled at the knees, and Joseph threw another punch to his side. Kopecny dropped, his right hand holding his side. Joseph stepped back, unable to catch his breath. He wheezed in an effort to breathe.

Melina remained at Joseph's side in the shop. He sat down, still unable to catch his breath, pale and sweaty. She wiped his face with a cloth as Cheryl returned to the house.

Kopecny was treated for broken ribs. His left side was taped, and he didn't work for a week. He was quiet during that time and stayed to himself. Nick saw him seated on a wooden crate in back of the shed where the dog had given birth to the puppies.

Nicole picked up dirty jeans, a halter top, a blouse, and soiled underwear off the floor of Bridget's room. She put them in the washing machine and added liquid detergent. Nicole's mother had had a crippling addiction to amphetamines and had spent hours washing and rewashing clothes. Then, after days of hyperactivity, she swallowed barbiturates with alcohol to help her sleep—until one day when Nicole found her lying on the sofa, her eyes open toward the ceiling.

But Bridget was different, Nicole told herself. She wouldn't take after her grandmother; she showed signs of recovery; she must recover.

While the clothes were in the washer, Nicole logged on to the computer and opened the Excel spreadsheets. Her accounting methods were smooth and highlighted with graphs. She looked at the notes Helen had taken on the finances of Jessup Carthage and the CCLC: overfunded insurance policies, loans and leases, gifts and donations, entities without a history. A spider web of activity, one web on top of another web, on top of another...Why had it not drawn anyone's attention?

Nicole left the computer on and returned to check the washer, then went upstairs to wake Bridget. She hoped Bridget would enroll in an adult-education program and earn her high-school diploma, but she was still lethargic and uninterested. Nicole's mother had gone through withdrawal several times, and each time she'd fallen back into addiction. She'd confessed to Nicole that she once had looked through her own feces for the remnant of a capsule to be reused.

Nicole coaxed Bridget into the shower then downstairs for something to eat. As a child Bridget had been a delight to be around. Nicole once had explained to her that money was really quite dirty: "Please don't put it in your mouth, honey. You don't know where it's been. So many people touch it." That night Bridget collected coins throughout the house and put them in a glass of water with a bar of soap. *Where is that little girl?* Nicole wondered. *Do we change on the inside the way our appearance changes through the years? Do we have so little control?* Nicole opened the refrigerator door to take eggs and butter from the inside tray, thinking, *Where did my baby go? Who is this person now in her body?*

"How long are we staying here?" Bridget said. She picked at her eggs.

"This is where we live," Nicole said. "Here. He's my father."

"Maybe he doesn't want us here. Maybe he's doing this out of guilt."

"Damn it, Bridget." She hit the counter with a wooden spoon. "I get so sick of your negative shit!"

"You don't know he wants us. We could go back to Baltimore."

"Goddamn it! Can't you shut up?" She threw the wooden spoon against the wall and went out the back door onto the patio. Tears welled in her eyes. A life here in this house with her garden and her father—that's all she wanted. There had been times when she'd fantasized about her mother's death just to escape the misery of living with her, and then, when her mother was finally gone, she didn't feel any sense of guilt but rather an unspoken relief. Not until much later did the memories of her mother become pleasant. *Sometimes,* she thought, *those who cause you pain have to be gone before you can love them.*

When Nicole returned to the kitchen, Bridget was gone. She'd returned to her room, and Nicole didn't have the will to coax her out again. She sat down at the table. The eggs and toast she'd prepared were cold; only a bite had been taken from the toast. She remembered Bridget as a little girl—playing Harry Potter, wearing a cape, and waving her magic wand. *Watch, Mommy. I can make Grandma come back from her sleep.* The memory of such innocence was all the more painful through its loss. Nicole wished Nick had seen her then, had known how delightful she was. The young woman upstairs—drug addicted, infected with HIV—wasn't her daughter. Someone else was living in her body. A stranger.

Her father arrived home in the early afternoon. The garage doors opened, and he pulled into the first bay. He appeared preoccupied, if not sullen, but his smile returned upon seeing Nicole, and his eyes sparkled. She wanted to ask whether he liked her. Was she welcome here? What did he really think of her?

"Have lunch with me?" he asked.

"Yes, of course." She searched his eyes for something more.

"I'll just be a moment," he said. "A quick shower and change."

"Where are we going?"

"The Ford House," he said. "The Cotswold Café."

Nicole changed into cream-colored slacks and a V-neck sweater of blue cashmere. She looked at herself in the full-length mirror. Why had he given her an American Express card if he didn't want her here?

She met him at the head of the stairs. He winked at her, and the gesture made her happy. In the car he said the Ford House and the grounds had a special meaning for him. He'd grown up only six miles away, but it might as well have been a universe apart. From Lake Shore Drive, they approached the entrance to the grounds.

"My father pointed the house out to me," he said. "We drove along here, and he said, 'That's the Ford House.' It meant nothing to me at the time. Not until my teens did I realize it was someplace very different."

Nick stopped at the gatehouse, and the guard asked whether they were going to the restaurant. Nick said yes, and the guard waved them through.

Nicole had expected the restaurant to appear old-fashioned, but it wasn't. It was modern, with the look of a glass atrium. They each ordered a glass of Riesling and cucumber sandwiches with cream cheese. Nicole was self-conscious, as though everyone knew she was from the wrong side of town in Baltimore. A woman and her daughter were escorted to their table and seated near them. The woman appeared close to Nicole's age. She was casually dressed yet quite smart and fashionable. Her hair was short and blond and combed away from her face. From the tilt of her head, the woman seemed to know all eyes were on her as she entered the room. To be the focus of attention seemed so natural for her. Nicole stared at her until the woman looked her way; then Nicole quickly looked the other way.

"Would you like to see the main house," Nick asked, "when we've finished?"

"Yes."

"The house and the grounds," he said, "give me a pleasant feeling. There are times I drive over here by myself just to go for a walk." He asked the waiter to refill their glasses.

"I have an old fantasy," he said. "I picture the house in December... Christmas Eve. There's a light snow falling through the bare trees. As you drive up, you can see the snow and the outside lights. Edsel and Eleanor are inside. They're waiting for Henry and Clara to arrive with gifts for the grandkids. Edsel is upstairs, and he's feeling quite anxious. Nervous. He has an idea to present to his father. But Henry isn't open to new ideas—especially as he's gotten older, and if the idea isn't his own.

"When Henry and Clara arrive, the chauffeur brings the gifts in and sets them under the tree. Edsel meets his father downstairs. But before coming down, Edsel chews breath mints to cover the drink he had. Henry doesn't believe in alcohol; in fact he sternly disapproves. He doesn't believe in this house either—or Grosse Pointe for that matter. He's highly critical of Edsel's decisions and choices. He does love his son, though; there's no doubt of that. Yet Edsel hears only criticism."

The cucumber-and-cream-cheese sandwiches arrived. Nick peeled his sandwich open to sprinkle salt on the cucumber. Nicole noticed the smartly dressed woman with blond hair glance at her father then away again. *Does she find him attractive? Does she know who he is?* Nicole wondered.

"But as the evening passes," Nick continued, "Edsel never presents his idea of installing power steering on all Lincolns to make it standard. He cannot bring himself to do it. He anticipates only rejection from his father."

"It sounds like it really happened," Nicole said.

"It might be an accurate paraphrase. The relationship was painful for Edsel. His father didn't love openly. He didn't know how to show it. But he did love his son."

"I always heard negative things about Henry Ford," Nicole said. "Racist, anti-Semitic, meanspirited."

"He accomplished a lot. He created an empire and amassed a great fortune. That often produces jealousy and envy. Let the *left* hand cast the first stone."

After lunch they headed out to walk the grounds. As they left the café, Nicole looked back at the smartly dressed woman. She appeared so confident as she chatted with her daughter. *Where does that come from?* Nicole wondered as she looked at the two women. *Where does confidence come from?*

"How did their relationship end?" Nicole asked, turning back toward her father. "Didn't Edsel die before his father?"

"Yes, Edsel died of stomach cancer. Henry took it very hard. He blamed alcohol, the food Edsel ate, Edsel's choice of friends, this house, Grosse Pointe. The loss of his son must've been immeasurable."

They walked along the path toward the pool house and gardens. As they came to the rose garden, her father walked a few steps ahead of her. He seemed unaware that she was now behind him, watching, as he walked among the roses.

Nick's mother took him to an afternoon movie, and later that evening, his father asked him about what had happened. "Did she talk to anyone there?"

"Oh, yes. Sy was there."

"What about the trip to Lake Huron? Was Sy there too?"

"Yes, he was there. He had to spend the night because the weather was bad, but he was gone in the morning. His boat is really neat looking, but I still like airplanes better."

"What about the hockey game? Was Sy there?"

"No, but there was a man there Mom went to school with. I like their uniforms, especially the white ones with the wheel and wing on the front."

Nick answered with the innocence of youth. The adult world happened without purpose; it was just there.

Nick was stacking canned goods on the shelf with Kevin on the day his father came to Sy's Market. He saw him at the front of the store. Sy and his mother were talking at the cash register and didn't notice him at the door, watching them. Nick saw how different the two men were; his father was short and blond with eyes the color of ice. Sy was tall and thin with shiny black hair and a white smile.

Nick wanted his father to meet Kevin. Kevin was going to go to law school at the University of Detroit. Nick wanted to go there too, but his father wasn't listening. Sy held his mother by the elbow as they talked. His father said something, and Sy turned. He looked surprised and let go of his mother's arm. Sy was always smooth with people, but this time he paused and said he'd be in the back if anything was needed. Then he left.

His father came forward and squeezed his mother by the arm and whispered something to her. As he let go of her, he pushed her into the cash register.

Kevin said his father looked mean; he didn't want to be on his wrong side. But Nick was used to it. It seemed normal to him.

His mother left the store early, and Sy told Kevin to cover the cash register. Nick got home much later, when it was already dark. His mother was at the kitchen table. He could see she had been crying. She had tissues in her hand, and when she saw Nick, she wiped her eyes and said she loved him very much. His father sat in a lawn chair in front of the outside fireplace. He stared at the flames and took a drink from a whiskey bottle. Nick never had seen his father drink before, ever. The bottle had been in the top kitchen cabinet for years. He threw the empty bottle into the fire.

His father went to the shop, turned the lights on, then turned them off. A moment later he got in the car. He backed out of the drive, and as he turned the wheel to back onto the road, the front tire went into the ditch. He rocked the car back and forth, with the engine racing and the back wheels spitting stones and gravel until the car was free, and he took off down the road.

Inside, Kathleena was frightened. She asked what was wrong, and Nick said he didn't know. She asked whether Mom had a boy-friend, and Nick said that was "ludicrous." It was a new word he had learned, and he didn't know where it had come from. He later lay in bed, thinking about the new word. He wondered how words popped into his head without his thinking of a way to use them first. He was pleased that it had happened.

In the early morning, Nick found his parents in the kitchen. He stopped when he saw his mother. Her eye was black and blue and swollen, and her lip was split open. She looked at him. "It's OK, Nicky. I had it coming. I did something wrong. I deserved it," she said.

Melina still visited his father in the shop and often stayed late into the night, just the two of them. His mother never went back to Sy's Market.

The news was sudden but not a surprise. Helen picked up the remote and increased the volume. Nick entered the office with a cup and saucer in hand. He stared at the screen. Helen looked at him. Neither said a word. The news reporter pointed toward the yellow tape around the crime scene and explained that the FBI had replaced local authorities.

The housekeeper, the reporter said, discovered the body in the early morning.

Helen set the TV to mute. "Monica called not an hour after he signed," she said. "Carthage knew."

"Of course he did. And he got it from Sylvia Blackwell."

"Where's Marshall's wife?"

Nick shook his head. "I don't know. I think she left him before he signed the agreement. I get the feeling she was at odds with him over it. But I don't know that. He never talked about her."

"Nicole said the CCLC finances are a puzzle waiting to be solved."

"It's not my puzzle," he said. "Not anymore. I'm no longer part of it. I don't care what they do."

"You think the Justice Department will pursue it?"

"With Marshall gone I don't know. He knew where the bodies are buried."

"What did Monica say when she called?"

"She said she hoped everything worked out well for the judge. She just wanted to let me know that they knew."

Within a few days, there was a clearer picture of Judge Goodwin Marshall's death. There had been no sign of struggle or forced entry into the house. The judge had been found facedown, as though he'd fallen forward from a kneeling position, and had been shot execution style in the back of the head. Investigators believed he'd known the person who shot him.

Sandy said it was fascinating the way everything pointed toward Carthage, but nobody talked about it. Or maybe everyone was just so used to the way those people killed one another that no one cared. But Nick *did* care. He'd liked Marshall—not in the beginning, but in their time together, he'd felt a shared sense of childhood, one that had guided each man to the realization that the law was anything he made it up to be. It was that simple.

"Yes," Sandy said, "but you have to have laws. You can't have people going about and killing each other willy-nilly."

"Well, don't we have those now?"

"Nicky! You know what I mean."

She took a nine iron from her golf bag in back of the cart and set up for her shot. She looked back at Nick. "You know, Edward has been coming around lately. He's been very nice to Mellissa. Personally I think he and what's-her-face he's married to aren't getting along." She turned back to the ball, started her backswing, and followed through. The ball soared high in a beautiful arc and came down on the green just a few feet from the pin. She looked at Nick. "See how well I play when my children get along?"

She set up with her putter and birdied the hole. Nick was on the green too, but he had a twenty-foot putt, and when it was finished, he was double bogey for the hole.

"Edward was there the other night," she said, putting her club back in the bag. "They were in the pool together. I think they'd been drinking. The underwater lights were on, and they were naked. At first it surprised me, but then it seemed normal enough. I mean, they're brother and sister; they've seen each other naked before." She paused. "You seem awfully quiet."

"It's nothing," he said. "My thoughts seem to wander." For a moment Nick considered telling Sandy about the sexual affair between Mellissa and her brother, but he couldn't bring himself to do it. What purpose would it serve? They were adults, and to Nick's thinking, it harmed no one. Why cause pain to everyone involved? Just let it be.

"Are you still going to that funeral?" Sandy asked.

"Yes. Will you come with me?"

"I don't know," she said. "They're all black; it's kind of creepy." She looked at Nick. "No," she said, "it's *uncomfortable*. That's a better way to say it."

"I'd like you to come with me."

"Why are you going? He's no longer a client. You can wash your hands of the whole thing."

"I liked him," he said. "I'm sad that he's gone."

"I've never known anyone who likes criminals the way you do."

"We are all criminals, Sandy."

"Oh, no. I'm not getting into that one again."

She took her driver from the golf bag and teed her ball at the ninth tee box. Nick watched her bend over. It was such a pleasant sight.

⊱✦⊰

The following day Sandy arrived in Grosse Pointe with her overnight bag. She was spending more and more time at the house. Helen's car was in the drive. She, Nicole, and Nick were on the patio. Sandy kissed Nicole on the cheek and squeezed Helen's hand. "Look at that face," she said, still looking at Helen. "It amazes me how beautiful you are."

Nick poured a glass of wine and handed it to Sandy. "Are you going to the funeral?" she asked Helen.

"No, I don't think so," Helen said.

"I didn't even know him," Nicole said.

Sandy looked at Nick. "It's just you and me?"

He nodded.

"How's Mellissa?" Helen asked.

"She seems fine," Sandy said, "but I wish she could find someone...someone special."

"Don't we all," Helen said. She seemed to notice the silence that followed and added, "I know what you're thinking...someone of age."

Nick smiled, and Sandy laughed.

"I don't know," Nicole said. "I saw this boy the other day—he couldn't have been all of sixteen. He was gorgeous. I wanted to jump his bones, I swear."

"Don't I know the feeling," Helen said.

"You know," Nicole said, "I was watching an interview on YouTube. That Huey Newton was really cute." She looked at Nick. "You said he might be the grandfather of Michael Carthage."

"I'm beginning to think the rumors are true," Nick said. "The resemblance is uncanny. Even the behavior."

"They're both drop-dead cute," Helen said. "I see why Bridget got so hung up on him."

Sandy shook her head. "Things are so different now. I don't like it. Things were simple when I was in school."

"I think change is good," Nicole said.

"No, it isn't," Sandy said.

"Well, if it weren't for change," Nick said, "you'd still be married to Edward."

"No, I wouldn't," she quickly added. "He's dead."

Helen stayed for dinner. They ate on the patio as the evening sun faded to a night full of stars. After dinner Helen helped Nicole wash and put away the dishes, while Nick and Sandy went for a walk. Bridget didn't leave her room. Nicole had taken a tray up to her before the rest of them ate. Sandy asked how Bridget was doing as she and Nick walked.

"She can't seem to get past her addiction," he said. "And she's HIV positive. It's depressing."

"Mellissa does seem a little better. I guess she could be taking pills again. But she doesn't have any money."

"How often does Edward come around?"

"He's very attentive lately. He comes by a couple times a week."

Nick wondered how much money Mellissa was getting from her brother.

Helen was gone when Nick and Sandy returned from their walk, and Nicole was in her room. Nick and Sandy showered together and got ready for bed. The next morning they left early to avoid the long procession to the cemetery.

There were news and camera crews at the cemetery, dignitaries from the NAACP and the State Bar of Michigan, and a line of mourners that stretched through winding lanes. Nick remained back from the proceedings at the grave site. Jessup and Monica Carthage were near the minister as he gave his last words. In back of Jessup Carthage were several members of the Nation of Islam in white shirts and bow ties.

As the service ended and the crowd dispersed, Sylvia Blackwell from the US Justice Department stepped forward and whispered something to Jessup Carthage. He nodded and looked toward Nick.

Blackwell stepped back and blended into the crowd again.

When Dale turned sixteen, Melina went back to work at a small parts distributor to buy him a car. She found a 1953 Ford convertible, mint green, with a black top. Joe Kopecny argued for a 1949 Ford, but Melina said she was paying for it, and her decision stood. The Cushman Eagle had been taken apart, painted, repainted, and reassembled. It was now for sale.

Once the car was paid for, Melina quit her job, but a year later, she went back to work because Dale wanted a 1957 Chevrolet. Kopecny hit the roof! He drove a goddamn '54 Pontiac, and the kid wasn't getting a goddamn newer car than his, he argued.

Nick was soon old enough to get his driver's license, so his father bought the Ford from Melina. Nick didn't quite understand why he needed a driver's license. What did it have to do with driving? His father explained to him that it kept unsafe drivers off the road. But why, then, were there so many accidents if unsafe drivers were kept off the road?

When his father wasn't around, Nick drove the car down to his grandfather's. His grandfather said he was a Chrysler man, but he had respect for old-man Ford. He'd built that company on his own.

His grandfather drove the Ford onto metal blocks he'd welded together, and he showed Nick how to drain the oil and clean the filtering system. It was important to keep a record of when the oil was changed and to clean the spark plugs at the same time.

His grandfather sent him to the shop to get a wrench, and as Nick looked for it, he saw the edge of a photograph sticking out from under a box. It was a picture of naked kids touching each other. He heard his grandfather coming, and he quickly put the photograph back under the box. His grandfather asked whether he'd found the wrench, and Nick said, "Not yet." He never mentioned the photograph to anyone.

Nick drove the car for almost six months before he got his driver's license. He stopped at the White Castle at Eight Mile and Gratiot and went inside. He looked back through the large window at his car. His grandfather had given him a can of paste wax, and the mint green now reflected the sun, while the windshield reflected a drifting cloud.

When he returned to the parking lot, a Detroit policeman was standing next to his car. Nick thought for a moment about walking back into the White Castle and pretending he knew nothing about the car, but he continued forward. The officer watched him approach. He stood next to the front tire, his elbow bent, with his forearm resting on the butt of his service revolver. With his head slightly tilted, as if in question, he asked Nick if he was Joe Winterstein's boy. "Yes," Nick answered. "That's my father." The officer said he thought he recognized him; he was Courtney Spangler, his father's first cousin. Nick asked whether that meant they were related too. Of course, the officer said. He put his hand on Nick's shoulder. They were second cousins.

They spoke a bit, and Officer Spangler said to tell his father he'd see him soon; but then he stopped, his hand on the door of the squad car, and said Nick had better not say anything to his father, or he'd know that Nick had been driving that Ford without a license.

A few months later, Nick got his driver's license, and it didn't feel any different to drive with or without a license. When he was younger, he'd been told what he could and couldn't do and what was right and what was wrong, but as he got older, nothing seemed to make sense anymore. Right and wrong were simply words; they weren't objects.

The day didn't start out right. He spilled a cup of coffee next to his computer in the study off his bedroom. Cleaning up the mess was one thing, but the idea of having spilled it—the mistake, the unexpected—was unsettling. The unthought-of event, the unconsidered, sometimes took on a life of its own. How do you plan for that?

Even after his morning run, after new oxygen had cleared his mind and fed his thoughts, a sense of melancholy still hung over him, and it was with him still when he heard the outer office door open and a man speak to Helen.

Helen stepped around the corner and said, "You'll never guess who's here. Robert Purcell. He wants to see you."

Purcell didn't wait to be shown in; he stepped around Helen. "Winterstein, got a moment?"

Purcell leaned against the windowsill in his shirt sleeves, one sleeve rolled higher than the other, his collar unbuttoned, his necktie pulled loose, and his thinning hair uncombed.

"Robert, do they ever say anything at the office about the way you look?"

Purcell looked down at his pants. "Look?" He still had his hands in his pockets.

"Nothing," Nick said. Purcell was oblivious to his appearance. "What can I do for you?"

"What did Marshall know?"

"I don't know," Nick said. "He didn't share."

"What did he know of the Nation of Islam?"

"He knew enough not to antagonize them."

"That's where the money is, isn't it?"

"Robert, I don't know. You have the resources. Look into it."

"It doesn't do any good. It gets stopped, derailed somehow by someone."

"Talk to Sylvia Blackwell."

"No," he said. "I'm not going there."

"You know about her connection to Jessup Carthage?"

"Of course we do."

"I can't help you, Robert. For me it's over. And I don't give a shit about Carthage."

"It's never over, Winterstein."

"It's become personal for you, hasn't it?"

Purcell didn't answer. He turned to look out the window, his hands still in his pockets. "Yes," he said, "and it pisses me off."

In his heart Nick knew Jessup Carthage was responsible for Marshall's death. The national media ignored any connection between Carthage and the Nation of Islam; they benefited from the image of Carthage as the champion of the downtrodden, but they kept their distance from the Nation of Islam for the same reason Marshall had.

It was still early in the day when Purcell left, yet Nick cleaned up around his desk, rinsed his coffee cup, and asked Helen whether she was coming by for dinner later. He was making an early day of it.

"Yes," she said. "Nicole and I are making lasagna."

The thought of having a favorite dish for dinner should have cheered him up, but it didn't. In his car he stared out the window then reached for his cell phone. But before he pressed the speed dial, the phone rang. Sandy's name appeared on the ID.

"Nicky, it's so terrible," she said, "and I feel responsible. Like I drove her to it."

"Sandy, slow down. What's so terrible?"

"Mellissa—she tried to kill herself."

"Where are you?"

"Beaumont Hospital," she said. "They're trying to revive her."

"I'm on my way," he said.

"Please hurry. I can't tell you how I feel. It's my fault."

He left the parking lot to take the freeway to Birmingham. Three blocks from the office, a Detroit fire truck was stalled at the side of the road. Smoke billowed from the engine, while several firemen stood in the street and watched. To put distance between his car and the smoking fire truck, Nick drove onto the sidewalk and passed it. He looked back in the mirror as the firemen watched the truck burst into flames.

He took the interstate to Birmingham then to Beaumont Hospital. Sandy was in the waiting room. She held wadded tissues in her hand, and her eye makeup was smeared. He sat her on the sofa and asked what had happened.

"I found her on the couch," she said. "Half naked. She was unconscious. She took a whole bottle of muscle relaxers with vodka. It's my fault. I thought they were hidden."

"Slow down. What was hidden?"

"The muscle relaxers. They were mine. I take one at night. She found them. God knows how much vodka she drank; it can kill her. She wanted to die, and I helped."

"How long has she been here?"

"An hour maybe—I don't know." She wiped her eyes. "Nicky, I didn't mean any of those things I said about her. I love her so much."

"Has the doctor talked to you?"

"Mellissa's in intensive care." Eye makeup ran to her cheeks. "On a machine to help her breathe. Is she going to live?"

A young intern came into the waiting room, and Nick saw from his face that the news wasn't good. He wanted somehow to stop the words he knew were coming.

"Is she OK?" Sandy asked him. "She's going to be OK, isn't she?"

"I'm sorry," he said.

"Sorry...No, it's not true. It can't be. Nicky, tell me it's not true!" Nick held her close as she cried in his arms. Over her shoulder he saw a young man enter the waiting room. From pictures he'd seen, he knew it to be young Edward. The man came forward and placed his hand on Sandy's arm. She turned. "Edward, she's gone."

Tears came to his eyes. He looked at Nick; although the two men never had met, they were not strangers.

Sandy turned to the intern. "I want to see her. Please?"

The intern looked at Nick and nodded. Then he led mother and son to the intensive care unit. Nick followed. They entered a room, and the intern pulled the curtain back. Mellissa lay, lifeless, on the bed. The monitors had been disconnected. Sandy took Mellissa's hand in hers. "Oh, my baby, my baby." She squeezed, clung to Mellissa's hand, until Nick pried her fingers loose and led her from the room.

In the waiting room, Edward said, "She can't be alone tonight."

"She's going with me," Nick said. "She won't be left alone."

"Should I stop at the house to get her things?" Edward asked.

"No, she has everything she needs."

Edward looked lost, dazed. Nick wondered what his thoughts were. Had he lost more than a sister? Had he lost his lover?

It was unspoken and understood that Nick would make the necessary arrangements for Mellissa. He told Edward he would be in touch the next day then led Sandy out to the car. Before getting in on the driver's side, Nick sent a text message to Helen. On the way back to Grosse Pointe, Sandy laid her head back on the seat and closed her eyes. She remained that way for several minutes then started to cry. Nick reached for her hand to comfort her. But there wasn't anything to say.

When they arrived at home, Helen's car was parked near the patio. She and Nicole were waiting inside. The terrible news was written on Nick and Sandy's faces as they entered the room. He poured Sandy a glass of brandy, and Helen poured one for herself.

Bridget came down the stairs and entered the living room. "What's wrong?" she said. She looked at Helen. "It's Mellissa, isn't it? She's dead…She said she'd do it."

"You knew?" Nicole said. "Why didn't you say something?"

Bridget looked at her. "Why? She's found peace."

They met at a summer-league baseball game in Bloomfield Hills. Sandy lived in Birmingham, and Nick lived in the far corner of Warren, on the border of Roseville and East Detroit. They lived in different cultures.

Their first date was the night they met. Nick was on the pitcher's mound, and his father was behind the backstop. Nick had a natural curve to his pitches, and his father was always there to watch. The Bloomfield Hills team had white uniforms with blue socks, blue hats, and shoes with metal cleats. Nick's team had red T-shirts with peeling numbers, sun-faded red hats, and canvas sneakers. The boys were all of the same age, but the teams were mismatched. The boys from Warren led twelve to zero at the fifth inning, and the coach took Nick out of the game to give John Zebercot a chance to pitch.

Sandy seemed to appear from nowhere. Nick was behind the backstop, talking to his father, when he noticed her a few feet away. She wore a blue varsity jacket with "Seaholm High" across the front. She smiled and said hi. Nick liked that he didn't have to say hi first. She asked where he went to school, and he told her

Warren High. His father said he was leaving and glanced at Sandy. His father walked toward his truck, and as he opened the truck door, he looked back at them. She asked Nick whether he had his own car, and he pointed to the Ford convertible. He said the top went down, and she said she figured it did since it was a convertible. Nick was proud to show her his car. He pointed out the teardrop skirts and the large red dice for radio knobs.

When the game ended, the people in the stands started to leave. A girl called to Sandy and said to hurry up. She asked Nick whether he could give her a ride home, and he said sure. The lights above the baseball diamond were turned off, one at a time.

Sandy gave directions to her house. She scooted across the seat to sit close to him. The streets were new to Nick, and the houses were large and made of stone. Even in the dark, the lawns looked well cared for and big. When he turned into her drive, she said to turn the headlights off so her mother wouldn't know she was out there. He left the radio on; Ricky Nelson sang "Young World."

She asked whether he knew how to French kiss. He shook his head; he'd never heard of it. She said, "You open your mouth and slip your tongue inside my mouth—then our tongues play together." Nick did what she said, and he liked it.

He didn't see Sandy again until one night in late September at Ted's Drive-In. The carhop brought two root beers on a tray out to his car. Betty Kleinhower sat next to him. A few cars away, a group of kids were standing in front of a car and talking. One of them was Sandy. She was showing the ring she wore on a chain around her neck. She was going steady with Eddie Wellington. A group of boys came out of Ted's, and one of them put his arm around Sandy. He was much taller than Nick.

Soon after, Nick and Betty were going steady, and she wore his ring on a chain around her neck until she broke up with him that same autumn. That January he saw Sandy at a swim meet against Seaholm High. The swim meet didn't count in the standings; it was just a practice meet.

Nick was on the diving team, and he saw Sandy in the stands. He was on the diving board, ready to make his approach, when he saw her. She was with Eddie Wellington.

It was a summer morning, and the sunlight was warm and still soft. Nick raked a few leaves from the backyard, while Nicole tended her garden. She wanted to know where all the rabbits came from; they'd been into the snow peas all summer. Sandy was on the patio in a summer robe, her bare feet tucked under her. She sipped from a cup of hot tea.

Nick carried a handful of leaves to the trash can. He noticed a few things at the bottom of the can as he dropped the leaves into it. He turned to continue raking, but then he stopped and went back to the trash can. He fished through the leaves to the bottom of the can and retrieved a clear plastic bag, the size of a quarter. He saw several more at the bottom. There was a brownish-white residue inside the plastic bag. He held it to his nose. It had an acidic odor. He asked Nicole whether Bridget was still in her room.

"I didn't notice," she said. "Come to think of it, I haven't seen her since last night…or early evening."

He looked toward the second-floor windows. The shades were still open, but she never closed them anyway. It was early afternoon before he saw her. She came down for coffee. It appeared she'd been living in the same clothes for days. Her blouse was only half buttoned, and underneath she didn't wear a bra. The back of her jeans showed a stain of dried blood near the crotch. She poured a cup of cold coffee and placed it in the microwave. Nick asked how she was feeling. She shrugged with her back to him.

"I don't know," she said. The microwave stopped, and she removed the coffee and sat down at the table.

"Why are you looking at me?" she said.

"No reason."

"No lectures," she said. "Please."

"Have I ever lectured you?"

"No." She wouldn't look at him. "But Mom does. I get so sick of it: 'You have your whole life ahead of you.' What a crock of shit. I have AIDS, for Christ's sake. All I have ahead of me is what happened to Mellissa."

"You don't have AIDS. You're HIV positive, and that can be controlled."

"You don't get it, do you?" She looked at him. "You really don't."

She got up to leave; there was smeared blood on the seat of the chair. It was against his better judgment, but he followed her to her room. She turned to face him. "What?"

"You're using again," he said. "How are you getting it?"

"What difference does it make? When I'm high, I don't care. I don't fucking care. That's all that counts."

"Is it coming from Carthage?"

"Jesus Christ!"

"Is it?"

"Yes!"

He left the room; how Carthage got it to her no longer made a difference. He stopped at the head of the stairs and gripped the railing. He squeezed in anger, his knuckles white.

Sandy came in from the kitchen. She looked at the top of the stairs. "What's wrong?"

He forced a smile. "Nothing."

"Come outside," she said. "I want your company."

He returned to the patio and to raking the lawn. He paused and looked toward the second-floor windows.

"Did you find Bridget?" Nicole asked, but her attention was on a vine of cucumbers she was tying to the trellis.

He didn't answer.

In the late afternoon before dinner, the three of them shared wine on the patio. Sandy had prepared a plate of hors d'oeuvres.

"You seem distracted," Nicole said.

Nick looked at her.

"It's Bridget," he said. "She's using again."

"I thought so," she said. "She won't take care of herself. I don't know what to do. I just want it to go away."

Sandy was quiet. The funeral had been only days before. She and Nick set the patio table for dinner, and Nicole called to Bridget from the bottom of the stairs to come down and join them. But Bridget didn't answer, and Nicole didn't pursue it. Her presence brought tension to the table. Avoidance was easier.

By evening there was still no sign of Bridget. Nicole went to check on her, while Nick and Sandy remained on the patio. The summer air and the quiet were pleasant in the fading light as the sun dipped below the trees.

"She's not there," Nicole said, returning to the patio. "I didn't hear her leave."

"She might have gone for a walk," Sandy said. "I'd give her a moment. It might be what she needs."

It didn't sound right, but Nick kept the thought to himself. The sky far above the trees was now indigo, and the first stars were visible. Bridget might have gone for a walk, but it was unlikely. He went up to his study and made a phone call from the landline, but there was no answer. He pulled on a bulky sweatshirt and removed a fanny pack from the bottom drawer of his desk. He clipped it to his waist and went downstairs.

"Where are you going?" Sandy said as the garage door opened.

"I have a hunch," he told her.

"Where are you going?" she asked again. She saw the fanny pack around his waist. "You have a gun, don't you?"

He didn't answer

"Take Helen with you," she said. "Please."

"I can't reach her. I tried. There's no answer."

He opened the trunk of the black Volkswagen, took a screwdriver out from the tool kit, and removed the license plate from the back of the car. He replaced it with the hand-painted license plate from the trunk: WJ-447.

"I don't know what you're going to do," Sandy said, "but I'm worried."

He held her for a moment then kissed her forehead and the side of her face. "I'll be fine," he said.

"At least wait for Helen."

"I don't know where she is."

She watched as he backed out of the drive. He drove south along Lake Shore Drive to East Jefferson into the city then turned right on Cadillac. There were no streetlights anywhere; none of them worked. He turned off his headlights and drove slowly to the corner of Kercheval, turned, and stopped at Hurlbut. The house he looked for was in clear view. There were empty lots on either side, and the windows on the second floor were smashed out and burned. The first floor was boarded up except for the front door, and a light was on in the basement.

He drove one street over to approach the house from the rear. Bewick was a one-way street, so he backed in from the intersection of Kercheval and parked at the curb next to an empty lot. There was a line of trees at the end of the lot, and on the other side of the trees was the house on Hurlbut. As he approached the trees, he heard voices from inside the house.

The basement windows at the rear of the house were boarded up, but on the side of one window was an opening through the boards. He lay flat on the ground to see through the opening. Bridget was on her knees in front of Michael Carthage, and there was another man with him. Her face was bloody, and she was crying. "It's not AIDS. It's different," she said. "Honest, it is."

"You gave me AIDS," he said. "You filthy bitch!"

"It's not." Tears covered her face. "You can take medicine."

"No, you can't. It's a death sentence!" Carthage raised a gun to her head and fired. Her head snapped forward, and she fell at his feet.

For an instant the scene seemed unreal, as if what he'd witnessed hadn't happened. It couldn't have—but it had. Bridget lay facedown in a pool of blood as Carthage stood over her, holding the gun. At that moment Nick was paralyzed, as if all the air had been sucked from his lungs. His eyes stared, unblinking. Thinking came to a standstill—until it came to him: there was nothing he could do. It was over. The moment to act had been seconds ago; nothing would bring her back. He stared through the tiny opening. Somehow this was his fault. He could have saved her.

Still lying flat on his belly, Nick pushed himself away from the window.

B etty wanted to go bowling, and there was a new bowling alley on Gratiot Avenue. There was a bar with a dance floor inside and live music on the weekends, but this was Wednesday. They rented bowling shoes at the counter, and Betty asked whether he knew how to keep score. Nick said he didn't. Betty laughed and said she did. "Just do as you're told, and we'll be fine," she said.

Nick picked the lightest ball he could find and inserted his fingers. It felt good, but Betty said it was a woman's ball. She said to choose one of the solid-color balls. He followed her suggestion, but the heavier ball pulled him off balance at the point of release. At the end of the frame, he went back to the lighter ball, and Betty rolled her eyes. By the end of the third frame, his approach and release were smooth, and he ended with a spare and a strike. Betty said his score was beginner's luck. Nick thought it was because of the lighter ball.

Betty threw two gutter balls in four tries. She removed the gold chain with his ring from around her neck and put it in her purse, because the damn thing was getting in the way. In the next several frames, she threw two more gutter balls. She sat down and said the whole experience had been ruined, and she wanted to go. She un-laced her shoes and tossed them to the side.

Nick returned his shoes to the counter and asked Betty for hers, but she said she'd left them back there. He returned to the lane, but the shoes were gone. The man at the counter said no shoes, no de-posit. "But that's five dollars!" Nick argued.

"Sorry, kid. That's the policy."

"But that's not fair."

"Fair? So sue me, kid."

In the car Betty said he'd let that man walk all over him. Nick didn't remind her that she was the one who'd tossed the shoes.

On Thursday nights the bowling alley was crowded. The bar and dance floor were closed, but the lanes were full of noisy bowl-ers. Next to the first lane was a walkway to the back of the lanes, to the pin-setting machines. Nick had been back there once before with Vito Battelinie, when Vito had worked part-time at the lanes after school.

In the back Nick counted seven lanes to the left. He then raised an extension ladder to the exposed steel beam. From his back pocket, he unfolded a cardboard sign and hung it from the ladder: DO NOT REMOVE. Under his shirt was a long rope, wrapped around his waist. He started up the ladder.

The steel beams ran the length of the lanes to the ceiling above the office. The asbestos ceiling tiles below the beams were loosely fit-ted. He saw the lanes and the bowlers below as he scooted along the beam to the office ceiling. Once over the office, he removed a ceiling tile, attached the rope to the beam, and lowered himself down.

The only light in the office came from under the closed door. Behind the desk was a tall filing cabinet. The top drawer of the cabi-net had a combination lock. He used a letter opener to pry open the door, with little resistance. There was a bag of coins and thirty-three dollars in cash. He counted out five dollars but then decided to take it all and stuffed it into his pocket.

He climbed back up the rope, drew it through the opening, and replaced the ceiling tile. He scooted back along the beam to the extension ladder. At the opening he lowered his head to see whether anyone was there, and then he went down. He removed the sign and replaced the ladder on the floor next to the tool closet.

As he left the bowling alley, he passed the counter. The man who'd refused to give him his deposit back was talking to a woman with red hair and red nails; she wore a shiny necklace like tiny mirrors on a string. The man tried to take her hand, but she pulled back. "You're so bad," she said, and giggled.

From the parking lot, Nick looked back through the glass door to the counter. The man was holding her hand.

The night was a series of naps with dreams and images of Bridget's death: he'd been given a puppy to watch on the grounds of the Ford estate, and a large wave from the lake washed over them and pulled the puppy away, but he was helpless to reach it. He turned over on the pillow. Sandy lay next to him. Her sleep was sound and without effort.

In the morning he called Helen and asked her to come by the house. "What's wrong?" she said. "I can hear it in your voice."

"Not on the phone," he told her.

From his study he heard Nicole in the kitchen. She no doubt knew that Bridget hadn't come home last night. But how could he tell her? And Bridget's body still lay in that basement. This seemed like the most difficult thing he'd ever faced. Why had he left her body there?

When he heard Nicole leave, he went down to the kitchen. He poured a cup of coffee and went out to the patio. Sandy soon joined him in her summer robe and slippers. She set her tea on the table and kissed the top of his head. "So tell me what happened. You were so withdrawn last night."

"When Helen gets here, I'll ask Nicole to join us. I'll explain then."

"Nicky, what happened? What is it?"

He shook his head.

"You're frightening me," she said.

He heard Helen's car pull into the drive. She parked in front of the first bay and got out. She came toward Nick then stopped. "What's wrong?"

"Nicole is upstairs," he said. "Would you ask her to join us?"

"Oh, my God," Sandy said. She put her hand to her mouth. "Tell me Bridget's OK."

Helen returned with Nicole. The two women sat down. Nicole looked pale. "It's something terrible, isn't it?"

"Bridget is dead." There was utter silence at the table. "There was nothing I could do," Nick said. "It happened within seconds." He and Nicole stared at each other.

"You saw it?"

He nodded.

"It's me," Nicole said, as tears filled her eyes. "If I hadn't been screwing everyone in sight, none of this would have happened."

Helen took her hand in hers. "Don't, Nicole. It doesn't help. It wasn't you."

"How?" Nicole asked. "How did it happen?"

"She was shot."

"Oh, my God! And you saw it?"

"Yes."

"But why? Who did it?"

"Michael Carthage. I don't know why."

"Oh, my God," Sandy said. "You saw it? Couldn't you have stopped it?"

He shook his head. "It happened too fast."

"Did you call the police?"

"No," he said, "but I'll take care of it." He looked at Helen.

"Where is she?" Nicole asked, tears coming down her face. "Where?"

This was the hardest part. How could he explain that he had left her body in that filthy basement? "She's still there."

"Where?"

"In a basement."

Nicole broke down, and Helen put her arms around her and held her close as she cried. She led Nicole into the house. A moment later Nicole returned to the patio, her face wet with tears. She looked at Nick. "I know you would have stopped it. I don't I blame you." Her face was covered with tears.

He went to her and held her close.

As the day wore on, the news of Bridget's death sank in, and the shock was less, but the pain was still there. Sandy changed into jeans and a T-shirt, but she wore no makeup. Nick sat on a lawn chair and drank wine, as though he were exhausted from hard labor. He and Sandy were together outside, while Helen comforted Nicole in the house. Helen offered Nicole a half a Valium, but she refused it. Sandy left Nick on the patio and went to the kitchen to put together a dinner of cold cuts. Nick sat by himself. The wine on an empty stomach helped ease his sense of guilt. He could have done something—fired a shot through the opening in the window, made a noise to distract them, anything—but it had happened so fast. He had to stop replaying it in his mind. He had to. It was making him sick.

A moment later Sandy came back onto the patio. "Nicky, come here! Look at this—on the news."

The TV on the island counter showed Michael Carthage wearing handcuffs and standing between two policemen. Helen appeared in the kitchen entry with an empty brandy glass. The three of them watched the screen.

"Michael Carthage, grandson of civil-rights leader Reverend Jessup Carthage, is being held in connection with the murder of a young woman on Hurlbut Street," the reporter said. "Reverend Carthage was unavailable for comment."

"Then her body's at the morgue," Helen said.

I t was an early summer day when the man arrived at the front door and asked for Joseph Winterstein. Nick and his sisters were in the living room, and his mother stood at the kitchen sink, washing dishes, when the man knocked. His mother turned and looked toward the door, but when the man asked her husband whether he was Joseph Winterstein and handed him the papers, she quickly turned her back to them.

His father stood at the door, reading the first page. He then turned to the second page and, while still reading it, returned to the living room and sat down in the armchair. He looked toward his wife, a smirk on his face. "Mental cruelty, the flaunting of infidelity? You haven't had a winter coat in ten years?" he said, as he read. He tossed the papers to the floor.

The following day Joe Kopecny was served divorce papers. Nick heard him through the open windows. "Divorce? What more do you want? You already screw everything in sight."

The thought of his parents getting a divorce wasn't upsetting on the surface. Nick knew he would stay with his mother, away from the fear of his father's judgment and disapproval. The thought of their divorce was a reprieve. Nick now kept the hours he pleased; his parents had the turmoil of their new lives to figure out. That afternoon he got into his car and drove with no destination in mind. He ended up at Sy's Lebanon Market.

The market had been sold, and Sy had retired to his place on Lake Huron. The new owners had expanded the business and the parking lot in the rear along a line of decaying trees. The new owner and his son cooked sausages on a hot plate behind the butcher's counter. The son put together a sandwich and offered it to Nick for free. He and Nick were the same age. It seemed a strange way to make a profit, but at the time, Nick didn't consider the meaning of profit and loss. The world was just beginning to reveal itself.

Nick sat in his car with the radio on and ate his sandwich. He didn't put the top down because it was more trouble than pleasure. The top never went down the same way twice, and when it was down, the sun was either too hot, or dirt and leaves blew into the car, and he didn't like the mess.

A 1932 Ford, a street rod, without headlights or fenders and with the engine exposed, pulled into the parking lot. It was the Lassider kid and his girlfriend. The Ford engine rumbled with a rough idle, and through the rolled-up windows, Nick saw Lassider yelling at his girlfriend as she pulled back from him. He pushed his hand into her face and pinned her head against the window then flicked it free. Lassider got out of his car and walked in front of Nick's car toward the store. He was well muscled with a slim waist. At school Nick had seen him grab a boy by the hair and punch him in the face until it was a bloody mess.

Lassider returned to the car with a paper bag clenched in his fist. He opened the car door and threw the bag inside. He yelled something at the girl, and she nodded, but she didn't look at him. She kept her head down. In a sudden rage, Lassider got out of the car and came around to the passenger side. He pulled the door open and dragged her out by the hair. She cowered and tried to cover her face. He drew his fist back and punched her; her head snapped back, and she fell to the ground. He stood over her and screamed at her to get up.

Nick got out of the car and grabbed a decaying tree branch that was the size of a man's arm. As though it were a baseball bat, he hit Lassider on the side of the head. The branch shattered, and Lassider staggered sideways. Before Lassider came to his senses, Nick had another branch and hit him in the rib cage at full swing. Lassider fell to his hands and gasped to breathe. Nick turned to help the girl, but when he saw her bloody face, he stopped. He turned back to Lassider and hit him again; blood trickled from his ear.

Her name was Bobbie and she lived at Fairlawn Trailer Park. Nick helped her to his car and gave her a red-and-blue handkerchief to put over her bloody nose. As he put the car in reverse and let out the clutch, he saw Lassider sitting on the asphalt, his hand covering his bloody ear. He looked at Nick, and Nick knew Lassider would come looking for him.

Bobbie lived with her mother in an older trailer with peeling paint and cinder blocks set at the front door for steps. All the window shades were down. Nick parked behind a maroon Studebaker with two flat tires, and she got out. He watched her walk up to the trailer, still holding the handkerchief over her nose.

When Nick got home, his mother was in her garden, and his father was in the shop with the garage door open. His father sat on a bench, a cigarette between his fingers, and stared out at the road.

Nick heard Kopecny across the yard. "It won't last a goddamn month—you'll be screwing someone else."

The Wayne County Medical Examiner's office was on East Warren Avenue. Helen and Nicole were in the backseat of the Lincoln, and Sandy was up front with Nick. He didn't want Nicole to see Bridget this way, but she insisted on identifying her daughter's body. As they got closer to the medical examiner's office, Sandy had reservations. She didn't want to go inside. She didn't want to remember Bridget this way.

"I can't bury her here," Nicole said. "This isn't her home. She didn't have one."

Nick looked at her in the rearview mirror. Nicole was looking out the window. "This is *my* home," she said quietly. "I was conceived here."

Nick looked in the mirror. He felt Sandy's hand on his forearm. He looked at her. It was as though she were reading his thoughts. "Cremation," Nicole said. "That seems the right thing to do." Helen took Nicole's hand.

The smell of death was in the parking lot, a stringent, acid smell that entered the nasal passage, the throat, and the lungs—the smell of dysfunction and decay. Sandy remained in the car with the windows up. Helen looped her arm through Nicole's and held her close as they entered the building.

Inside, the smell was even worse, as though you had a sore throat while trying not to breathe through your nose. Nick identified himself, and they were led to a viewing room. There were silver-colored body bags on stretchers along the hallway. A gurney was wheeled into the viewing room, and the silver body bag containing Bridget's body was unzipped to the waist. Nicole nodded; yes, it was her daughter. She touched the side of Bridget's face. Tears came to her eyes. She leaned down and kissed Bridget's forehead as her hand rested on the lifeless body. "I'm so sorry, my baby. I'm so sorry…I did everything wrong." Helen placed her hand on Nicole's arm. Her face covered with tears, Nicole looked at Helen.

Helen led her from the room, but Nick remained for a moment longer. The coroner had done little to clean her up. The bullet had entered the top of her head and come out through her chin. "I'll take care of this," he whispered to Bridget. "It will not go unanswered."

Nicole signed the necessary papers, and Nick arranged for the transport of her body to a private crematorium. In a few days, further decisions would have to be made, but they were for Nicole to decide. She had her father's support.

Late Monday afternoon it was announced on the local news that Michael Carthage had been charged with first-degree murder. The news reporter was in front of the house of Jessup Carthage.

"The fingerprints of Michael Carthage were found on the gun reportedly used to kill"—the reporter glanced at her notes—"Bridget Winterstein, the granddaughter of noted Detroit attorney Nicholas Winterstein." She looked into the camera. "It seems that friends and former associates of Mr. Winterstein were unaware that he had a granddaughter or any family for that matter."

The camera cut to a taped interview with Joshua Bellingham, a former associate of Winterstein and Associates.

"No one knew of a granddaughter or daughter or any family," he said to the interviewer. "It's news to me. To all of us."

The interviewer asked whether he thought Mr. Winterstein was a secretive person.

"Secretive? I don't know," he said, considering the question. "But he certainly is a lone wolf. He does things his own way," he said, shaking his head. "He and I never agreed on much."

"Why is that?" the reporter asked.

"He doesn't think like the rest of us. Personally I think he needs help."

The camera cut back to the live broadcast. The young reporter looked up from the monitor. "So far Reverend Carthage refuses to make a comment," she said into the handheld microphone, "and his office has yet to release a statement."

Nick turned the TV off and sat back in his chair. It had been a few days since they retrieved Bridget's ashes from the crematorium. The ashes were in a small urn on the mantel above the fireplace in the living room. Nicole had asked to have lunch at the Cotswold Café at the Ford House as part of a personal service for Bridget. She wanted Sandy and Helen to join them.

Nicole placed the urn in an embroidered bag she carried over her shoulder. Nick watched from the hallway. He didn't ask any questions.

They drove to the grounds of the Ford estate, and as Nicole stepped out from the car in the parking lot, she again carried the embroidered bag over her shoulder. Once seated in the café, she carefully placed the bag next to her chair. They ordered light sandwiches and a Riesling wine.

"When I was a girl," Helen said, "I knew this place was here. It was pointed out as we drove by. But I never really saw it. It was like a fairy tale in the distance."

"I was here once," Sandy said, "when I was a little girl. With my father. He worked for Cadillac, in advertising. I think all the car people knew one another. I have no idea why we were here."

"Dad had an interesting story," Nicole said, "the last time we were here, about Henry and his son."

"It had more to do with their relationship," Nick said, "the conflict between father and son. I think it's pretty common, no matter who you are. It exists between—"

"Mothers and daughters," Sandy said.

"Yes," he said, "between mothers and daughters too."

"What was the story?" Helen asked.

"I can think of another one," he said. "An anecdote with the same point." He took a sip of wine. "Henry returned from a trip and discovered that Edsel had been developing a new car. They had fallen behind General Motors. GM was giving customers what they wanted. But not Henry. The customers got what Henry gave them. That was it. His way or no way.

"Well, the engineering department was involved, and the design people and marketing. Edsel hoped his father finally would see the need for a new model. They created a life-size clay model. But when Henry discovered the model, he supposedly stood there with his hands on his hips without saying a word, and then he walked around the model, looking at it. I'm sure there was enough tension in the room that you could have cut it with a knife.

"Well, the old man blew up. He grabbed a tool and started ripping into the clay model. Edsel stood there and had to watch, humiliated in front of everyone."

"We all do that," Nicole said. "We love them to pieces, yet we hurt them terribly."

"Henry loved his son very much. He was devastated when Edsel died, and I'm sure there were events and things he had done and said to Edsel that haunted him all his life. To this day I wish I had *my* father back so I could love him with my words and my deeds. And tell him I blame him for nothing."

Nicole reached for Nick's hand and squeezed it. "You're a good man."

Nick shook his head and started to say that no, he wasn't, but this wasn't the time.

At the finish of lunch, Nicole said she wanted to walk the grounds again—and did he mind? "No, of course not," Nick said. "We'll all go. It's a pleasant walk."

They followed the path from the café to the walkway past the great house. Nicole led them to the rose garden. She continued past the fountain and into the garden. Nick stood at the garden entrance and watched her. She removed the urn from the embroidered bag and sprinkled Bridget's ashes into the rich soil among the flowers.

His father rented a house in Mount Clemens, and Melina moved in with him. The divorce required that the house on Frazho Road be sold and that the money be divided between his parents; but until the divorce was final and the house was sold, Nick and his mother lived there. His mother continued to garden and worked at a small factory on Groesbeck Highway, while Nick attended Wayne State University. He earned his tuition through day labor and an occasional story sold to the *Saturday Evening Post* under a pseudonym. He wrote stories about his father without mention of Melina, in a world of his own making.

His sisters chose to live with their father. This fact was painful for his mother, and she seldom spoke of it, as though it were a scarlet letter she had to wear until her early death.

His sisters seemed content in the house near the river. The backyard was overgrown with weeds, and the boat was set on blocks above them. The outboard motor was corroded in one position, while the bilge filled with melting snow and rain. His father never mentioned the airplane anymore. But Nick still flew and maintained it, and he worried it might be sold with everything else. His grandfather never had seen the airplane, but he always had a suggestion for any problem Nick described regarding its maintenance.

Nick came several times to visit his father at the house near the river. His father appeared tired and sad. He had lost weight. The biceps that once had flexed under the slightest pressure were gone. His decline was too painful to see, and Nick looked for reasons to cut his visits short. Whenever Nick left the house, he couldn't recall having spoken a word to Melina. Although there was eye contact, nothing was ever said. There was only a silent, cold stare.

After one such visit, he returned to Roseville along Gratiot Avenue and pulled into the A&W drive-in. He backed into a parking slot, and a carhop came to the side of his car to take his order. He watched her walk away, and she turned to look over her shoulder at him. They smiled, each caught in a second glance.

There was a notebook and a textbook, *History of Roman Law,* on the seat next to him. Nick opened the notebook. He had just put a thought down on paper when he heard the engine rumble of a street rod.

It was the Lassider kid. He stopped in front of Nick's car and glared at him. He put the street rod in reverse, backed into a parking slot across the way, and got out. Nick understood this was no time for posturing. Hurling threats and insults, Lassider came across the open lot. Nick gripped the inside door latch, pulling it back, but didn't open the door. He held it for the right moment. When Lassider reached the right distance, Nick threw the door open. The edge of the door caught him at full impact in the groin and stomach. He staggered back, and now Nick was in front of him, his fist drawn back. The punch was solid, and Lassider went down on his butt hard. Nick waited for another move, but Lassider sat there, stunned, with his hands on the ground for balance. Blood dripped from his chin.

Nick got into his car and started the engine. The carhop was on her way across the lot with a mug of root beer on the car tray. She stopped when she saw Lassider. Nick put the car in gear and started forward. In the side-view mirror, he looked back at Lassider, who was still sitting on the asphalt. He didn't think Lassider would look for him again.

N ick was at the office late into the afternoon. He was usually gone by this time. He no longer worked long days, even nights, seven days a week. His modest fortune had been earned; it now worked for him. The memory of his granddaughter, executed in front of him, now drove him. Over his shoulder a moving cloud blocked the sun though the window. He very seldom drank hard liquor anymore, but a glass of bourbon was on his desk in the emerging sunlight. Helen picked up the glass. "May I?" she asked.

"Of course." He smiled.

She took a sip, then a second, and placed the glass back on his desk. She sat down on the sofa. "If he's convicted, he'll get life. You'll never get to him then."

"I know," he said. "I've thought of it, over and over again."

"I know what you're going to do," she said.

He nodded.

"Can it happen?" she asked.

"If the family insists I represent him and the court doesn't object, it'll happen."

"So it's up to Jessup Carthage?"

"In the end, yes. The decision will rest with him."

Helen closed the office, and Nick drove home to Grosse Pointe. Sandy was on the phone as he came into the living room; she seldom returned to Birmingham since Mellissa's death. She covered the mouthpiece and whispered that she was talking to Edward. His marriage was near an end, and he needed reassurance over his decision to divorce. He'd never wanted reassurance when forcing Sandy from Wellington Industries, but now he was lost.

"He's like a child," Sandy said before dinner. "I don't say that out of anger but sympathy. The last days Mellissa was alive, the two of them were like children together."

Nicole joined them for dinner, but it was a quiet occasion. The air was still tender with loss.

From his study Nick later made a phone call on his cell. It rang several times and was then answered by Monica Carthage. "Hello?"

"Monica? This is Nicholas Winterstein."

"If you're calling to make threats, I'm hanging up. I won't speak to you."

"No, don't hang up. I'm calling to help. I'm on your side."

"Is this some kind of joke? Some cruel—"

"No, please listen to me. I don't believe Michael is guilty."

"You don't? But it was your—"

"I know…But think about it. Why would I offer to help if I thought he did it?"

There was a long silence. Nick waited.

"You mean that, don't you?" she answered. "I don't know what to say."

"If the charges stick, if there isn't a dismissal, I'll defend him. And I can win."

"You're serious, aren't you?"

"I've never been more serious in my life."

"Have you talked to my father?"

"No, but I will. I'll explain it to him, and there won't be a bill—nothing."

"Why are you doing this?"

"Because," he said, hesitating, "it's the right thing to do."

Nick waited until the next day to call Jessup Carthage. He was sure Monica would call her father as soon as she finished talking to Nick. He wanted to give them both time to think about it. They would have to approve the choice of counsel to represent Michael Carthage, and if they weren't convinced of Nick's sincerity, their choice might go to some hack instead. An effective attorney must understand he's playing a fool's game. He must wear the emperor's new clothes, as ridiculous as he might feel.

The next day Helen was at the office ahead of Nick with coffee and croissants. She had worked hard at preparing the wrongful-death suit, and as she explained, the last thing she wanted was for the whole thing to end up in court. In her preparation she was careful to leave an attractive opening to an out-of-court settlement.

"It's not a matter of greed," she said. "A few months' rent will do."

Nick cut a croissant in half. "Make it easy and cheap," he said, "and everyone goes to lunch happy."

Nick looked for the right moment to call Jessup Carthage, but when the office phone rang and Helen answered it, he knew it might be him calling first. The light for line one went from solid to blinking as Helen put the call on hold and stepped around the corner to Nick's office. "It's him," she said.

Nick picked up the line. "Nicholas Winterstein."

"Winterstein, it's Jessup Carthage. Monica told me of your offer. You think you can win this?"

"Yes, I can."

"Why?" His tone was serious and without pretension. "Why are you so sure of yourself?"

"I've defended seven clients charged with murder, and I've won all seven."

"How many were plea bargains?"

"No one went to prison. That's the important thing."

"I've already talked to someone else," he said.

"May I ask who?"

"Kwame McGinley."

"So your mind is made up?"

"You represented Marshall and—"

"He had a guarantee of immunity. That is a victory."

"We know how that worked out." The unspoken had been mentioned. A silence followed, as if Carthage was waiting for Nick to speak in defense or accuse him of something, but there was nothing. "I've got to think about this, Winterstein. My grandson is at stake. His whole life," he added, and hung up.

Nick stood there, holding an empty line. He looked at Helen. "Now what?" she said. "You think he'll call back?"

"I don't know."

Nick wasn't ready to think of an alternate plan. Even if Carthage chose McGinley, there was a chance he might seek Nick's advice. It was too soon to consider a new course, but how long should he wait?

He went home in the early afternoon to busy himself in one way or another. He first washed his car then reorganized things in the garage, but there was little to do there. If an object was seldom or never used, it was discarded, except for his parents' tools. His mother's garden tools were now Nicole's. They were cleaned and organized; the rakes, shovels, and hoe hung on the wall, and the hand tools lay on a bench along with gardening gloves. His grandfather's genes lived within her, as they did in himself.

The next morning, on his way to the office, his day was still without purpose until he knew what Carthage intended to do. Helen was at her desk when he arrived. His uncertainty was visible.

Later in the morning, Nick managed to distract himself with work. He made notes in the margin on the second page of a brief then looked up. He heard the front office door open, followed by a man's voice—a moment later Jessup Carthage stepped around the corner. His bodyguard followed. Helen stood behind him, her hands spread as if to say, *I couldn't stop them.*

"Winterstein…"

It was the first time Nick had been face-to-face with Jessup Carthage. He appeared older than Nick thought him to be, while the graying temples gave dignity to a history of anger and perceived arrogance. His face was full, puffy with age, and his eyes appeared tired yet still energetic. Seeing him for the first time, Nick felt a sense of respect for the man.

Nick stood. "Jessup…" It crossed his mind to address him as Mr. Carthage or Reverend, but now wasn't the time for pretense. "Please have a seat."

"I'm fine," he said, with a brief wave of the hand.

"Would you care for anything to drink?"

"No," he said. He looked at Nick. "I don't know your motive in this. And I'm not sure I trust you. But I do believe you can help. Why you would want to," he said, "I don't know. It's your granddaughter he's accused of killing. It's bizarre."

Nick considered giving some reason, but the less said the better.

"Winterstein, I don't care if Michael is guilty or not. I will not let the system—the white system—have him." He spoke without cameras or cadence of speech or audience; it was just two men on opposite sides of the fence. "Look around," he said. "You see a city full of drugs and murder, and you people say to each other, 'It's the way those people live.' Well, it's not our choice. But you can't see that, and you never will. I watched my brother being murdered in front of me by white policemen. It's indelible. You can't erase it. It's something I'll always see."

But Nick did understand it. In his mind he saw Bridget kneeling in front of Michael Carthage as he shot her in the head.

"I do understand," Nick said. "There are some things you cannot erase." The two men looked at each other. "Let me defend Michael. I can win this. I will win it."

For Carthage it was a win-win: two chances at acquittal for the price of one. If Nick lost, a successful appeal was almost guaranteed. Carthage would argue he was biased; Winterstein wanted a conviction. The prosecution certainly wouldn't object to Winterstein's representation of the defendant, and there wasn't a court in the state that would deny Carthage the counsel of his request. Politics are law.

"Somehow I believe you," Carthage said. He nodded his approval but didn't offer his hand.

Carthage left the office. His bodyguard went first through the outer office door and waited for the elevator. Carthage did not look back.

Bill drove a truck for one of the many factories in Detroit. He was thin and wiry with a dark crew cut. Nick's mother introduced him as a special friend, but Nick wasn't impressed. Bill didn't have the suave, handsome manner Sy did. He appeared false and eager to use, but his mother needed the attention. Within a week's time, he moved in, but Nick was seldom home; he worked three jobs to pay tuition and often studied and sometimes slept in his car between jobs.

Nick stopped at the house to get clean clothes and sometimes to sleep in his old bed. His mother still ironed his shirts and starched the collars, though she worked at the factory on Groesbeck Highway and maintained her garden. She hoed weeds from between the rows of vegetables, while Bill sat on a lawn chair and watched with a cold beer in his hand. He called out comments to imply her efforts were silly, "since you can buy a stupid ear of corn or a tomato down at that Arab store."

Bill learned that Nick knew how to fly airplanes and asked why Nick would do such a stupid thing. No one knew why people stayed up in the air to begin with, and sometimes they didn't and crashed on top of their ass. "Then where are you?" He took another swig of beer then laughed as if considering the humor of his own remark. Nick looked toward his mother; their eyes met, and she looked away. Bill asked Nick what he was studying at school, and when Nick said he intended to go to law school, Bill made one lawyer joke after another until Nick left the house to work on his car.

Bill drove a truck at night and sometimes several days at a stretch until it was necessary to do a layover in Cincinnati or Louisville before returning to Detroit. One afternoon Nick returned home to see his father's truck in the driveway. Through the screen door, he saw his father in the kitchen with his mother. His father reached forward to take her hand, and she took his; they looked at each other, his thumb gently rubbing the top of her hand. Tears rolled from her eyes. Nick stepped away from the door to leave their private moment.

He waited at the side of his car. The Kopecny house was empty and for sale. The lawn was uncut, and the door to the toolshed hung open. A moment later his father left the house and came toward the truck. There were tears in his eyes. He saw Nick and said, "Hello, son." He placed his hand on Nick's shoulder, and Nick hugged him.

His father backed the truck to the end of the drive and waited for traffic to clear. They looked at each other through the windshield; then his father backed onto the street and drove off.

A few weeks later, Nick received a note at school, relayed through the front office, to call Melina at this number. He saw no hurry or desire to call her and pushed the note into his hip pocket. The next day he called from a pay phone. The call was received at the switchboard of Lapeer County Hospital. He asked to speak to Melina Winterstein, and the operator asked, "Which department, please?" Nick was confused; a sense of worry rushed over him. He gave his name and the circumstances of the call, and she said to please hold for a moment.

Melina came on the line and said his father had suffered a severe heart attack and was in intensive care. She said he hadn't been conscious for two days. Nick said he could be there by late afternoon and left immediately to tell his mother what had happened.

When he arrived at the house on Frazho Road, Bill's car was in the drive. He could see that she already had heard the news. Her eyes were red. She asked him to wait for a bit before he left for Lapeer County. She intended to tell Bill he had to move out that afternoon, and she wanted Nick there when she told him. She didn't know what to expect.

Bill hung his head and said he knew when he wasn't wanted, and he would take his lumps like a man. But he would be fine, he said. He could sleep in his truck or maybe, if it wasn't too cold, on the beaches of Lake Saint Clair; he'd get along, all right—he'd be fine. Nick rolled his eyes.

It was dusk as Nick drove out to Lapeer County. The autumn clouds were tinged with orange and stretched along the horizon. Brown leaves blew from the trees and across the highway.

When Nick arrived at the nurses' station outside the intensive care unit, three nurses stood and watched him approach. There was no greeting, only silence. One nurse said she was very sorry as she reached for his hand. She said his mother had asked to see the body. In a cold tone, Nick said she wasn't his mother.

⋯

Soon after the funeral, Cheryl-Ann disappeared altogether from peripheral view. Then one day Nick received a letter from her, one paragraph that stretched over four pages without periods.

> I married Loren he looks so much like daddy it takes my breath away the same color eyes and hair and he even smells like daddy but I'm scared because I cant always do all the things he wants in bed and he likes the girl across the street a lot, maybe the girl can be my friend, I know the holy spirit will protect me

Cheryl-Ann married three times in search of her father's love, now buried beneath the cold earth.

Kathleena was bitten by an evil cupid. She married a man who humiliated her with a never-ending string of public paramours. While her heart bled with impotent rage, she endured the "wishes of Jesus" to bear the humiliations of having been touched by an older man as a child.

California now claimed them both. Cheryl-Ann found contentment in a religious order of its own label, while Kathleena gave public lectures to cuckolded women on the sanctity of marriage.

Nick found further contact with them too painful to endure.

The police responded to a 9-1-1 call in which the caller said there were multiple gunshots going off. But when the police arrived at Hurlbut, the street was quiet. No one appeared on the street, and only two houses on the block had their lights on; while a third house, between two empty lots and with the upper floor boarded over, revealed a single light in the basement. The responding officer said it was a known drug house, but at the time of the call, the house appeared empty.

A second officer arrived at the scene, and the two of them entered the first floor with service pistols drawn. From the hall entry, a basement light was visible. At the top of the stairwell leading down to it, the first officer saw a woman's foot turned sideways on the basement floor. He called out for anyone in the basement to reveal himself or herself, but no one answered. Both officers started down the stairs and found the body of a young white woman. She had been shot in the head.

A later search of the house and outer premises found a patchwork of wiring that tied into a live connection hanging from a utility pole; they also found a .40-caliber pistol under a mattress on the first floor. The shell casing found next to the body matched the pistol. The ballistics report from Lansing revealed it was the same gun used to kill Bridget Winterstein, and the fingerprints on the gun identified Michael Carthage. The prosecution indicated there was a witness who had placed the victim in the company of Michael Carthage on the evening of her death. When asked to provide the name of the witness, the prosecution said it would appear on a revised witness list.

⚊⚊

Seated at a table, Michael Carthage looked up, his hands clasped in chains.

"If I'm going to help you, Michael, I have to know." The look in Michael's eyes was almost humble, if not frightened, as the situation became clear to him. "There's no death penalty in this state," Nick said, "but you could spend the rest of your life in prison. Think of it: the most common freedoms taken away—a walk outside, the company of a woman. Gone forever."

Michael shook his head. "I don't know who saw anything. I didn't do it. And I don't know about fingerprints that got on a gun I don't know about."

"Forget about that," Nick said. "It doesn't concern me. I want to know who might have seen you with Bridget that night." Nick thought of the young man who had stood next to Michael when he shot her. "Try to remember. Did anyone see you with her?"

"No, I tell you—I didn't see her that night. I don't know how she got there."

Nick placed his hand on Michael's shoulder to reassure him. "It's OK, Michael. I believe you." He squeezed his shoulder in a fatherly manner. "We'll deal with that later when we learn who this person is."

At this point Nick was more concerned with bail. He must argue for a reasonable bail while obtaining a guarantee that it would be denied. He felt certain that once free, Michael would jump bail. Jessup Carthage had enough influence in West Africa to provide asylum in Nigeria, the Ivory Coast, or across the continent in Kenya.

A bail hearing was set for the following week. Sandy and Nicole were upset and confused that Nick was defending Michael Carthage. "I don't understand this, Nicky. Why? You saw him do it!" Sandy said.

Nicole was near tears. She tried to ask the same question—why would he defend him?—but nothing came out. Helen took Nicole in her arms. She whispered, "Please, sweetheart, trust your father. He knows what he's doing."

Nick went to the refrigerator to pour a glass of wine. It was painful to keep his reason for defending Michael Carthage from them. Sandy followed him. "Nicky, why are you doing this? You owe her that much."

He set his glass on the counter, gently took her face in his hands, and kissed her forehead. "Carthage is going nowhere," he said. "There'll be an end to him. I promise."

"Then tell Nicole. Reassure her."

"Helen can do that much better than I can. She trusts Helen, just as Bridget and Mellissa did."

"Then you're not going to tell me either?"

He raised her chin to look into her eyes. "I'll let nothing harm you, Sandy—nothing. That includes keeping you innocent."

Sandy asked to attend the bail hearing, but Nick convinced her it wasn't a good idea. Helen was the only one he needed at this point, the only soul privy to his intentions. On a piece of scented stationery, Helen sent an anonymous note to Robert Purcell. In a clear hand, she laid out a fictitious plan to carry Michael Carthage to West Africa once bail was granted. Passage from Detroit to Florida and to Cuba then on to Nigeria by cargo ship was described in convincing detail. The US Attorney's Office wasn't involved in the prosecution of Michael Carthage, but the name "Carthage" would cause Purcell to hand-carry the note to the Wayne County Prosecutor's Office.

The chances of Michael Carthage being released on bail were slim, but Nick had to give a convincing argument to grant bail. The hearing was held in the courtroom of Judge Chantal Littleton, whose reputation was one of leniency in matters of bail. Monica and Jessup Carthage were in the courtroom. Jessup appeared tired, with dark circles beneath his eyes, his hair even grayer at the temples than when Nick had last seen him a few weeks earlier; while Monica, in a dark suit, appeared tense and agitated, her eyes going from her son to the judge and back to the attorneys for prosecution.

The prosecution argued that Mr. Carthage "is not only a threat to the community, as demonstrated by a record of convictions, but also has the financial means to flee and the very real potential of gaining asylum under foreign sovereignty if he does flee, of which the state is convinced." The state strongly urged that bail be denied.

While the prosecution argued against bail, Judge Littleton appeared inattentive to the argument as she read several pages in front of her on the bench. She glanced through one page and then another and didn't look up while the state made its argument. "The court is not concerned with what the state is convinced of," she said without looking up. "Please present what is known and substantiated, nothing more.

"Mr. Winterstein," she began. She looked up from the papers in front of her. "The court has had an opportunity to read not only the pretrial-services report but also the memorandum and supporting documents filed by the defense. Is there anything more the defense wishes to add?"

"Your Honor, the defense wishes to restate the strong ties Michael Carthage has to this community and his connection to his grandfather's ministries, in which he is deeply involved. As for risk of flight, he is of such a high profile that there isn't a place on the planet where he could remain hidden. The state also would have the court believe he is a threat to the community. I believe the court has the twelve character references, as filed. There is nothing in those letters, Your

Honor, including the statement of Reverend Jessup Carthage, to indicate the slightest risk to the community or of flight. Any terms or surety the court may require for bail, the defendant and his family are most willing to meet. Thank you, Your Honor."

Judge Littleton announced an adjournment until 1:00 p.m. the following day, at which time the court would present its ruling.

As Nick gathered his papers into his briefcase, Helen stood next to him. "Good argument," she whispered. "I hope it doesn't backfire."

He looked at her. "Pray it doesn't."

That evening Nick and Sandy and Nicole sat on the patio for coffee and a light dessert after dinner. Nick still felt the effects of the extra glass of wine before dinner when his cell phone rang. He reached for his pocket to answer it. He paused and looked at the caller ID.

"Yes, Monica?"

"I wish to thank you," she said. "Your argument was so heartfelt. My father was impressed too. I know Michael is in good hands."

"Thank you," he said, then listened for a moment longer. He again repeated, "Thank you for your confidence." He folded the phone and slipped it back into his pocket.

"Monica Carthage?" Sandy asked.

"Yes. She wanted to thank me."

"I'm not sure what you're doing," Nicole said, "and I'm not sure I want to know either."

"Helen seems confident," Sandy said. "She simply said to trust you."

"Helen's such a strong woman," Nicole added. "I've never known anyone like her."

The following day at the hearing, Judge Littleton read the court's decision. Monica and Jessup Carthage were in the same seats as the day before. Nick noticed Robert Purcell at the back of the courtroom. The prosecution didn't appear confident. The two attorneys seemed tense; Marsha Rose doodled on the edge of a yellow pad. She glanced over at Nick. They might have already known the court's decision. Helen looked over her shoulder for a second time at Robert Purcell.

The bailiff asked everyone to rise as Judge Littleton entered the courtroom and took her seat at the bench. She wasted little time. "Considering the charge of murder in the first degree and the very real risk that the defendant may flee the country, bail is denied."

Arthur Zimmerman was twenty years older than Cheryl Winterstein. He had three grown daughters and two grandchildren. He worked in a factory at a skilled position, and as a young man, he'd lost his right index finger in a metal lathe.

Zimmerman wasn't exactly a shy man, but he was secretive. He lived in Highland Park in a three-bedroom house with his three daughters and grandchildren. He'd converted his workshop, just off the kitchen, into a bedroom. The workbench was cluttered with tools, and the walls were lined with shelves that held glass jars filled with nuts and bolts and screws as well as nails, washers, and drill bits. He had cleared a space against the wall for a cot, and a wooden crate, turned on its side, served as a nightstand for a radio, lamp, ashtray, and clock. On the nightstand lay a two-inch threaded bolt and matching nut. He found twisting the nut on and off the bolt to be a relaxing pleasure, which he repeated several times before turning off the lamp, as he thought, *Such a simple invention, the nut and bolt.*

Cheryl refused his first invitation to dinner. He was too old, and there was nothing romantic in his odd manner. Not until the third invitation did she sense a simple honesty in him. Several dinners, movies, and time to talk and observe each other gave Cheryl a trusting view of him. This man was truly honored to have her company.

Nick finished school in the spring, and while he waited to take the entrance exam to law school, Cheryl and Arthur Zimmerman were married. The house on Frazho Road had been sold, and Arthur Zimmerman arrived with a flatbed truck to move the furniture and belongings to Highland Park. The daughters had moved out to make room for their father and his new bride. The girls told Cheryl they'd never seen their father so happy.

Nick remained in the house on Frazho Road while he awaited his exam results for law school. There were a few items left in the house and time remaining until the closure of sale. His mother insisted that he live with her in Highland Park while he was in school, but Nick said he had other plans. She expressed concern: where would he live? He told her his grandfather had offered to pay room and board through law school. His mother looked at him in disbelief. "When did this come about?" she wanted to know.

"Last Sunday," Nick said, "at dinner."

Art Zimmerman and Nick's mother drove to Chicago for their honeymoon. They left Sunday morning and planned to return at the end of the week. Nick worked full-time through the summer at a construction site, backfilling foundations with a shovel. The work was hard and mindless. He passed the time in daydreams and anticipation of his test results. The results finally arrived in the Friday mail. His mother was due home that evening. He opened the envelope to find an excellent score.

That night Nick waited for his mother to return from her honeymoon. He had such good news to tell her. He watched Johnny Carson on a small black-and-white screen, with a single lamp on in the living room, when a sudden knock came at the door. It was his grandmother. He opened the door. Her eyes were red from crying, and when she looked at Nick, she started crying again. He helped her inside, asking what was wrong. It was his mother, she said, barely able to speak. She'd been killed...in a car accident.

Jury selection was slow, and the revised witness list never appeared. Nick had to know the name of the new witness. He felt certain it was the man who had stood next to Michael Carthage the night he had shot Bridget. It was the only witness the prosecution had for a certain verdict of guilty. Helen was sure Robert Purcell knew who it was, but the thought of persuading him to reveal the name was unpleasant.

The prosecution wanted a jury of racial balance, and Nick wanted an all-black jury, but he was careful not to offend potential white jurors. There was little doubt that a few whites would be seated, and in the end, he needed their support. He searched for issues of anger against a parent, a boss, an undeserved traffic ticket, all of which are symbols of authority. And it was the *symbol* of authority that had Michael Carthage on trial. Here he could find and nurture sympathy for his client.

At the end of the third day of jury selection, Helen learned from Robert Purcell the name of the prosecution's star witness.

"How did Purcell know?" Nick asked.

"I didn't ask," she said. "But I found a picture of him on Facebook." She handed him the printout. "Anyone you know?"

He studied the picture. "Yes," he said. "It's who I thought it was."

"His name is Tobin Jefferson. He's twenty-three."

"How'd you get the name?"

"Friendly persuasion," she said.

"You spend the night with Purcell?"

"No, just thirty minutes. I like my boys a little more fastidious."

"He's not quite a boy."

"Almost," she said. "More like a little boy chasing frogs in a muddy pond."

"Has a deal been offered to this guy? Why would he turn against Carthage?"

"I don't know," she said. "Once Bobby zipped up his pants, he quit talking."

"I can't let this guy testify."

"I'll look into it," she said. "You can't be seen anywhere near him."

Of the jurors selected, four were white, one of whom was in her early fifties. She revealed that she was a Christian, never had married, and saw the world in terms of right and wrong, with nothing in between. Authority gave structure to her life, and as long as there was structure, there was never any reason to think. Her behavior was laid out for her like a set of clothes to wear.

There was also a woman of medium complexion with her hair drawn straight back in a tight bun. She appeared to be the same age as the white woman and was also a Christian and mentioned indirectly the need for forgiveness. There was a warm, if not charismatic, manner about her that drew the attention of the other jurors. When she spoke the other jurors turned their heads to listen, a few of them nodding in agreement. This was the juror Nick needed. He would mold his argument and behavior to her way of thinking. She would do the rest.

At the end of the third day of jury selection, Nick relaxed outside on the patio with a glass of wine before dinner. Sandy no longer questioned why he was defending Carthage; there was an understanding between them. Nicole too had come to realize that her father was dealing out his own sense of justice. In the beginning his ways were odd and opposed to her idea of right and wrong, but as she lived with him, she saw him differently. His ways had become hers, as though it always had been her way of thinking and was just now becoming clear to her.

Once the trial was underway and opening arguments had been presented, the prosecution promised proof beyond any doubt that Michael Carthage had killed Bridget Dean, recently known as Bridget Winterstein; here the prosecution glanced at Nick as if asking, *Why are you defending this man?*

The physical evidence was presented to the jury. The weapon used was a .40-caliber pistol with Michael's fingerprints all over it. Ballistics also had matched the prints on the bullet casing found near the body, and two witnesses testified that Bridget had been in Michael's company the night of the shooting.

"He most certainly had the opportunity," the prosecutor said, "and the motive. Ms. Winterstein knew about the drug money that was laundered through the campaign funds for the election of Monica Carthage. The night she was executed, she pleaded with"— he pointed to the defense table—"this man, Michael Carthage, to spare her, promising she would say nothing. But there was no mercy. He executed her in cold blood."

Witnesses did indeed testify that Bridget was in Michael's company the night she was murdered, but Nick didn't cross-examine them. He passed on both of them. That she was, at one time or another, in the company of Michael didn't prove a murder. But the eyewitness had yet to testify—the witness who could state that he had seen Michael Carthage kill Bridget Winterstein. Court was adjourned until Monday morning.

On Friday evening Nick phoned Helen several times without an answer. He left a voicemail asking her to call him. By Saturday morning he still hadn't heard from her. He felt confident everything was fine, but worry distracted him throughout the day. When Sandy or Nicole said something to him, it seemed he wasn't listening. He was off in another world.

"Something's bothering you," Sandy said. "What's wrong?"

He forced a smile and shook his head. "Nothing."

When Helen arrived at the house Sunday morning, there was relief in his eyes. Sandy saw it. Nick and Helen looked at each other but said nothing. That evening on the news, it was reported that there had been three shootings Saturday night. One man was in Henry Ford Hospital in critical condition, and one had been pronounced dead at the scene on Detroit's west side. A third victim, a male in his early twenties, had been found slumped over the steering wheel of his car in Palmer Park. He'd been shot in the head. He was identified as Tobin Jefferson.

On Monday morning in court, as Nick removed a few papers from his briefcase, he glanced up to see the lead prosecutor staring at him. Their eyes met. Nick smiled and said, "Good morning." Silence followed.

By the end of the second week, the prosecution had pieced together a case that didn't place the hand of Michael Carthage on the trigger at the time of the shooting. The jury was asked to believe that simply because fingerprints were on the same weapon used to commit a murder, the fingerprints were necessarily that of the murderer.

"But where is the proof?" Nick asked. "And what about the other set of prints? The fingerprints of Tobin Jefferson were also on the gun. Did he do it? Did he kill Bridget Winterstein? But we'll never know," he said.

In a closing statement, Nick looked at the jury, pausing for a moment to make eye contact with each juror. "How can you say, with certainty, it was Michael Carthage? You cannot. You cannot imprison this young man for the rest of his life simply because he was at a certain place at a certain time." He paused. "Where do we draw the line? When someone can say, 'Yes, he did it. I saw it'? But that's not the case." He turned his back to the jury and stepped toward Michael Carthage, seated at the table, then turned to face the jury again.

"Ladies and gentlemen, we know who the victim was in this terrible murder: my granddaughter, Bridget Winterstein. Do you think I could defend her murderer? It's absurd to even consider it. I am defending Michael Carthage because I know him to be innocent, and I trust with all my heart that you will too." A moment passed. "Please, look at me, ladies and gentlemen"—his hand was now on Michael's shoulder in a fatherly manner—"and know he didn't kill her."

Nick returned to his seat. He looked at Helen then at the court. "The defense rests, Your Honor," he said, and sat down.

The jury was given further instructions and then filed from the courtroom. Nick didn't expect a lengthy period of deliberation, nor did he expect anything too soon. Monica was encouraged, but she had her own concerns with an ongoing investigation into campaign funds. Jessup Carthage appeared tired and more lethargic than Nick had seen him in years. Time was catching up with him.

Helen came by for dinner Saturday evening, but there was little or no talk of the trial. She and Nick seemed to speak in glances, as though preoccupied with another matter. Nicole appeared much better. The heavy sadness that lay in her face had lifted. Helen squeezed her hand. Nicole confided that she was going to enroll in night school at Wayne State. There were a few math courses that fascinated her. "Math," Helen said. "My Lord. If I can't spell it, I don't understand it."

"Math," Nick said. "M-a-t-h."

Helen looked up. "What a snot." She laughed.

Sandy slapped him on the rear. "Be nice. You know what she means." The weekend was pleasant and passed quickly.

On Monday nothing was heard from the jury; then on Tuesday afternoon, they sent word that they were deadlocked. This wasn't good. There were jurors who obviously thought Carthage was guilty. The judge ordered them to continue deliberation. Late Thursday after-noon the jury reached a verdict.

Within a few hours, everyone had reassembled in the courtroom. The verdict was passed to the judge. She read it and passed it back.

The foreman of the jury read, "We, the jury, find the defendant, Michael Carthage, not guilty."

Relatives and spectators were jubilant. Monica Carthage hugged her father as he wiped tears from his eyes. Friends and supporters celebrated until the noise seemed to get out of hand and the judge called for order in the court, but still the celebrating went on.

Helen covered Nick's hand with hers. "He's all yours," she said.

His grandfather gave Nick a check each month to cover expenses while in law school. Nick rented a room by the week at the Normandie Hotel in Highland Park. He parked his car across the street from the hotel in an empty lot. His glove box was stuffed with parking tickets. Street prostitutes solicited business from the empty lot and sometimes removed the tickets from his windshield to write down phone numbers or an address. Most often they got in their customer's car, parked in the lot, and conducted business.

He took his meals at the Howard Johnson coffee bar on Woodward Avenue. He often spread a book and notepads on the counter and studied. He occasionally looked up at Woodward Avenue through the large plate window to watch the cars and pedestrians. As long as he didn't have to interact with them, he found comfort in their presence.

Law school wasn't difficult. The course work was easy, and after an argument or two, he'd learned not to discuss the philosophy of law with certain faculty members. Where Nick saw natural order, others saw, without human intervention, only chaos. "You must intervene," he was told, "and set moral codes and laws, without which you'd have anarchy."

"Since man has existed longer without laws than with laws," he asked, "how did we get here in one piece?"

He was told he simply didn't understand the complexities of human nature.

Among the participants at Faculty Hall was a math student from Wayne State. He suggested that human complexities might be better expressed in a mathematical equation. A young woman sat next to the math student. Her short hair was dark with a natural wave, her eyes blue, and her skin porcelain-like. Her name was Janice. The way she stared back at Nick caught his attention. He later ran into her again between classes. Each time he glanced at her, he found her looking at him with a smile in her eyes. He suggested they have coffee together. Her behavior had seemed quiet and demure, but when she arrived for coffee, she was animated and talkative. She intended to go into family law—and maybe contract law too, because wasn't marriage a contract? The two went together. She added cream to her coffee and two spoons of sugar. Nick wondered about the sudden change in her behavior. Where had the quiet-mannered girl gone?

Their first date was with another couple. They went to a secluded dance hall north of Dodge Park. They drank beer at a picnic table in the moonlight. Janice took two white pills from her purse and swallowed them with beer. She saw Nick watching her. She said they were aspirins. But less than thirty minutes later, she was animated and talkative, and when the other girl suggested they go back to her house, someplace inside, Janice quickly agreed. The other girl said her parents were out of town and they could all be alone. She swatted a mosquito on her arm.

The house was in Lincoln Park, and the young girl, now hostess, soon produced a bottle of rum from the liquor cabinet. Janice removed another pill from her purse. She said it helped relax her. She swallowed it with rum and Coke. The other couple disappeared into the bedroom, and a short time later, Nick led Janice by the hand to the other bedroom.

In the morning they all had scrambled eggs and toast, and there was another trip to the bedroom before Nick drove Janice to her aunt's, where she lived while in school. He continued to see Janice for the next few months. The relationship was convenient and didn't distract him from his thoughts. When Janice took a few pills, she did all the talking. All Nick had to do was nod and continue thinking of other things.

At the end of law school, days before graduation, Janice told Nick she was pregnant. His denial was instant. It couldn't have been him. It wasn't his baby! What about the math guy, he asked, whom she had been seeing too? He might as well have called her a whore. The hurt was in her eyes. Days after graduation her parents drove up from Baltimore to take her home.

Nick didn't think of her again until one Sunday while sitting at the coffee bar at Howard Johnson's. He saw the marriage announcement of Sandy Vermeer to Edward Wellington of Birmingham. The thought of marriage brought Janice to mind. He looked up from the paper and through the plate window at the pedestrians and traffic on Woodward Avenue. It was the first time he'd admitted to himself that the baby was his.

Nick turned onto Rochelle Avenue and crossed Gratiot to Joann Street, then drove to the middle of the block. He parked in front of a boarded-up house with charred siding and a detached garage. Across the street were empty lots, overgrown with weeds and small trees. He looked in all directions then got out of the black Volkswagen and walked up to the garage. He pushed open the sliding door and looked inside. It was empty. From the trunk of his car, he removed a power drill, a handful of screws, and a hasp and padlock. He attached the hasp to the garage door and locked it.

That weekend he picked Helen up at her apartment building. She wore Western boots and tight jeans. In the car she removed a blond wig from her shoulder bag. "After tonight," she said, "this gets retired."

"Did you use it for—?"

"Yes," she answered before he could finish. "It almost went badly."

"You haven't talked about it."

"It was a little frightening," she said. "I was the only white woman in the bar. All the hostility came from the women. He was easy, at least in the bar."

"How'd you end up at Palmer Park?"

"I told him to follow me. He thought he was getting laid. I pulled into Palmer Park near the fountain, and he parked next to me. When I got into his car, he started getting rough. He grabbed my hair and tried to pull my head down as he unzipped his pants. I bit his hand. He screamed and reached back to hit me. He froze when he saw the gun."

Just north of Lake Orin, Nick pulled into a gravel parking lot with a stand of trees at one end. At the other end was the Desperado Saloon and Grill. The parking lot was full. Near the saloon entrance, a handicap parking sign had been knocked over. A Ford F-150 was parked on the mangled sign.

Helen put on the blond wig and adjusted it in the mirror. She traced her lips with dark-red lipstick and put on a pair of glasses with a slight tint. "Follow my lead," she said. "It's all ad lib from here. If I leave in a vehicle alone, we'll meet on Joann Street."

She got out of the car, walked toward the bar, and disappeared through the doors. Fifteen then twenty-five minutes went by—then forty-five minutes. She finally emerged with a man in his fifties, barrel-chested, in a Western-style jacket with white piping on the sleeves and collar. He had a ring of keys in his hand. She reached up to kiss him quickly on the lips and said something to him. He turned and looked back at the door. She tilted her head as if to say, *Please?* As he started back toward the door, she stopped him and took the keys from his hand then playfully slapped him on the rear.

She turned toward the parking lot and activated the remote. The headlights on a white Ford SUV flashed. Nick watched her hurry toward the SUV, start it, and drive off the lot. He followed her to Joann Street in Detroit, where he unlocked the garage and she drove the SUV inside.

On Sunday morning Nick helped Nicole in the garden, while Helen helped Sandy prepare breakfast on the patio. Helen had been spending more and more time at the house and less time at her own place.

In the afternoon Nick called Monica Carthage on the pretense of asking how she was holding up. An indictment had been issued against her for the misuse of campaign funds, money laundering, filing a false tax return, and seven counts of wire fraud.

"Do you know this Robert Purcell?" she asked.

"Yes," Nick said.

"It's not me he wants, is it? He wants my father."

"I've seen the indictment, Monica. It doesn't look good."

There was a long silence on the other end. "Can you do anything?" she asked.

"I don't know," Nick said. "I can look into it," he lied. "By the way, how's Michael these days?"

"He's been keeping to himself. He doesn't stay in the city. He's somewhere in Warren."

"So I've heard."

Michael Carthage had been using a house on Frazho Road. The house had been condemned by the city, but it was well suited as an exchange and drop-off point. Nick had developed a feeling for Michael's schedule and had called Monica just to confirm Michael's whereabouts.

On Wednesday evening Nick drove to Joann Street, parked the black Volkswagen in the garage, and backed out in the white SUV. He drove north on Gratiot Avenue to Frazho Road and turned left. The sun was at a soft angle to the west. The seasons had changed. It had been a year since Bridget had been executed in the basement on Hurlbut Street.

As Nick approached the house on Frazho Road, he slowed down. The driveway was empty, but he noticed a reflection through the front window, movement in the house. He pulled into the driveway. The neighborhood was quiet.

The side door had been padlocked, but the hasp was torn from the frame. He pushed the door open quietly with his foot and stepped inside. He heard movement in the other room. He removed a nickel-plated revolver from under his belt and activated the laser sight. He stepped from the utility room to the kitchen. Through the entryway to the living room, he saw Michael Carthage kneeling next to a black satchel filled with cash, his fingertips touching the money.

"Hello, Michael."

Nick's voice startled him. When Carthage saw who it was a slow smile of condescension came to Michael's face.

"Surprised to see me?" Nick said. "You shouldn't be."

"What the fuck you doin' here? Don't point that gun at me." The red laser dot moved to his forehead. The smile went away. "You crazy fuck…I been acquitted. I didn't do that killing." His eyes showed panic. Nick drew the hammer back with his thumb. It clicked in place.

"You can't do this! It's like double jeopardy. It's against the law."

"The law? The law is anything you make it up to be, Michael. There's no math involved."

"Jesus Christ! You're crazy."

"Did you know that slavery was once the law of the land? Now what does that tell you about the law?"

"OK, listen, we can talk about that. Anything you want, OK? Just point that the other way."

"Talk? OK. We can start with who killed Marshall."

The question caught him off guard. He hesitated, thought for a moment. "I did. But I didn't kill that girl."

"That girl?" Nick stretched his arm forward. The laser dot came to a steady rest on Michael's forehead. He slowly squeezed.

"Listen to me—"

The shot was sudden and loud. Michael's head snapped back, and from the knees up, his body went limp. He fell forward onto his face. Blood pooled on the floor. Nick stood there, looking down at the body. He heard tires roll onto the gravel drive out front.

He looked through the side window. A police car had pulled up behind the SUV. A young officer with a blond crew cut stepped from the squad car and came toward the side entrance. He removed his service pistol from the holster and carried it at his side. Nick stepped into the tiny bathroom near the side door. Through the opening between the door and the hinges, Nick had a clear view to the kitchen.

He heard the officer step inside. As he passed the narrow opening between the bathroom door and the hinges, he carried his service pistol, aimed in front of him, with both hands. As he came to the kitchen entry, he stopped. The body on the living-room floor was in his line of sight. A red laser dot came to a rest on the back of the young officer's head, and Nick fired. The young officer lurched forward, his knees buckling.

Nick pushed the bathroom door open, stepped forward, and stood over the dead officer. He heard a second set of tires on the gravel drive. He stepped around the corner wall into the living room. He saw the second squad car park behind the first one, and the second officer was coming toward the same entrance on the side of the house. From behind the living-room entryway, Nick had a clear view of the side door. He waited, the laser dot pointed above the entrance.

The officer appeared as a silhouette in the open doorway. Nick quietly exhaled and held his breath as the red dot focused between the eyes. He fired. The silhouette jerked back then fell to the floor hard, as though his knees had been cut out from under him.

Nick stepped from the entryway and walked toward the second officer. He stood over him, then looked back at the first officer, then at Carthage lying in a pool of blood. He looked up. He saw his mother standing at the kitchen sink; he heard his father's electric saw cutting through wood out in the shop. How had it all come to this?

Had it all been written before it happened?

After law school Nick worked for General Motors in the department of contracts and negotiations. The older attorneys had told him it was a good place to work. It was secure, and you were safe from the kind of screw-ups and blunders that could cost you your job and a future retirement of ease. Just keep your head down and look busy. From the first week on, he started saving to go out on his own.

That summer the Detroit riots erupted in 1967. The Michigan National Guard set up roadblocks on Woodward Avenue to stop traffic from reentering the city after curfew. Nick was returning from Birmingham when he was stopped at Eight Mile and Woodward. The young guardsman said the area was under lockdown. Nick explained that he lived at the Normandie Hotel, just past McNichols. The young guardsman said, "Sure, go on."

As Nick returned to his car, a young woman stopped behind his car and got out of her vehicle. The guardsman told her to get her black ass back in the car and turn around. The young woman looked stunned. She started to say something, but Nick shook his head subtly, as if to say, *No, don't. You can't win this.* She looked at Nick and returned to her car.

The next day Nick used the riots as an excuse not to go to work. He returned to Birmingham. He stopped at a coffee shop on Old Woodward. Seated at a table by herself was the young black woman from the night before. She gave a slight smile, and he asked whether he could join her. Her name was Valerie Brown, and she was an attorney for the state of New York. They had coffee together and talked late into the afternoon. By evening they had a disagreement over the cause of the riots in Detroit. The argument became heated, and Nick implied she was a racist. She was outraged and demanded an apology. He refused, and the argument continued into the night. The next morning they awoke next to each other in a motel north of Birmingham.

The following year Nick resigned from his position at General Motors. Huey Newton had just been charged with first-degree murder in Oakland, California. The case caught his full attention. Valerie had accumulated vacation time, and she drove with Nick to Alameda County, California, to witness the trial. Her interest in the trial was emotional; Nick's concern was academic.

Huey Newton was indeed a violent individual, but he was also handsome and charismatic, with a boyish appeal. To hear him testify in a soft, seductive voice—it was nearly impossible to think of him as violent. His cause was political, not one of personal gain, and the officer he was accused of killing had shot him in the stomach. In the end the officer had been killed with his own weapon. The gun had never actually been placed in Newton's hand, nor had a paraffin test been performed. There were many holes in the prosecution's case.

When the jury returned a verdict of manslaughter, Valerie was near tears. Nick recounted the many openings the defense had missed. Too much time had been spent on politics and not enough on appealing to the jury. Convince the jury they are superior to the proceedings they are judging, and you own them.

When they returned to Detroit, Valerie wanted to make their relationship permanent. She wanted marriage. Nick said he couldn't do that. There was no room in his life for marriage, not now, not for a long time.

Valerie seemed to disappear after that. She returned to New York, and he never heard from her again.

Months later the investigation into the murders on Frazho Road was concluded. It was near Thanksgiving, and the first snow had dusted the ground. It was a dry, powdery snow that swirled along the street and collected at the curb. From his office window, Nick saw Helen's car pull into the parking lot below. As she hurried from her car, she carried a white pastry bag and pulled her coat collar close to her neck. She entered the security code at the door and opened it.

Helen set the pastry bag in the kitchenette and put her coat in the closet. Minutes later she carried a tray with a pot of coffee, cups and saucers, and a plate of pastries into Nick's office. She set the tray on the coffee table in front of the sofa. She noticed a copy of the investigation on his desk.

"Are you coming to Thanksgiving dinner?" Nick asked.

"I wouldn't miss it. I've talked to Sandy. She said Judge Weatherly and her husband will be there."

"Yes, and Allen Rotheim, and Adele."

"I ran into Nicole," she said. "She was with her new friend. Do you think it's serious?"

"I don't know," he said. "But I'm happy for her. When I first met her mother, she too was dating a guy from the math department. A doctoral candidate. Wayne State."

"So is this guy, isn't he?"

Nick nodded. "Yes. But I only met him once."

"What did you think of him?"

"He seems genuine. Matthew."

"I like the name." She handed Nick a cup of coffee with a pastry next to it on a saucer. She glanced down at the report. "What do you think about that?" she asked. "They made quite an effort to tie it altogether. And no mention of HIV—nothing. No loose ends. I'm sure they don't want to revisit it."

"No," he said. "Not with the name Carthage attached to it."

"So he really was related to Huey Newton?"

"The DNA seemed conclusive. Jessup paid for the whole thing. There's political mileage in it. Grandson of Jessup Carthage *and* Huey Newton. Spike Lee is no doubt writing the movie script right now."

"But they chalked it up as a drug deal gone wrong. Where's the romance in that?"

"Violence," he said. "Guns, outlaws. Newton was charged with two murders: a police officer and a prostitute. It ended in several mistrials, and he walked free. Now he's seen as a hero."

"But then he was shot."

"Again it was called a drug deal gone wrong." Nick put his cup back on the saucer. "It seems Newton was robbing drug dealers, and someone shot him in the face. Michael followed the same path."

"Like father, like son," she said. "Or daughter for that matter."

"Behavior is genetic," he said, "as genetic as the color of your eyes."

Helen laughed. "Some would argue hard against that one."

"I know," he said. "The Flat Earth Society."

www.ingramcontent.com/pod-product-compliance
Lightning Source LLC
Chambersburg PA
CBHW030029180626
46810CB00001B/286